Flight

A novel by
Darren Hynes

© 2010, Darren Hynes

 Canada Council **Conseil des Arts**
for the Arts **du Canada**

Canada

 Newfoundland
Labrador

We gratefully acknowledge the financial support of the Canada Council for
the Arts, the Government of Canada through the Book Publishing Industry
Development Program (BPIDP), and the Government of Newfoundland and
Labrador through the Department of Tourism, Culture and Recreation for our
publishing program.

Cover design by Eric Walsh and Todd Manning
Layout by Todd Manning

Published by
KILLICK PRESS
an imprint of CREATIVE BOOK PUBLISHING
a Transcontinental Inc. associated company
P.O. Box 8660, Stn. A
St. John's, Newfoundland and Labrador A1B 3T7

Printed in Canada by:
TRANSCONTINENTAL INC.

Printed on acid-free paper

Library and Archives Canada Cataloguing in Publication

Hynes, Darren, 1972-
    Flight / Darren Hynes.

ISBN 978-1-897174-66-1

 **Mixed Sources**
Product group from well-managed
forests and other controlled sources
www.fsc.org Cert no. SW-COC-000952
© 1996 Forest Stewardship Council
FSC

I. Title.

PS8615.Y53F55 2010   C813'.6   C2010-904538-6

Flight

A novel by
Darren Hynes

St. John's, Newfoundland and Labrador
2010

"This slender volume is a gripping read, literally a page-turner from start to finish. The stakes are high, and the situation both familiar and dire."

– The Telegram

For Michelle

MONDAY

EMILY WAKES TO KENT PRESSING HIMSELF AGAINST HER; his warm breath on the back of her neck, his strong fingers beneath her nightgown gripping her hips, his grunts in her ear.

She shifts farther to her side of the bed, unwilling to let go of the sleep she's somehow managed for the first time in months.

He latches on to her again, tighter than before. Almost all of him, it seems, wanting inside.

"Don't," she says, thrusting her pelvis forward. "I'm so tired."

Any farther now and she'd be on the floor.

She listens to his breathing, sensing him close still.

She waits.

Waits some more.

Then, just when she expects him to grab hold of her again, he flips over on his back and kicks off the sheets. Gets up and leaves the room.

She struggles to hang onto the sound of his footfalls down the hallway.

It's still dark. Plenty of time yet before his blaring alarm. Why's he up?

Although she tries, she's unable to lift her cheek from where it's practically glued to the palm of her right hand.

She thinks she hears footsteps again, the opening of a cabinet door, the running of water, but then dismisses them.

What was the dream that he'd interrupted? Yes, she'd been standing near the stern of the ferry, gripping the rail so tightly her hands had turned white; Lynette, her youngest, holding her around the waist; Jeremy, older than his sister by four years, off to one side, hands cupping his mouth, shouting into the wind, *She's stealing us away, Dad!* A lone figure in big boots and a blue parka standing on the receding dock. Him. Kent. Hands partway in his jean pockets, and hair, though balding at the crown, blown askew in the gale. The sound of the churning engines widening the gulf between them. The first hints of freedom warming her belly like strong whiskey.

I should get up, she thinks, but sleep snatches her away before she gets the chance.

1

* * *

EMILY BOLTS AWAKE. Inhales sharply. Sits up.

In the dark room it's the whites of his eyes that she notices first. Then his nakedness. He's peering down at her, and holding the good crystal jug.

"Next time it'll be Coke," he says.

She runs her hands over her face, through her wet hair. Nipples hard through her now-soaking nightgown. "What'd I do?"

"You know."

He comes closer, his upper thighs pressed against the side of the bed, the jug in front of his penis.

Why the good crystal jug her mother had given them? Why not the stained plastic container underneath the sink for the sugary Tang or lemonade? That would make more sense, wouldn't it? But to get *this* one he'd had to reach behind the fancy wine glasses on the top shelf of the cabinet.

"You couldn't get enough of me once," he says.

Looking at him now she can hardly believe there was a time when that was true. Like teenagers they had been.

She imagines digging what're left of her nails into the flesh of his chest, etching bloody rivers down the whole of him, right to his belly button.

"I'm just tired," she says.

He's standing there, looking down at her.

She doesn't move. Or breathe even.

Suddenly he turns and walks out of the room. Slams the door so hard that the family photo on their night table nearly topples over. She listens to his bare feet slapping off the hardwood, then him opening and closing the bathroom door. Running the shower.

She wonders if he's woken the children. Probably not Jeremy. He's like his father that way, could sleep through jet planes. But little Lynette is a light sleeper; cutting bread is enough to rouse her. Once woken, she'd come in, pajama bottoms covering her tiny feet, and that ratty, stuffed giraffe, as always, tucked underneath her left arm.

Emily sits in the near dark, waiting. Then gets to her feet. Wipes the wetness from her cheeks with the back of her hand, then walks over to her dresser, pulling open the bottom drawer. She lifts the wet nightgown over her head and tosses it through the open doorway of the closet, not caring if it finds the clothes hamper or not. The dry one she finds in the drawer feels warm against her skin.

The alarm clock on Kent's side of the bed says 5:30 a.m.

Although lately she pretends to be sleeping, his wet kiss usually wakes her – hot lips smelling of coffee and baloney against her forehead, his right hand resting delicately against her left cheek. Then the sound of his footsteps in the hall, him opening and closing the front door, the turning of the ignition, pumping of the gas, rocks spitting out from underneath the heavily treaded tires. Two horn blasts. Then the stillness.

At the window, she makes a space in the blinds to peek through with a forefinger and thumb. The sun is on the cusp of slicing upwards out of the bay. In the distance a trawler floats listlessly, as if timid about venturing too far from shore.

"Four more sleeps," she hears herself whisper to the windowpane. One year of saving sixty bucks a week. Three tickets on a seat sale: $1,755 with $1,125 left over. All of it shoved under a loose floor panel in the basement near the washer and dryer. Even now, because the rectangle of wood blends so nicely with the others, she has trouble finding it. Every payday she spends a minute or two on her hands and knees like a dog, her fingertips gliding along the floor in order to find the ever-so-slight ridge. Because of her chewed nails, she sometimes needs a butter knife to wrestle the wood out of place.

She leaves the bedroom and goes out into the hall. Moves towards the kitchen, deciding that it's better to make coffee and fry him baloney rather than lie in bed.

She covers the coffee grinder with a drying towel to muffle the sound. Breathes in the aroma of freshly diced beans. As she drops six heaping tablespoons into the filter, she realizes that Kent's shower has stopped. In her mind, she sees him hauling aside the shower curtain and stepping onto the matt near to the tub: strong calves and a still-trim waist to match his firm arms and chest. Then snatching a towel off the rack and drying himself so roughly that his skin turns red. His long-fingered hand wiping the steam from the mirror. Nose hairs to pluck, a few on the lower lobes of his smallish ears too. Then his chin dropping onto his chest so he can get a better view of the thinning hair on top. Frustrated breaths before he combs what's still lush on the sides and back.

He's right there when Emily turns around.

"Oh," she says.

The towel's tight around his waist, water from his hair running down his cheeks, past his neck and onto his collarbones. His eyes right on her.

3

He takes hold of her. Hugs too tight. Always too tight.

"I'm sorry," he says.

She allows herself to be held, ignoring the impulse to push him off, her left cheek pressed against his chest, his heartbeat in her ear.

"Did you hear me?"

She nods. "I heard you."

"You sorry too?"

She knows the list is long with the things she's sorry for. "Yes."

He kisses her forehead. Squeezes her behind. Lets her go. Smiles. Turns around and heads back the way he came.

She hauls out the baloney and some butter, places the frying pan on a burner and cranks up the heat to almost max. Plops in more butter than she'd prefer, but that's how he likes it.

The aroma of sizzling meat and dripping coffee fills the kitchen now, and her one hand holds onto the spatula; the other arm is crossed just below her breasts, its hand tucked into the opposite armpit.

After a few minutes, she flips the baloney, then turns around to look out the window above the kitchen table: the sun is inching higher on the horizon, the bay alive with ripples.

A flick of grease from the pan strikes her neck. Except for a rushed intake of breath, she doesn't make a sound. Doesn't even bother covering the burn with her hand.

She lowers the heat on the burner and flips again, the meat a stiff purplish red. Not fit to eat. Perfect for Kent though.

She smells him before she sees him. Old Spice. Even before his union job, when, like the others, he'd gutted whatever fish they happened to haul from the now-empty waters, he'd splashed a little on. Laughed at the things said behind his back because of it, Emily knew, so confident he was about moving up. First it was shift leader to foreman, then union representative for Lightning Cove, and finally union head for the whole of the northeast coast. No one laughed at him anymore. All nods and 'yes sir.' Eyes could barely stay trained on him now. Hers couldn't.

"I thought I smelled coffee," he says, as casually as if she were a buddy from work. As if it was someone else who'd thrown a jug of water in her face not more than twenty minutes ago.

She forces a smile without looking at him, the pulse throbbing in her neck.

"Baloney, too," he says, wrapping his arms around her waist. "Aren't I a lucky one?"

His scalding lips suck momentarily on her neck.

"Don't."

He stops. "You're not still mad, are you?"

She shakes her head.

"I said I was sorry – "

"I know."

He grips her tighter. "Do you love me?"

She doesn't answer.

"Do you?"

She nods.

"Say it."

"I love you."

"Love you too, baby. So much."

If he squeezes her any harder she'll pass out.

"Sit down," she says, "I'll bring over your breakfast."

He lets her go and sits down at the kitchen table. She watches him: tan chords and black cashmere sweater, clean shaven and too much gel in his combed-back hair. Because it had been thick, wavy, and parted in the middle, they'd called him 'Vinny Barbarino' in high school. The dimple in his chin along with his height helped the nickname stick until well after graduation.

With a fork, Emily stabs at the crusted-over baloney, dropping it on a plate. Pours his coffee, then brings everything over to him. Before he has a chance to ask, she grabs the bottle of ketchup and the cream from the fridge, laying both beside his plate. The sugar is already on the table.

She sits down.

"You'll have a cup with me," he says.

She rises and pours her own, then sits beside him again.

The ketchup makes a fart noise when Kent squeezes the bottle. He squeezes again and again until his plate is a collage of red and brown, like the insides of some wild animal.

Emily turns her face away, looking out the window. She finds herself paying extra attention to his clicking jaw and his sticky saliva as he chews, suddenly conscious that, soon, she will no longer have to listen, or look at him.

After he finishes eating he sits back, his thick fingers around his cup. He brings the lip to his mouth and sips. Scrunches up his face. "That's strong." He drops in another spoonful of sugar and more cream. Tries another gulp. Puts it back down.

Emily notices his eyes lock onto the centre of the table. She waits for him to look up at something else, the view outside the window perhaps, or at her, but he doesn't. He's left her and she knows it.

She glides a fingertip along the top of one of his palms. "Kent?"

By the look on his face, it's like she's not even in the room.

She slides her chair closer. "Kent?"

She wishes now that one of the children were up – Lynette, so he could throw her up in the air and then catch her, or Jeremy, so they could talk hockey or weightlifting. They could bring him back, she thinks.

She takes her hand away. Slides back in her chair. Is he thinking about earlier? Had the cold water in her face not been enough after all?

"Kent?" she says. "What's wrong?"

He looks up, finally. Right at her. Back from wherever he'd been.

It's Emily now who looks away.

"They're announcing the layoffs this morning," he says. "'More workers than there is fish,' the crowd from St. John's says. In their fancy suits and ties they were. The Minister of Fisheries and Oceans with a goddamn flower on his breast pocket." He goes silent again, this time casting his glance out the window.

Other than the thinning hair and the few lines in the corners of his eyes, she thinks he looks exactly as he did in high school. His body even better. Hard not to be, with all the exercise he does. Five nights a week he lifts weights in the garage with the stereo blasting. The other two evenings he's on the treadmill. Comes back in the house then soaked in sweat and plays with the youngsters before their bedtime. Jeremy likes to wrap his hands around Kent's flexed bicep. Lynette on her daddy's shoulders, her long blonde hair down to the middle of her back.

"Myles is finished," he says, still looking out the window, "and him with another young one on the way."

In the silence, she gets up and returns with the coffee pot. He speaks as she's refilling his mug. "I dare say there won't be a woman left by day's end. Not enough seniority."

She lays the pot on the table and sits back down.

"Young Alan Cross says he's taking his wife and getting the hell out." He doesn't use the spoon for his sugar this time, just tips the jar. "Can't imagine many wanting to stay after this." Thick waterfall of cream. The clinking of the spoon inside his cup as he stirs. Licks it off after he's done with it.

He leans toward her. "I shouldn't be saying any of this, but there's talk about shutting her down. 'Too expensive to keep it going,' the St. John's crowd says." He pauses long enough to suck in a big breath before letting it out slowly. His forehead is suddenly creased with wrinkles. "There may not be a Lightning Cove by the end of the month."

She holds his gaze for a second before looking down at her coffee, then wraps both hands around the mug, enjoying the warmth in her palms. Takes several sips in quick succession, but doesn't put the cup back down after she's done. Just keeps it below her bottom lip, in front of her chin.

"Nothing to say about it or what?" he says.

"Hmm?"

"I said, you've got nothing to say about it?"

The town can sink into the bay for all I care. "What's to say?"

He leans in closer. "Lots, considering we live here."

Another sip before she says, "What difference what I think?"

After a moment he sits back in his chair. "I'm glad it's not you fighting for us."

She finds the air between them growing thinner, lately. Can barely fill her lungs. Suffocating. The pillow over her face being pressed down harder.

There are footsteps in the hall, quick and light, like a puppy. Lynette. Emily imagines her daughter's feet: big toes curled in and longer than average baby ones with nails always in need of trimming. She imagines Lynette's walk too, her reed-like body thrusting forward as if through pounding wind, her little darling never getting to wherever she needs to be fast enough.

Lynette's hair is all tangles when she comes into the kitchen, her giraffe trapped at the neck between her ribcage and the nook of her left elbow.

"Always in a rush, my little darling is," Emily says, prodding a forefinger under Lynette's armpit.

Because Lynette's nightgown doesn't go past her knees, it's easy to see the fresh glob of blood on her right knee where, last night, a scab had been. She walks into the space between Emily's parted thighs and gives her mother a hug, easily interlacing her fingers at the base of Emily's back.

"Good morning, my love."

"Morning, Mommy."

"What did I tell you about picking that?" Emily says.

"Give your dad a kiss," Kent says, splaying his arms.

"It was itchy," Lynette says, letting go of her mother and moving over to her father.

Kent kisses and hugs her, reaches into his trouser pocket and hauls out some tissue. He dabs at Lynette's knee.

"Ouch!"

"All done." Kent balls the tissue up, then looks for somewhere to put it.

Emily grabs it and throws it into the garbage by the porch door. Stands there long enough to watch her husband take Lynette into his arms, then bounce her on his knee.

"What are you doing up so early?" he says.

All the bouncing is making Lynette giggle.

"Wanted to see your daddy before he went to work, did you?" He kisses her on the cheek before putting her down. "Daddy's got a big day today." He disappears the same way Lynette had just come.

Emily is standing near the porch door. "Sit down and I'll give you some Honeycombs."

While Emily is pouring the milk, Kent comes back in, putting his cell phone in its holder on his belt loop. Though his sport's jacket matches his pants, the look doesn't quite work. Too much tan, she thinks. Or maybe it's just that now he looks too 'done up.' Too perfect. *Too perfect,* she thinks. Too perfect for those at his work, and the friends he goes fishing with; too perfect for the guidance counselor at Jeremy and Lynette's school, and Sonya at the Royal Bank, and Pat Gullage at the marina; too perfect even for her own mother. Too perfect for everyone but her. Water in her face, and then he's the sweetest thing going. Tomorrow it'll be a slap across the mouth, or his body pinning her against the wall before his: "I love you," his: "I didn't mean it," his: "Let me take you out for dinner."

He comes over and grazes the base of her neck with his lips, then says, "Best not to plan on me for supper."

She nods. "I'll put some aside."

He pats her bottom, then blows Lynette a kiss.

"Bye, Daddy."

"Bye," Emily says.

He slams the door. There's the sound of a turning ignition and pumping gas.

8

She listens to the sound of crunching rock and the two quick horn blasts as he backs out of the driveway. Listens too for the single one he insists on halfway down their street. *Too perfect.*

2

JEREMY'S JAW CLICKS WHEN HE CHEWS, just like his father's. She watches him as she sips coffee. He overloads his spoon like Kent does too, then opens his mouth wider than necessary to accommodate the food. He's most focused during mealtimes, his nose so close to the plate sometimes it looks as if he might dip his face in it.

"No one's going to steal it," she says.

He doesn't bother looking up at her.

An appetite nearly as big as his dad and not yet twelve years old. It's not uncommon for he and Kent, during *Hockey Night In Canada*, to devour a whole extra-large pepperoni pizza. They'll go piece for piece like it's some game, every so often showing each other the contents of their mouths. Some evenings Jeremy will go into the garage with his father to watch him lift weights. Although Kent says his boy is still too young, Emily knows he sometimes lets Jeremy do a little. More than once she's peeked through the garage window to see Kent instructing him, both of them with their shirts off, bandanas wrapped around their heads and soaked with sweat.

Jeremy finishes and then dips his spoon in Lynette's bowl.

"Get out of it," Emily says. She yanks the spoon from his hand. "Get an apple if you want something else."

"She's *not* eating it."

"She is too."

"Can I have a toasted strudel then?"

"Is it Saturday, Jeremy?" It suddenly occurs to her that, by then, the three of them will be in British Columbia. She needs a second to allow the nervousness in her stomach to pass.

"How come only Saturday?" he says.

"Because they're loaded with sugar, I said. Now either you eat an apple or you go and get dressed."

"I don't want a stupid apple."

"Go then."

"I don't know what to wear."

"Your clothes for today are on top of your dresser like they are every morning. Best not to try my patience."

Jeremy stomps through the kitchen and down the hall to his bedroom. He's been getting into fights at school. Lately, he's been hitting his sister.

Emily looks out the window. The sun is just above the surface of the bay. After such a long winter, these spring days are a relief. She sees the Lightning Cove ferry in the distance, loaded with cars. Passengers as tiny as ants taking the forty-minute ride to the main part of the island. Emily and the children will take that ferry too this Friday, then find some way to get to Gander by ten to catch their eleven o'clock flight. She figures she won't breathe until the layover in Toronto.

"Eat!" She says to Lynette.

"It's soggy."

"Whose fault is that?"

Lynette is the opposite of her brother. Instead of eating, she'd rather be drawing pictures of trees and houses in her sketchbook, or finger painting in the basement. Eating is like an intrusion on her day. Mature beyond her years though, Lynette. Everything is *why* with her. Why is there a sun during the day and a moon at night? Why is the water closer to shore than other times? Why does Jeremy get to stay up later? Why does Daddy get quiet?

"Four more spoonfuls, okay?"

"Why?"

"Or no colouring this evening."

Lynette forces the cereal in, nearly gagging.

"Good girl. Now go and get dressed. I'll be right in."

Emily watches her go, then gets up and takes the cereal bowls to the dishwasher. She squeezes in some dish liquid and turns it on, then stands with her belly against the machine, letting its vibrations settle her stomach. She breathes in, lets the air out slowly, her mind on Friday.

3

SHE'S HOLDING LYNETTE'S HAND. Jeremy is walking a few
feet ahead. Despite the clear day and a sun that is close enough to
touch, it's chilly. So the children are wearing spring jackets over their
sweaters. A purple knapsack hangs on Lynette's back. Jeremy carries
a math book and a green scribbler in his right hand, pressed against
his waist. Too cool, even at eleven, to carry a bookbag.

They take a left on Trinity Street away from the water and toward
the centre of town. Hanrahan's Seafood, on her right, has a special on
trout and shrimp; Anique's Antiques has a gorgeous oak rocking chair
and a grandfather clock for sale on the front stoop.

Jeremy kicks at rocks on the shoulder of the road. Lynette hums
a melody that Emily has never heard.

"What's that song, baby?"

Lynette stops humming and gives her mother a look. "Miley
Cyrus, Mom."

She feels old. And it's not because of the way Lynette said *Miley
Cyrus*, either. Some nights she lies in bed and tries to remember being
young: running through the waist-high grass in her mother's garden,
filling salt-beef buckets with blueberries, riding her bike along back
streets and trails in the woods. She'll often check in the groceries of
women much older than herself and wonder how they can seem so
much younger, so free with their laughter, so animated when they talk,
how they can be loaded down with bags yet still walk lightly.

They pass the Royal Bank. She sees Sonya, one of the tellers,
through the glass. Sonya waves while giving fake *Oh, they're so sweet*
looks to the kids. Emily waves back. Sonya's the main reason why Emily
decided against opening up her own account. Better to take her
chances in the basement rather than have her husband hear about
her weekly sixty-dollar deposits from Sonya or one of the others. Kent
prefers all of the money to flow into and out of the same place. Should
have been a banker, Emily sometimes thinks, considering the attention he pays to their joint account.

Underneath her jacket, she wears a blue button-up shirt with Hodder's Grocery and Convenience written over the right breast pocket.

Over the left is her nametag. As if anyone needs their name written on their chest in this town. Her black pants end at her black sneakers. Come Friday she can part with them, too – maybe throw them in the trash or leave them lying on the bed. Something for him to remember her by. Perhaps she'll leave her nametag in his coffee cup.

She almost forgets there was a time she'd dreamed of studying at the university in St. John's: social work, or something to do with children. Becoming pregnant with Jeremy dashed those plans. As did the ring in its black casing Kent had presented to her on that day in September eleven years ago.

"Jeremy, wait for us!" She was unaware that he'd run off already. That's how consumed she is in her own thoughts. The other day she'd left the house with the stove on, then forgot her phone number when she went to call Kent and warn him.

Jeremy doubles back, joins them. "I can walk myself, you know."

"But Mommy likes to go with you." It's not a lie. The fifteen-minute walk with them to school each morning is the only part of her day she loves. The chance to be alone with them away from that house. For so long she's imagined taking the right onto Glover Street instead of Trinity, walking past the Anglican Church and the Parish Hall, Pete's Fish n' Chips and The Dock Marina, along the gangway and onto the ferry. Jeremy holding her right hand; Lynette her left. Them walking to the bow of the boat towards the mainland. Not once looking back.

Years of weather have faded the orange-brown elementary school at the end of the street. With the rise of marsh, and stilted, windblown trees beyond it, the building seems out of place, like a scar. Children in open jackets and sneakers run and laugh in the courtyard. Some red-faced girls chase some red-faced boys. Others kick a soccer ball.

"Can I go now?" Jeremy asks, his eyes on the boys with the ball.

"Not before you tell me what you have to do."

He's like a dog being held back from a steak. "Hold Lynette's hand."

"That's right. What else?"

"Mom!"

"What else, Jeremy? When are you allowed to let go?"

"When we get to the house."

"That's right. Don't you dare let go until you're turning the doorknob. I shouldn't be much later than four today."

Emily wishes she could kiss him goodbye like she used to do up until six months ago. But something in her boy has changed since this past Christmas. Not only can she not kiss him in public, she can't hold his hand either, or walk too close.

"Go on then," she says to him.

He takes off without so much as a goodbye.

Lynette still likes her mommy's kisses though, and she'll take a hug afterwards too.

"Have a nice day at school," Emily says, watching her baby girl walk away, purple knapsack flopping side to side with each step, and golden hair in two long braids with green buckles at their ends. Instead of joining the other children in the schoolyard, Lynette goes to the main entrance. Emily waits for the limp wave that her daughter gives her every morning before she pulls open the doors. Lynette doesn't disappoint. Emily imagines her youngest going to her locker, then to her homeroom, not feeling the need to linger in the crowded corners, or gossip by the water fountain. Such a practical little girl. Twice her age it sometimes seems.

Jeremy is hogging the soccer ball. A few boys give chase, but can't get it away from him. Athletic like his dad, and bigger too than most of the other kids his age.

"Fine morning," says a voice behind her.

She turns around to see a pregnant Irene Baker – hands, one on top of the other – resting on the impressive bulge beneath her long sweater.

"Chilly though," Emily says.

"When isn't it in *this* place?"

"There's a whole week in late August, I think."

They both laugh.

"Where's your boy?"

"Chasing yours." Irene points.

"She doesn't want to come out, does she?" Emily indicates Irene's belly with a jut of her chin.

"*He*. And no, he doesn't. Nearly two weeks overdue now. Myles says with everything going on the baby's better off staying inside."

In the silence, Emily remembers what Kent had said to her earlier: *Myles is finished.* "Perhaps it won't come to layoffs," she says.

"There'll be a lot of angry men if it does. That's what Myles says."

Emily nods but doesn't say anything.

For a while both women watch their children.

Finally, Irene says, "Some bite to that wind."

"Goes right through you, doesn't it?"

"To the bone." Irene tucks a sliver of red hair behind her ear. Turns to Emily, hesitates before saying, "Has he said anything?"

"Hmm?"

"Kent. Has he said anything?"

There might not be a Lightning Cove by the end of the month. "No."

Irene keeps her eyes on her for a long time before finally turning back towards the schoolyard.

Another long moment passes and, just as Emily's about to say goodbye, Irene says, "Not a skill does he have."

"Sorry?"

"Myles. It's either the plant or nothing."

The school bell rings. Children scatter.

It rings again.

"I should be getting to work," Emily says.

"Go on, my dear, don't let me keep you."

"Have a good morning." Emily turns around and starts walking. Then stops long enough to say, "I hope the little one comes soon."

"He'll have to, won't he?"

She doesn't get very far before she hears Irene's voice again.

"It's good news."

She turns around. "What is?"

Irene smiles. "No news."

Emily does her best to smile back.

4

TERRY GRINS AT HER through the glass doors of Hodder's Grocery and Convenience – exposed gums above tiny teeth. He reaches inside a trouser pocket and pulls out his keys. Inserts one and then turns the deadbolt. Pushes open the door. "Morning."

She rushes past him. "Sorry I'm late."

He smells like Mr. Clean.

"Hardly late," he says, looking at his watch.

She goes to the cash and takes off her coat, stuffing it into the cubbyhole underneath.

"Early if anything."

She stops and looks at him. "Am I?"

He nods.

"That's funny, thought I was late." She looks down, notices that Terry has put her till, along with the two hundred dollar float, into her register. "You don't have to keep doing this," she says.

"I don't mind." He puts the deadbolt back in place and goes over to her. Stands on the other side of her checkout counter with his hands in his pockets.

"You don't do it for Heather."

"That one needs all the practice she can get."

Those are new pleated slacks he's wearing, she thinks. His dress shirt is new too, buttoned up to just below his Adam's apple, the veins is his neck about to pop. The same shoes, except polished now. See your reflection in them. She pushes in the till and then runs a little receipt paper through. Tears off the top and tosses it in the garbage near her feet.

"Put a new roll in not ten minutes ago."

"Oh," she says. "Thanks."

"You're welcome."

He takes another step towards her, his lower half pressed against the counter. "There's coffee downstairs."

"Had some already."

"Oh. Well, you know where to find it if you change your mind."

She nods.

He just stands there.

Jutting her chin towards the store's entrance, she says, "You going to open?"

"In a minute."

Emily nods, then reaches towards the magazine rack for a *Newfoundland Herald.*

Terry rushes over and grabs one before she gets the chance. He hands it to her.

"Thanks." Emily rests her bum against the cash register and opens the magazine. Searches through the table of contents for something interesting. There's an article on page forty-eight: "The New Province of Newfoundland, Labrador, and Fort McMurray," the caption says. She flips through until she finds the page.

Terry's still standing there.

"You just going to watch?" she says.

He takes his hands out of his pockets only to put them back in again.

She closes the magazine. Pushes her pelvis forward so that she's standing at full height. Moves closer to him. "Something the matter?"

"Why do you ask?"

"I don't know. You're acting strange."

Terry shrugs. Fumbles with the loose change in his pockets. "It's nothing."

"Tell me," she says.

He doesn't.

"Tell *me.*"

He releases a breath. "Okay, but you don't have to worry, you're still a hundred times the worker that Heather is."

"Oh my God; what did I do?"

"No big deal – "

"Tell me."

He hesitates, then says, "You left without cashing out yesterday."

She doesn't say anything.

"The till was left on the counter with all the money in it."

Still she doesn't speak.

"No biggie. Who's going to steal it around here, right?"

She goes back to yesterday in her mind. Ten customers the whole day. Maybe less. Donna Rowe with her two young ones; and Peggy Flynn with the dirty hair; Reverend Parsons, his basket loaded with Vachon Cakes and Canada Dry (To mix with his whiskey, no doubt);

Alan Cross's pretty wife, Marlene with the dimples and nice figure. Emily can even remember the clothes they wore, so why can't she remember leaving out the money?

Terry swallows so hard it's a wonder he doesn't snap the top buttons of his shirt. "It's not the first time."

She pauses, waits for him to go on.

"Monday of last week it was."

She lays her palms on the checkout counter to keep herself upright. Breathes deeply, right down to her toes. Exhales, then says, "Why didn't you mention it *then*?"

"Because you'd never done it before. And who doesn't make a mistake every now and then, right?" He takes his hands out of his pockets and rests them on his hips. "Sure, not that long ago, I closed up without shutting off the lights."

It's the tiredness, she thinks. The worry. The weeks – since she's decided to go for good – of pretending everything's perfect. *Weeks? Years* more like it. Her *whole life*.

Terry's saying something, but she has to ask him to repeat it.

"No harm done, I said."

Emily looks past his shoulder towards the door and can swear Kent's standing there with his face pressed against the glass, fogging up the window with his breath.

"Emily?"

She can't turn her face away.

"Emily?"

Finally she's able to. Looks down at her hands, wondering when it was that Terry had placed one of his over top. She lifts her chin to meet his gaze. "What?"

"You're so pale."

She slips her hands out. "Who isn't in this place?"

"You look beat."

"You try raising two youngsters."

"Perhaps you should take the day off?"

"I'm fine."

"Are you sure?"

"Open the store, Terry."

They're silent for a moment.

He walks around the cash, intending, she thinks, to join her in the cramped space behind it. She sticks out her palm. "That's far enough."

Terry stops.

"We're right in front of the window," she says.

He looks to it, then back at her.

She imagines Kent's fists. Those empty eyes.

Terry goes to the front door and inserts the key and turns the deadbolt. Flips the sign around to Open. Turns back to face her. "You sure everything's all right?"

She nods.

Another silence. Then Terry says, "You're not just any employee, you know."

She doesn't say anything.

"Not to me."

She holds his gaze for a moment, then picks her *Newfoundland Herald* back up. Opens it and pretends to read. When she turns back to look, Terry's gone.

5

EMILY AND HEATHER ARE SITTING on overturned milk crates behind Hodder's Grocery and Convenience. An Orange Crush with a lipstick-stained straw is pressed between Heather's thighs. Emily's leaning back, her face tilted towards the midday sun, wondering how Jeremy will react once he finds out his father won't be coming with them this Friday. He'd always been closer to Kent, even as an infant. She'd spend hours trying to coax her sore nipples into his mouth while he screeched. It was only when Kent would come home and lift him into his arms that the tears would stop.

"I wish there was something stronger in this," Heather says. She takes a draw before handing the cigarette over to Emily. "Anything to get me through this shit day."

Emily grabs it and then takes her own puff.

"How does he even stay in business? There's hardly been a soul in the place all week."

"Be worse after the layoffs," Emily says, throwing the smoke to the gravel before dabbing it with the toe of her sneaker. "If people start moving away."

Heather sucks on her straw, then says, "Better off sinking this shit-hole town into the bay."

Emily imagines herself standing on some other shore, watching as the last of Lightning Cove sinks beneath the ocean: the cross atop of St. Paul's; the dome of the parish hall where, by now, the layoffs have already been announced; the last of the jagged rock peppered along the hill behind Jeremy and Lynette's school. She sees Kent's face slip beneath the water too. Him along with this life she's been living.

"We should get back, break's over." She goes to stand up, but Heather reaches out and grabs her wrist.

"Place won't fall apart if we take a few more minutes."

She sits back, wishing she were less tentative, braver, like her younger co-worker. Might have left Kent ages ago if she were, she thinks.

"Terry's probably got his chubby hand wrapped around his stop-watch by now wondering why we're not back at our tills." Heather squeezes the now-empty Crush can, throwing it into the bin beside the back door.

"He's okay."

"Never said he wasn't, just anal is all."

In the silence, the young woman jams the ball of her tongue ring into the space between her front teeth.

Emily points to her own tongue. "It hurt getting that?"

Heather shakes her head. "The guys love it."

"How do you mean?"

A grin lifts one corner of Heather's lips. "Are you serious?"

"What?"

"You don't know?"

Emily shakes her head. "Know what?"

Heather simulates giving a blowjob.

Emily watches for second. "Oh."

"Apparently the stud feels good against the head of the guy's dick."

She nods slowly but doesn't say a word.

"The last guy I did it to made such a racket I thought his bag caught fire or something."

There's a second of dead air before the laughter comes. Emily bends forward, her hands pressed against her stomach. There's the fight to try and breathe then, tears running down their cheeks, feet pounding the ground. Finally, when it seems like they've gotten themselves back under control, Heather adds, "The best twelve seconds of his life." This sends them into fits again, stomachs burning, tight jaws, hands gripping upper thighs.

After the second bout of laughter recedes, and they've caught their breath, Emily says, "Perhaps *I* ought to get one."

Heather looks across at her. "Your hubby could use it, that's for sure."

"What's that mean?"

"Oh come on, he's that wound up I'm surprised he hasn't given himself an aneurysm or something."

Emily looks away. After a moment, she says, "It's the plant business. All those people getting laid off and him not being able to do anything about it."

"Yeah, well, nothing lasts forever, right?"

Tell-it-like-it-is Heather, she thinks. Younger than herself by six years and yet she already knows so much more. Perhaps it has something to do with Heather being in a rock band, Emily thinks, having the freedom to hop in a van and take to the open road and play in nightclubs and Lion's Club halls in every little town from here to St. John's. Standing centre stage with all eyes on you and all ears open to the sound of your voice as it's amplified through thick black speakers.

Emily tries to remember the last time she went anywhere. If not for work, and walking the kids to school, she thinks she'd never leave the house.

The sound of her name snatches her from her thoughts. "What?"

"Where'd you go?"

"Hmm?"

"I said your name three times."

"Did you?"

"Yeah."

"I'm a bit out of it, I think. Barely slept last night."

"Me neither." Heather smiles.

"What did you want?"

"I was wondering if we could do a shift-swap."

"When?"

"You take my Friday and I'll take your Saturday – "

"Can't. "

"The manager of the bar we played in last night booked us for another show – What? You can't? Is that what you said?"

Emily doesn't answer.

"What's the matter?"

"Nothing. I'd switch with you if I could, but I can't this Friday, that's all. Sorry."

In the silence they both slant their faces towards the sky, the gathering breeze against their young skin, the sun warming the tops of closed eyelids, their noses alive, finally, to the smells of spring – black earth and grass and dog shit and the sea.

A car with a dying muffler roars past. A distant shout from a mother beckons a playing son in for lunch. A dog barks, then stops. Barks again.

"Why don't you eat?" Heather says.

Emily looks at her. "I do."

"Really? When was the last time I've seen you eat something?"

"Come inside then and you can watch me eat a bag of ketchup chips."

"Just tell me that you don't have an eating disorder."

"What?"

"You heard me."

She can't help but laugh as she gets to her feet. "We should go back in."

"It's not funny. An old drummer friend of mine used to be into that shit and she almost died. Eighty fuckin' pounds she was."

Emily sits back down. "I don't have an eating disorder."

"Explain all the weight you've been losing then."

"A few pounds, that's all." Closer to ten, she knows. Worry weight. Nearly 130 three months ago. "I haven't had much of an appetite lately."

"Swear to God?"

"Swear to God." She takes Heather's wrist and pulls her to her feet.

They walk towards the back door.

"I should have you over to my place for supper some time," Heather says. "Mom'll put five pounds back on you with all the butter she uses."

Emily pulls open the door, stepping aside to let Heather pass before going in herself.

6

SHE CAN'T GET THE NEEDLE INTO THE FABRIC. She gets up from the kitchen table and goes over to the stove, flicking on the light above it. Tries again. Still can't get the needle through. It's her hands; they're shaking. "Goddamn it," she says, throwing the cross-stitch onto the floor. "Goddamn this." She jams her hands inside her pockets to steady them. Fights the urge to cry. Not too long ago, she could finish a decent sized one in two or three nights. How long now has she been working on this one, she wonders? Two weeks? Three? And this one simpler too than the others.

A deep breath in before she reaches down and picks it up, then goes back over and sits again at the kitchen table. She lays the cross-stitch down in front of her. All that's done is part of the log cabin and the hill beyond it. There's still the sea and the sky and silhouetted birds flying in front of a reddish sun to finish.

She imagines herself behind the cabin's walls; her children, in light sweaters, running through the fields in back, their echoing laughter, a fire in the wood stove and a cup of tea on her lap. Then the children coming in, their heavy breathing and red faces. "Come sit with me," she hears herself saying, "I'll read to you." They doze as she reads, the smell of earth and sea on them. She imagines herself looking to the door, expecting him to burst through, looking for a place to unload his torment. But not even Kent can find her here.

The sound of Kent's tires in the driveway make her jump. Between the heavy wheels on the crushed rock and the idling and then shutting off of the truck's engine, she manages to grab his macaroni and cheese from the oven and put it on the table. By the time she hears the slamming of the driver's side door, she's already removed the tinfoil and fetched him the ketchup and a Canadian from the fridge. She fills a tumbler with water as his steps travel up the stairs and then along the porch. Water spills over the edges of the glass and onto the hardwood floor as she carries it to the table. She lays it down just as she hears him grip the doorknob. A cool breeze from outside rushes in and brushes against her face when he pushes it open. She's there at the entrance of the foyer when he steps inside.

"You're so late," she says. It's too dark to see his face.

He kicks off his shoes and pushes by her. Not bothering to take off his jacket, he goes straight for the bottle of beer. With his back to her, he twists the cap and then takes a gulp.

There's a tingle in her stomach, numbness on the soles of her feet. She moves towards him, slowly. "Are you all right?"

He slams the bottle on the table, freezing her in midstride, then turns in her direction.

She notices an open gash above his right eye, blood trickling from the wound.

When did her hands go up to her mouth, she wonders? "Oh my God! What happened?" She's unable to move. Wonders if she ever will again.

Kent touches the cut with a few fingers, covering the tips with fresh blood, then lowers them to take a look. He wipes the mess on his good pants. "Everything I've done for them and this is the thanks I get."

She can barely make out his words.

Between his open jacket, she notices a tear along the neck of his cashmere sweater, and three red lines just below his Adam's apple. Nail marks, she thinks.

He pulls out a chair but doesn't sit in it, makes to grab his beer again but doesn't pick it up.

"Let me wash it," she whispers.

He doesn't say anything.

She *is* able to move after all, slipping past him like a stranger, through the kitchen and down the hall. Each creak of the floor, each crack of ankle or knee, or wind against the windowpanes, or her own breath, she hears as if for the first time.

A door opens. She turns, knows who it is despite the dark. "Go back to bed."

"Daddy home?"

"Yes. Now go back to bed."

"I want to see him."

She's able to grab her daughter's shoulder before Lynette has a chance to move towards the kitchen. How familiar her tiny body is, Emily thinks, every toe and finger, every scratch and bruise she knows as if they were her own.

She drops to her knees and turns Lynette around so that she's facing her. "Remember how sometimes Daddy needs to be by himself?"

25

Her face is in shadow, yet Emily sees her nodding.

"This is one of those times, sweetie."

"But –"

"I'll tell Daddy to come and wake you first thing in the morning. How's that?"

"But I want to see him now –"

"No!" Emily shakes her, then picks her up and carries her back to bed. She pulls the covers up to just below her daughter's neck. Goes to kiss her cheek and tastes salt on her lips. These are the times she hates him most, when she has to grab and shout to protect them. "I'm sorry, baby. Mommy didn't mean it." She wipes the tears from Lynette's face, then swipes at one of her own. "Give me a hug."

Lynette does.

"I love you."

"Love you, too."

* * *

HE'S PACING THE KITCHEN WHEN SHE COMES BACK IN, his face pointed towards the floor, mumbling to himself, oblivious to her.

She stands at the threshold, watching him, Polysporin and a wet cloth in her hand. Never before has she seen him this way, unraveled. She moves to the table and slides out a chair, her free hand resting on its back. "Please sit."

He stops pacing and looks over at her, surprised to find someone else in the room.

"Won't you?" She moves around to the side of the chair.

He approaches. There's a dried rivulet of blood all the way down to his chin. The chair's wood groans under the weight of him as he drops onto it.

Using the damp cloth, she wipes away the blood on his chin, along his cheek, and to the place above his eye. The wound is deeper than she'd expected. "This'll need stitches."

"No."

He doesn't even flinch when she presses the cloth directly onto the exposed flesh. An inch lower, she thinks, and he'd have lost his eye.

She crouches between his parted legs and, in silence, washes and then applies a thick coating of Polysporin. How stale his breath is, like sickness, against her face. His forehead slick with sweat despite the

26

coolness of the room. The trousers she'd given him last Father's Day covered in dirt.

On her haunches now, a palm on each of his knees, she surveys her work. Blood still trickles from the cut's corners. "You *need* stitches –"

"No, I said."

She takes her hands away from his legs. "I'll get some Band-aids."

Returning, she finds him leaning forward in his chair with his face in his hands. A long time passes before she says, "Tell me what happened." She takes several steps towards him.

He doesn't move.

"Please."

More silence passes until, finally, he lifts his face to look at her, half of him in shadow. "On the hall steps they were, calling me down to the dirt." His voice is low and gravelly, almost parched.

She comes closer, so if she'd wanted, she could reach out and touch him. "Who?"

"Them from the plant. Who do you think? 'I'm not the one who stole your Jesus jobs,' I said."

How many meetings in St. John's had he gone to in order to get them better wages, she wonders? And a full year maternity leave instead of the six months? How many times had he taken from his own pocket to help someone who'd just been laid off? Groceries for one, a light bill for another. Sure, hadn't he paid half of Carl Rideout's mortgage last year? "You can't provide for them all," she'd had to say to him.

"The St. John's crowd got out through the back, so then they turned on me. 'Boys, it's *me!*' I said. An empty Pepsi bottle hit me then." Kent points to the still bleeding spot above his eye. "Knocked me right off my feet. I had too many demands, they said. Can you believe that? 'I asked for what I thought you deserved,' I said. Some grabbed hold of my hair then. That's when Myles Baker and Tom Bennet and a few others broke it up. 'That's enough,' Myles said."

He sits back on his chair, letting his breath out slowly, like an old person.

She takes the Band-aids out of their wrappers and sticks them length-wise along the seam of the wound, then sits close to him.

After a time, he says, "This place is finished."

She reaches out to him, from that place inside of her that cannot bear to watch him suffer. *Still.*

His hand meets hers halfway, covering it like a second skin, resting them on his lower thigh.

How well she knows this hand, she thinks: its large knuckles; its fingers, so accustomed to work; the fat vein on the back that she's traced a thousand times with her forefinger; the perfectly clipped nails.

"Try and eat something," she says finally, indicating the cooling plate of macaroni and cheese with a thrust of her chin.

"How?" He turns his face towards the window despite there being only blackness. "How can I?" With his free hand he wipes beneath each eye.

The last time she'd seem him cry was just after Jeremy was born. He couldn't look at her then either.

It seems like a long time before he's able to meet her gaze. He lets go of her hand and gets to his feet.

She does too. She smells the earth and sweat and his deodorant, feels his fingers running through her hair.

"I love you," he whispers.

"I love you," she says.

He holds her for a long time. Then says, "I'm off to bed. Coming?"

"Not yet."

"All right."

She watches him move along the kitchen. At the threshold of the hall, he turns back to her. "Snuggle up to me when you come?"

"I will," she says.

7

SHE CARRIES THE CORDLESS PHONE through the kitchen and into the foyer. Doesn't bother putting on her shoes as she grips the handle of the front door and pushes it open, looking back over her shoulder as she does. She steps out onto the porch and eases the door shut.

The night is cold. Goosebumps on her bare arms, her breath like smoke. She turns back towards the door, thinking she can see his silhouette within its frame, but when she turns away and looks back, he's gone.

She enters the number, then puts the phone to her ear. One ring goes through, then another. She swallows during the third ring, chews the inside of her cheek as the fourth and fifth come and go. On the sixth she goes to hang up, but then she hears a voice. She brings the phone back to her ear. "Hello?"

"Hello?"

"Jackie?"

"Who's this?"

"It's me, Emily." She realizes that she's speaking loud enough to wake the whole house.

"Oh, Emily. Hi."

She turns again in the direction of the door. "Can you talk?" This time she's whispering.

"Yes."

"Okay."

Jackie pauses, then says, "It's late there."

Emily glances at her watch, realizing it's almost midnight. "What time's it in Vancouver?"

"Nearly 7:30."

"I keep forgetting it's such a big difference – "

"You sound far away."

"What?"

"You sound far away. Must be something wrong with the connection."

Her eyes still on the front door. "I'll speak up." She moves to the stairs and walks down a few, but then static's on the line, so she has to go back to where she was.

Jackie says something, but she misses it.

"I didn't hear you," Emily says.

"No, I was talking to Stephen."

"Oh."

"He wanted to know how many cranberries to put on the salad."

"You're eating? I'll call back."

"No, we're not. Not yet. The chicken's nowhere near to done. How many times have I told him to defrost before baking? But you know, in one ear out the other, right?"

Emily tries to imagine Kent stuffing a chicken, then sliding it into the oven to bake. Basting it halfway through. Sprinkling cranberries on a leafy salad.

"So?" Jackie says at last. "When are you coming?"

She cups her hand over her mouth and the receiver. Stares so hard at the door that she's likely to burn a hole through it. She breathes in. "Friday." Exhales.

Jackie doesn't say anything.

"It's short notice, I know."

"That's like, four days."

"I would have called sooner, but I was trying to find somewhere else to stay. You know, so we wouldn't be in your way, but everything was so expensive. Even the shitty places."

"Vancouver's not Lightning Cove."

The bathroom light comes on. She nearly drops the phone. "I might need to call you back."

"What's wrong?"

"Nothing." She takes the phone away from her ear and waits, her thumb hovering over the 'end' button.

"Emily?"

The faint sound of the toilet flushing, then the light going out. She looks to the front door expecting him to walk through it.

Jackie's voice then, as if coming from a dream. "Emily? You still there?"

She waits. Listens for his footsteps, but he doesn't come to the door.

Probably wasn't Kent at all. One of the children instead. Jeremy most likely, all that bloody Dr. Pepper he drinks. She puts the phone back to her ear. "Jackie?"

"Yeah."

"Sorry. Thought I heard one of the children crying."

"Oh."

In the silence, she thinks about cutting the call short and forgetting she'd ever bothered her old high school friend in the first place. She imagines going back inside and putting the phone back in its cradle and walking down the hall to their bedroom and slipping underneath the covers beside him and forgetting the whole Jesus thing.

Jackie's saying something.

"What?" she says.

"I said, I'm sorry. I was just surprised to hear that you're coming so soon."

"Don't be sorry. It was stupid of me to suggest we stay there – "

"It *wasn't* stupid, and I want you to come. We both do."

She sees herself and her youngsters asleep on the living room floor of Jackie's condo. Stephen having to tiptoe over them in the morning. "No, it was a bad idea."

"Look, just come. We'll figure out the rest later."

Emily says nothing.

"You can't stay *there*," Jackie says. "Not with Kent the way he is." Then, "I'm still in shock to tell you the truth. Just can't believe it."

Sometimes *Emily* can't believe it. Happening to someone else.

"Hold on a sec, Stephen's saying something."

She waits. Tries to pick out what Jackie's husband is saying, but can't.

Jackie comes back to the phone. "Stephen says he knows lots of people here. Might be able to find you a sublet or something."

"Really? That would be wonderful. Thank him for me."

Jackie does, then says to Emily, "He says you're welcome."

Silence for a moment.

"What time on Friday? We'll pick you up at the airport."

"No, I'll grab a taxi or something. Is there a bus?"

"Emily, we'll come and get you. It's no trouble. We actually live quite close to the airport."

She pauses briefly, then says, "Okay. Seven-thirty. In the evening."

"Let me just write that down. And what airline?"

"Air Canada."

"Air Canada. Alright, got it."

Neither woman speaks for a moment, then Emily says, "I should get off the phone now."

"Hold on."

"What?"

It seems like ages waiting for her friend to speak. Finally, Jackie says, "He'll want to know where his kids are, won't he? Eventually."

Again she thinks about hanging up. Hanging up, and then tossing the phone into the yard.

"Have you thought about that?" Jackie says.

No. In fact, it just occurred to me that second when you mentioned it. She's lost nights thinking about it. Whole afternoons. Days. "I have, yes."

Quiet for a minute.

"And?"

"And," Emily whispers, "you're only aiding and abetting if you're complicit in it, which you're not, right?"

Silence on her friend's end.

"I mean, as far as you and Stephen are concerned, I'm just coming out for a little visit. To take in the sights, right? A drive up to Whistler, a ferry across to Victoria, maybe."

"My God, I didn't even consider that," Jackie says. Then, "No, I was thinking about you. About Kent calling the cops or something. Having you arrested."

"Arrested for taking my own kids."

"They're his too though, right?"

Emily doesn't say anything.

"I know you're doing what you think is best," Jackie says. "I'd just hate for you to get into trouble, that's all –"

"I'm scared, Jackie."

"What?"

"I said I'm scared."

"I know."

"No you don't. I'm sorry, but you don't."

Jackie stays quiet.

"It's different now."

Jackie's breathing, then her saying, "What's different?"

"I don't know. Him, I guess. He's different. What he's capable of is different."

"And what's he capable of, Emily? You've never really said."

She goes to speak, but stops herself. Breathes, then tries again, "So much that I'm willing to risk anything to get away. To just get away."

Neither woman speaks for a long time.

Finally, Jackie says, "Okay, see you Friday."

"Alright." Then, "I really should hang up."

"Okay. Jesus, please be careful."

"I will. Thanks, Jackie."

8

SHE GLANCES UP AT THE WALL CLOCK. Past one but she isn't sleepy. Exhausted maybe, but not sleepy. Hard to imagine there was a time she didn't know the difference.

She sits back, letting the chair take her weight, savouring the silence. So still she sits. Closes her eyes. Opens them a minute later to realize it's not completely quiet after all. Faintly, from all the way down the hall, and despite their closed bedroom door, she can hear his deep breathing, it somehow reminding her not to enjoy the moment too much.

Getting to her feet takes more effort than she expects, leaving her slightly dizzy. After it passes, she moves along the kitchen and down the hall to Jeremy's room. Inches the door open slightly, just enough to fit her head through. He's on his back, his *Simpson's* pajama shirt hiked up to just below his chest, exposing soft, unblemished skin. Red cheeks and hair damp from sweat. Beside him, lying scattered, are PlayStation games: *Mortal Kombat II, NHL Hockey,* others she can't make out the titles of. The remote control still in his fist and the television left on. She tiptoes over and shuts it off. Slips the remote out of his hand and lays it on his dresser beside the picture of him and Kent, taken last year when they'd gone fishing, each of them holding a trout by its gills. Could their smiles be any wider? Hats on backwards, and hip rubbers. The lake behind them and the sun beaming down. Father and son. She wonders how she'll stop Jeremy from telling Kent where they are. Nothing at all for him to pick up the phone. "Vancouver, Dad," she imagines him whispering late at night from Jackie's living room. "*Vancouver!*" Kent goes. "Yeah, you know, the *Canucks.*"

Just get him away first, she thinks. Work the rest out later.

Lynette's curled into a ball when she pushes open the door, her stuffed giraffe pressed against her cheek and her night light casting her body in a pinkish-red glow. Mouth slightly open and the tip of her tongue resting on her bottom lip. If not for the steady rise and fall of the sheets above her, she'd wonder if her daughter was breathing at all. An angel sleeping. Before leaving, she walks over

34

and pulls the comforter up to just below Lynette's chin, then kisses her forehead.

Back in the kitchen, she grabs a small pot from a cupboard, fills it with 2% milk and puts it on the stove. In a drawer beneath the cutlery, she grabs the same wooden spoon she always uses – its tip blackened from overuse – and dips it in, stirring absent-mindedly, envisioning all those angry plant workers, their hands all over her husband, pulling and grabbing. Curses loud in his ear. How often had she wished for this very thing? So he might know a little of what it feels like to be her. Someone's hand slapping his face, or him forced onto the ground, palms pressed against the back of his head. How strange then, now that it's actually happened, not to feel the slightest vindication.

The milk bubbling over the sides of the pot brings her back. She takes it off the element, the smell of burnt milk filling her nostrils. How did she not notice? Not hear the sound of it boiling? No point drinking it now.

She pours it down the sink. The bottom of the pot is charred black, so she drops in a little dish liquid and fills it with hot water, deciding to let it soak overnight.

Instead of going to bed after switching off the stove light, she goes to the window over the kitchen table. Peers out into the night, wondering if the sky will be the same out west. Will the moon be brighter or duller? The stars more plentiful or fewer? Will she still be able to smell salt on her clothes after coming in from outside like she can here?

She knows that, while she longs to go, a part of her is frightened, too. That's why, lately, she can't stop her hands from trembling, why at night, despite being bundled under heavy blankets, she can't get warm.

Suddenly feeling short of breath, she slides open the window, sucking at the night air, imagining that it's the Pacific instead of the Atlantic she's hearing. Imagines too being woken by the birds outside her window instead of by Kent's weight on top of her, his hot lips and coffee breath, his fingers through her hair.

She shuts the window and walks through the kitchen and down the hall. She opens their bedroom door and goes in, so light on her feet she feels weightless, like a ghost.

He's curled in a ball, his hands cupped and jammed between his thighs like a little boy. She'd often found him beautiful this way.

She moves toward him. Stops near the bed. It's hard to believe the things he's done. Every now and again she'll wake and think it's all been a dream and, for a moment, will feel such relief. But then the truth will settle over her like snow, and she'll wish for the years back. To start again.

She pulls the sheets over him before sliding in herself. Rests her head on her right palm. Stares at the still ceiling fan. *And what's he capable of, Emily?* Jackie had asked earlier. *You've never really said.* For a moment, during that conversation, she thought she might tell her friend about the last time she took the kids. How Kent, after realizing she'd gone, had shown up at her parents' place. How he stood in her father's kitchen and promised never to lay a finger on her again, how he shook her dad's hand, and kissed her mother on both cheeks, and how later, as they leaned against the rail of the ferry waving goodbye to her parents, he'd bent down and whispered in her ear, his breath melting her eardrum. "If you ever take my kids away again, I'll kill you." Her heart had almost stopped. Then the boat started to drift away from the dock, and her mom and dad started walking back to their car.

She turns over onto her side.

And what's he capable of, Emily? You've never really said.

Before slipping into sleep, she imagines a new answer to Jackie's question. *Killing me. That's what.*

TUESDAY

SHE WAKES TO THE SOUND OF WIND and rain against the window. Although her eyes are encrusted with sleep, she doesn't feel rested. Every joint and ligament aches. She's running a fever, she thinks. It hurts to swallow. The pounding inside her skull is relentless.

The only remnants of Kent are wrinkled sheets and dried blood on his pillow. All last night he had slept with his arm around her and his face pressed between her shoulder blades, his scalding breath burning a hole in her back. Half the night she had to put up with his mumbling, his jerking limbs. Twice his knee had come up and hit hard against the back of her legs. Another time, the arm draped over her had smacked against her forehead. She'd rammed her bum against him then in frustration.

No parting kiss again this morning, she realizes. It occurs to her too, that, for the first time in ages, she's slept through his engine revving and horn blasts.

She reaches across Kent's side of the bed and twists the clock around. 7:30. How could she have slept through the alarm as loud as it is? She turns over on her back, willing the energy to get up. She kicks off the sheets, and sits on the edge of the bed. They'll have to walk tightly together this morning, she thinks, seeing as there's only one umbrella. Jeremy will love that.

She slips her feet into her slippers and stands up, then waits for the dizziness to pass.

The clouds outside her bedroom window are a fat purplish grey and so burdened with moisture they look as if they might fall from the sky and wash away the whole town. She welcomes the thought.

Is that coffee she smells? Probably left over from what Kent had brewed.

Despite her fever, she's shivering. Definitely a cold, she thinks. As if she doesn't have enough to worry about. On a hook behind her closet door, she grabs her robe and puts it on, tying the knot tightly around her waist. Walks to the bedroom door and pushes it open.

Out in the hall she thinks she smells bacon. Perhaps Kent had wanted something different from baloney for a change.

In the bathroom, she resists the urge to look in the mirror on her way to the toilet. She sits slowly. The porcelain is cold against her backside. Elbows on her knees and her chin cupped in her hands.

Although she's finished, she stays sitting, wishing she could skip this day and move on to Wednesday. Better yet, to Friday. Get it over with. She imagines her cushioned Air Canada seat, its back reclined, and a book in her lap. Jeremy on her right; Lynette, her left. Their table trays down with glasses of Coke sitting on top, the light through the plane's windows reflecting in the ice cubes.

She grips the edges of the toilet bowl, like someone arthritic, and gets to her feet. She can't stop herself from looking in the mirror as she lathers her hands with soap. It wasn't so long ago, she thinks, that she saw herself as pretty. Not someone who could turn heads or anything, but attractive all the same. She could do a lot worse than her tiny nose with the curved tip, and the wide cheekbones, the slightly crooked teeth, and the far-set eyes. Even the two noticeable veins converging in the middle of her forehead, and her largish ears have never really bothered her.

There's nothing desirable about her now, she thinks, rinsing the soap from her hands. Dark bags under tired eyes, and pasty skin that used to be golden. Sunken cheeks too.

She dries her hands and makes her way to the kitchen. There's the sound of utensils banging against bowls and plates now, and scattering feet. Jeremy, she notices, is not in his bed when she opens his door. Nor is Lynette. "What are you two up to in there?" she says, quickening her pace.

She isn't prepared for what she sees when she emerges from the hall: Kent's at the stove, a spatula in his hand and his back to her; Jeremy's beside him, standing on a stool and stirring what she thinks are eggs. The shuffling of feet, she realizes, is Lynette, busy setting the breakfast table.

"What's all this?"

Lynette pulls out a chair. "Sit here, Mommy."

"You're not at work."

Kent turns to her. "The ship will stay afloat a few minutes without me."

"Mommy, *sit*," Lynette says again.

She goes over and sits down.

"I'm making scrambled eggs," Jeremy says.

"Wow."

Lynette pours her some orange juice.

"Careful not to spill, baby," Emily says.

"I won't."

"There's fresh coffee," Kent says.

"Juice is fine."

Kent scoops a pancake out of the frying pan and lays it on top of an already piled plate. "I'm ready for the eggs."

Jeremy lifts the bowl and pours.

"You want to make them?" Kent says.

"Can I?"

"Sure can. Mind not to burn them."

"Okay."

He comes over. Bends down and kisses her on the lips. "Good morning." The bandages she'd put on his cut last night are still there.

"How is it?" she says.

"Needs stitches."

"You don't say."

"I'll stop at the clinic on my way to work."

He pulls out a chair and sits beside her.

Lynette fills his glass too.

"Some waitress, you are," Kent says.

"Daddy fell getting out of the truck."

"I know, sweetheart," Emily says. She sips her juice, glancing at him over the lip of the glass. They're silent for a while after she puts it down. Finally, she says, "You seem happy."

"Why shouldn't I be?"

"After last night."

"The bruises'll heal. So will their tempers." He takes a sip of his own juice. "If not yesterday, the layoffs would have happened eventually. It's the same all over the island. Why do you think so many are off in Alberta?" He turns to Jeremy. "How are those eggs?"

"Almost done."

He looks back at her. "It was a losing battle. I did my best." He hesitates for a moment, then says, "Thanks for taking care of me."

She tries to remember the last time he'd thanked her. Or made her breakfast. Her whole life has been about pleasing *him*, she realizes. Dinner on the table when he walks in the door, his clothes ironed and folded, her parted legs whenever he's in the mood. It's all been for him. Everything. *Son of a bitch.* "You're welcome."

"They're ready," Jeremy says. He scoops them onto a plate and brings them over, a big smile on his face.

"Wow, honey, they look wonderful," Emily says. "Sit down now, sweetie," she says to Lynette who's in the process of transforming the last of the napkins into a swan.

Everyone, with the exception of Emily, grabs at buttered toast, pancakes and bacon.

In the middle of plopping eggs on his plate, Kent says, "Aren't you hungry?"

"I'm sorry. You all went to so much trouble."

"What's wrong?" Kent returns the spoon to the scrambled eggs.

"Bit of the flu, I think."

He reaches out and feels her forehead. "A bit! You're burning up."

She leans back.

"No work for you today."

"I have to."

"Why?"

"Because it's inventory, and Terry trusts no one else but me to do it."

"Let him do it himself."

"He's got the store to run."

"I'll call him and tell him you're sick – "

"No – don't. Look, I'll get some Tylenol Cold and Flu and some Halls at work. If I'm still feeling bad after that, then I'll come home."

Kent stares at her for a minute. "More than I'd do for ten dollars an hour."

She takes a sip of her juice. Puts the glass back down.

"It's not like you need the money."

She thinks of the old Adidas sock stuffed with bills underneath the floor panel in the basement. "It gets me out."

Kent puts a piece of bacon in his mouth. Chews. "You can go out whenever you want."

She looks down at her hands. "Perhaps I like making my own money."

He laughs despite his mouth being full. "Get a paper route. Outside all you want then, and more money at the end of the week too."

She raises her glass again. Gulps till it's gone.

"More, Mom?" Lynette asks.

She shakes her head.

His stare stays on her for a long time before he goes back to his food. "You should try and eat something."

Trapped within the sounds of clicking jaws, slurping, fork prongs scraping along plates, and Lynette's soft humming accompanying her own chews, Emily manages to swallow a few bites of pancake and egg – her stomach clenching in protest. Jeremy is there to eat what she can't, dumping what's on her plate onto his own like a starved orphan.

"I'll drive you this morning," Kent says, after having ordered the children to their rooms to get ready for school.

"You should get to work. We can walk."

"In the rain?"

"It does me good."

"You want to catch pneumonia too?"

She doesn't answer.

"I'm driving you and that's that."

2

EVEN WITH THE WIPERS ON TOP SPEED it's still hard to see straight ahead. He's got the heat on blast to stop the windshield from steaming up. She thinks she'll suffocate.

The radio's on low – Willie Nelson's, "Mammas Don't Let Your Babies Grow Up To Be Cowboys."

Jeremy and Lynette are in the back seat, both staring out their windows.

"The town's going to flood," Jeremy says.

"Will it, Mommy?" Lynette asks.

Emily turns around to face her daughter. "No, sweetheart. It'll stop before too long."

"Bet we all drown," Jeremy says.

"Mom!"

"Ignore him, baby, he's just teasing."

Kent reaches across the seat and takes Emily's hand. "And you wanted to walk in this."

He puts the truck in park just outside the main doors of the school. A few other vehicles are parked too, wipers and hazard lights going. Little children – raincoats of green and yellow and orange – hop out and start running, water splashing around their rubbers with each step. The girls are screaming, the boys laughing.

Emily makes to open her door, but Kent stops her by squeezing her hand. "I'll take them," he says.

She leans over the seat and kisses Lynette. Jeremy doesn't want one, but Kent makes him. She reaches down and grabs the umbrella between her feet, handing it to her husband.

"On the count of three," Kent says, popping the umbrella open.

"That's bad luck," Jeremy says.

Lynette's worried now that they'll all be struck by lightning.

On three, Kent flings open the door like it's made of paper, and moves to open the back one. He swoops Lynette into his arms, then waits for Jeremy to hop out and join them. He sprints to the entrance, Jeremy running at his thigh, Lynette pressed against his torso and jiggling like a rag doll. They're getting soaked despite the umbrella over them. It almost seems to be raining from the ground up. They're all laughing.

Just inside the glass doors, she watches him put Lynette down and kiss her, then offer Jeremy his hand to shake. Jeremy puts his whole shoulder into it.

How long before Lynette and Jeremy stop hating her for taking them away, she wonders? Or will they ever? She imagines them grown and not answering her phone calls. Holidays spent alone. Dusty pictures in an old photo album.

Mavis Callback, the principal, is standing there directing water-logged children to their respective lockers and homerooms. Something Kent says makes her throw her head back in laughter and then rest a hand on his shoulder. He laughs too, covering the older woman's hand with one of his own.

Still the charmer, Emily thinks. The boyish smile and mischievous wink. His way of standing right in front of you, his body slightly forward at the waist, his thumb and forefinger clasped around his chin, his eyes right on you as if nothing in the world were more important than your words. Who else but him to run the union? Who else but him to sway the people? Could turn a mother against her own son, he could. A father against his daughter. The ultimate actor, Kent is. Two selves. The one he presents to the world, and the one he is at home.

The sound of him opening the driver's door brings her back. His trousers are soaked. "Jeremy might be right," he says, throwing the umbrella in the back seat, "perhaps we *will* all drown." He runs a hand through his damp hair. Turns the ignition and pumps the gas. "You're sure you want to go into work?"

She nods.

He pulls away from the curb.

Will she forget the cuts and bruises over time, she wonders? The finger marks on her throat hidden beneath turtlenecks; the swollen eyes made less obvious with makeup and wide-rimmed sunglasses; the bald patches where he'd yanked out her hair covered by woolen toques and baseball hats; the limps caused by charley horses made less noticeable by sitting more, calling in sick for work? How about the ruptured kidney from when he'd thrown her down the basement stairs? "I tripped," she'd said when they asked. "One of the children's toys, I think. I said, I tripped. Thank God Kent was there." The whole time him seated next to her hospital bed, his hands covering the one of hers she'd allowed outside the blanket.

45

* * *

THERE'S A REPRIEVE IN THE RAIN by the time Kent pulls the truck up to the main entrance of Hodder's Grocery and Convenience. Won't last long by the look of the sky though, she thinks.

Terry's squirting Windex on the inside of the door.

Kent presses the horn, letting it go on longer than necessary.

"Stop," Emily says.

Terry looks up and waves, then goes back to spraying the glass.

"Why does he make you come in so early? You don't open till nine."

She doesn't answer.

Kent looks at his watch, then back through the windshield at Terry. "That's another forty minutes."

She feels a tightening in her chest. "There's stuff to be done."

"Like washing the door with Windex just to have customers put their grubby fingers all over it the minute he opens?"

She says nothing.

Kent shakes his head. "Should have stayed in Corner Brook where he belongs."

She reaches for the handle of the door. Pushes it open.

"Hey." He's pointing to his lips.

"I'm sick."

"I don't care."

She moves over and presses her mouth to his. He touches the tip of her tongue with his own.

After they pull apart, he says, "If you start to feel worse, call me and I'll pick you up."

"I will."

"Wish me luck," he says.

"Why?"

"Because we're negotiating a severance package with those St. John's bastards today."

"Okay then, good luck."

She's halfway out the door when he says, "Love you."

"You too," she says.

46

3

TERRY'S STANDING IN FRONT OF HER, holding the Windex bottle against his chest, his forefinger on the spray trigger. A roll of paper towels in his other hand. "Odd to see him drop you off."

"The rain," she says, coming closer. She holds out her hand for the Windex, "Let me – "

"No." He raises the bottle over his head though she's nearly as tall as he is. "I'll do it."

She doesn't bother reaching for it.

Silence then, both of them just standing there.

The rain starts again, pattering against the roof, against the windows.

He's done something different with his hair this morning, she thinks. Given it the 'messy' look.

Finally, she says, "I hope the wind doesn't change."

"What?"

"Or else you'll end up that way."

He lowers his hand. Smiles. "The silly stuff that youngsters say."

In order to clear a path to the cash register, she has to step around him. Once there, she takes off her raincoat and stuffs it underneath.

"There's coffee," Terry says from his spot in front of the door.

"Maybe later."

"Okay." He turns around and starts spraying the windows next to the entrance.

She leaves the till and makes her way to the back of the store where the small supply of over-the-counter medication is kept on display: a few bottles of Pepto Bismol, some Vicks Vapour Rub, five or six containers of Absorbine Junior, and one small box of Shield Condoms, caramel flavoured. There's no Tylenol Extra Strength, so she settles for regular. She hates cherry-flavoured Halls, but that's all there is. She takes two packs.

Terry's right behind her when she turns around.

"Oh," she says, "you scared me." She thinks that the word in the dictionary would read: *Scared: See Emily.*

"I just wanted to give you this." He hands her the inventory list. Looks down at the medicine in her hands. "Sick?"

"Touch of the flu, I think."

He takes a half step towards her. "Perhaps you ought to lie down. There's that fold-out in my office."

"I'm fine."

"You sure?"

She nods. "Let me just pay for this and then I'll get started."

"It's on the house – "

"Terry – "

"You're doing the *inventory*, it's the least I can do."

She notices flecks of dried blood on his neck from where he'd shaved. He's put on too much aftershave, its sharpness makes it hard to breathe. To escape it, she makes to go. "I'll start downstairs."

"Wait."

She stops.

"You'll need some water to wash down those pills."

She watches him walk away – too much weight planted on the out-sides of his feet, as if chaffed inner thighs prevent him from keeping his legs together, his hands plunged into trouser pockets where they can fiddle with loose change, his head tilted slightly to the right, as if in a perpetual state of trying to make sense of things. Nothing at all like her husband's walk, she knows: the lifted chin, expanded chest, confident arms hanging lazily at his sides, and the huge amount of space he covers with each step.

She touches her forehead, feeling the heat in her fingers, think-ing that people reveal so much about themselves just by sauntering up the road or down to the store. Not hard, for instance, to notice Terry's indecisiveness. Or Kent's boldness. What does she give away, she wonders? Is fear there every time her heels strike the pavement? Worry, in her bowed head? Regret, in the way her eyes stay on the space in front of her feet?

In her mind's eye, she sees Kent's *other* walk. Most people just have the one, but not him. This one is slower, deliberate, like a cat about to pounce. A bend in each elbow and the furrowed brows and the chin pointed downward.

"Emily?"

She looks up. Terry's standing in front of her. "Oh."

He's holding out a bottle of Evian. "You okay?"

She nods, embarrassed that she missed hearing his footsteps.

He hands the water over. "Best to keep hydrated if you're sick."

As she makes her way through the 'Employee Only' door, she hears him say,

"Take lots of breaks." And, "There's a sweater on the chair in my office if you find it chilly."

She passes through the cluttered back room, narrowly avoids banging her shin against a pail of dirty water sitting in the middle of the floor. Before continuing on, she puts her Evian on the floor between her feet and then searches her pocket for one of the packages of Halls. Rips it open and pops one into her mouth. It tastes like cough syrup. She lets the lozenge slip beneath her tongue before picking up her water and starting down the stairs.

* * *

SHE PICKS UP THE NEARLY FILLED-OUT INVENTORY LIST, bringing it close to her face. Notices that the five she'd marked in the box across from the Carnation Milk looks more like a squiggle. The seven, across from the Chef Boyardee, is even worse, as if a Parkinson's sufferer wrote it. There are other numbers she can't make out at all. Is that a nine beside the Kraft Dinner, or a four?

Putting the list aside, she clasps her hands together in order to stop them from trembling. Tries to slow her breathing. Shoots a look towards the stairs, half expecting to see Kent walking down them.

She's just swallowed the last of her first package of Halls, her throat numb now instead of sore. The three Tylenol she took earlier are making her feel light-headed, like she's floating a few inches off the floor. The coolness of the basement, she thinks, is keeping her fever in check.

Again her eyes go to the stairs – "Stop it," she says to herself. "Just stop it."

She stands up, starts walking towards Terry's office. He's left his door wide open, as usual. It's dark inside, the air a mixture of burnt coffee and black licorice. Near his desk, she fumbles about for the lamp switch. At last she finds it. The light casts an eerie glow against the far wall.

She walks around his desk and, before taking a seat in Terry's swivel chair, drapes his knitted sweater over her shoulders. There's a lever on the side of the chair that adjusts its height, reclines it either forward or backward. He prefers to sit forward and high up.

Not a picture on his desk. No mother or father, no siblings, no girl-friend, not even a dog or a cat. Pries into *her* business all he wants, Terry does, but doesn't say a word about his own family life. All she knows is he was born in Corner Brook, and that his parents divorced when he was still a youngster, his father off with some young thing down in Florida somewhere, his mother living alone in the house where he was raised.

He moved here not even five years ago. People *leave*, they don't come, she'd thought back then when he'd waved to her from the front window of the old dance hall. Had it renovated in a few months, then changed its name and opened for business. Bought some land about seven miles outside of town and had a house built. Too big for one person. Sometimes she'll see him out walking, hands behind his back like a poet, or a tourist with nothing but time. She'll see him every now and then at the marina too, when she's with Kent and the kids. Terry'll raise an eyebrow from across the way, then sip his coffee, slurp his chowder from a big spoon. She'll pretend he's not there.

His paperwork is in a neat pile in the centre of his desk beside a mug filled with pencils and pens. There's a notepad near to the phone on the right, and a book of crossword puzzles. No computer. The stained oak is dust free, shined to a luster, smooth against her finger-tips when she runs them along it.

She reaches inside her pocket and hauls out an old, already-paid electric bill. Flips it over to where she'd written the number down. Picks up the phone. Dials nine to get an outside line, then punches in the 1-800 number. She waits for the call to connect, then listens to the rings going through. Tells herself that she's safe, that no one can hurt her here. Still though, she keeps her focus on the door, as if, at any moment, Kent might come barreling through, his heavy breathing and unblinking eyes, no colour in his face, those pounding steps just behind her as she tries to get away, the hand gripping her hair, haul-ing her backwards and to the floor, all of his weight bearing down.

All the operators are busy the recorded voice says, first in English, then in French, and that her call is important and for her to stay on the line.

She waits while music comes through on the other end. A piano with an accompanying woodwind instrument. A saxophone? Heather would know, she thinks.

Her eyes go to the small filing cabinet, then rest on the nearly full pot of coffee on top, a container of Maxwell House beside it with its lid off, and a plastic spoon submerged. Like drinking maple syrup that coffee would be now, she figures. There's a plant beside the filing cabinet, a fern or something that, despite the lack of natural light, appears to be thriving.

For the first time in ages she feels hungry. Imagines her mother's goulash, topped with mozzarella cheese. Blueberry tart for dessert.

Someone human comes on the line. "Thank you for calling Air Canada. How may I assist you?"

"Hello. I'd like to confirm my reservations for this Friday," Emily says, her voice low.

"Confirmation number, please," says the female voice on the other end.

It's on her plane tickets, she bets, but they're underneath the basement floor. "I don't have it on me. Can you find my booking by my name?"

"What is it, please?"

"Gyles, G – Y – L – E – S, first name, Emily." There's a tapping of computer keys in her ear. She takes a pen out of the mug.

"That's Emily Gyles?"

"That's right."

"Traveling with a Jeremy and Lynette Gyles?"

"My children – yes."

"Departure time from Gander airport is 11:00 a.m., Friday, the eighth of May, arriving in Halifax at 12:05 p.m. before departing for Toronto at 12:45 – "

"Sorry, departing when?"

"Departing from Toronto at 12:45."

"Okay. Got it."

Arriving in Toronto at 3:00 p.m., and then departing for Vancouver at 5:30. Arrival time in Vancouver is 7:30 p.m."

The information is already on her plane tickets, but Emily scribbles it all down, her fingertips white from holding the pen so tightly.

"Did you get all of that, Miss?"

"Yes. Thank you."

"Alright. Take this down too. It's your confirmation number."

"Okay."

"Are you ready?"

"Yes."

"It's J –K – "

"I'm sorry, but didn't you say it was a number?"

"It's a combination of letters and numbers."

"Oh."

Emily listens hard, writes the confirmation in block letters along the bottom of the bill.

"Best to check that everything's on schedule several hours before departure time. Quote the number I've just given you. Is there anything else, Miss?"

"No, that's all. Thank you."

"Thank you for flying Air Canada. Have a nice day."

She returns the phone to its cradle, but keeps her hand hovering over the top, the pad of her palm nearly touching. She exhales the breath she's been holding. A shiver goes through her. She feels its journey from her toes to her heels, up her calves and hamstrings, along her spine, and into her head.

If it's the right thing to do, then how can it suddenly feel wrong?

She tries sitting back only to find herself leaning forward again, her right elbow on the desk while its hand takes the weight of her forehead.

Will Lynette and Jeremy be better off, she wonders? Is she helping by taking them away, or just making things worse?

She jumps when she sees the shadow along the floor. Looks up to see Terry standing in the doorway.

"Didn't mean to scare you," he says.

How long has he been watching? What's he heard?

"You shouldn't sneak up like that." She wonders if his feet touch the floor when he walks. You turn around one minute and no one's there. The next, Terry's standing right behind you.

"Sorry."

The less anyone knows about her trip to the west coast, the better, she thinks. All it takes is one slip up. One misstep. Like a chip in a windshield that turns into a crack and runs the whole length of the window. "What do you want?" she says at last.

Terry shoves his hands in his pockets, fiddling away with his coins. "Nothing. Only that the rain has stopped and would you maybe like to join me outside for a bit of fresh air?"

She grabs the electric bill off the desk, folding it in half and shoving it in her pocket.

"I'll be right up."

Terry lingers a second before going.

Although she's just put it there, she slides her hand back in her pocket to be sure. That's her way, lately, doing something and then not trusting she's done it. How many times in the basement at home, for example, has she wedged her fingernails beneath the floor panel to be sure that the money she'd just put there is there? How often too, has she written down the plan only to rip it into tiny squares a moment later?

7 a.m.: Wake.

7:05: Wake children.

7:06: Get money from basement.

7:10: Fruit Loops for Jeremy; Honeycombs for Lynette.

7:15: Wash face and hands. No time for bathing. And on and on.

Sometimes, on her days off, she'll take the children down to where the ferry docks to watch the passengers get on and off. Other times, the three of them will make the forty-five minute ferry journey themselves, for practice, although she'd never tell them as much. Soft-serve in cones. Chocolate for Jeremy; a mixture of strawberry and vanilla for Lynette. Then up to the second level to watch the ferry pull away from the dock, their hands gripping the railing. They'll ask why their dad's not with them. "This is just for us," she'll say.

She takes off the sweater and reaches over to switch off the desk lamp, then just sits there in the dark.

The last time she took the ferry she was alone. Three weeks ago. The children in school; Kent in meetings. The day off from the grocery store. Her father waiting there in his car. The whole way to Gander he played the radio and tried talking but he's terrible at talking, so eventually he shut up. At the kitchen table afterwards, over tea, her mother patted her knee and asked if everything was okay at home. She nodded, said things were fine. "You know what would be perfect with this tea?" she said then, "Peek Freans."

"No Peek Freans," her mother said. "I've jam jams though." Emily asked her father for his car keys then, so she could go to the store and get Peek Freans. Her dad wanted to go and get them for her, but she raised her voice and he sat back down. Nearly forty-five minutes by the time she got back. The tea was cold and her father asleep on the chesterfield. Her mother forced her eyes away from the *Young and the Restless.* "Go to St. John's for the Peek Freans?"

"Christ," Emily said. "I forgot the cookies." Her mother's eyes right on her. "If you didn't get the Peek Freans what in the name of God were you doing all this time?" Emily sat on the edge of the sofa where her father's feet didn't quite reach. "Driving. Just driving." Her mother went back to her show, and her father snored himself awake. Tucked inside her jacket pocket were three plane tickets to British Columbia. Three weeks from Friday.

∗ ∗ ∗

TERRY'S DRYING OFF A MILK CRATE with paper towels when she pushes open the back door.

He turns to her. "One second."

She stands there watching him, her hand in the pocket that has the old electric bill.

He wraps the paper towel around his pinky in order to get at the rainwater that has fallen between the crevices.

Though the clouds have lost their purple tinge, they still look like they have more rain to unleash. There's wind too, chilly enough to raise gooseflesh, strong enough to mess her hair. The air is a mixture of dog shit and tree bark.

"Okay," he says, a thumb pointed towards her now-dry seat.

She goes and sits.

"Not too cold, is it?" He says it like it's just occurred to him.

She shakes her head.

"Because we can go inside."

"It's fine."

"I'd hate for you to get sicker – "

"I'm *fine*, Terry."

"Okay."

He doesn't pay half as much attention to his own milk crate before dropping the soaked paper towels into the garbage pail beside the back door. He comes back over and sits down. Lifts his bum and inches the crate forward so that he's closer to her.

She notices how he can't get comfortable, moving forward till his backside is almost off the seat, then sitting back again. His greenish-grey eyes rest on her, then move away.

"I'm almost done down there," she says finally.

He smiles. "I'll count the rest, don't worry."

She looks away. *Don't worry.* Worry's been with her longer than her children. There to wake her in the middle of the night, and to keep her looking over her shoulder; worry's the relative she never sees but knows is there, the taste she can't get rid of, the message on her answering machine she can't erase. *Don't worry?* She wouldn't know how.

In the silence, she watches him pick the calluses on his right hand, every so often pulling away bits of dead and dried skin, letting them fall discreetly between his feet.

"You want to say something," she says.

54

He rips off another piece and tries releasing it without her noticing. Looks towards the door and then back at her again. Shifts forward some more so that his knees are nearly touching hers. He makes to stand up. "I'll bring you my sweater."

"No."

"But you're shivering."

"Tell me," she says.

He sits back down. Looks at her. At last, he says, "I just wanted to tell you that I'm sorry about yesterday."

The air's colder suddenly. She feels heavy in her belly despite nothing being in it.

"I shouldn't have mentioned anything," Terry says.

"I made a dumb mistake. You had every right to say something."

"It upset you."

"It's okay."

A peck of rain lands on her forehead. She wipes it away.

Overhead, a flock of seagulls pass, their squawks half drowned out by the building wind. Candy wrappers that had once lain on the top of the garbage bucket are being whipped around in the gale, scattering around their feet, just above their heads.

After a moment, Terry says, "You happy?"

She doesn't answer, choosing instead to tilt her face towards the sky. Another raindrop lands on her cheek. "Starting to rain again."

Terry looks up too. "Lightning Cove in May for ya. We're lucky it isn't snowing."

They go quiet. Then Terry says, "Did you hear what I just asked?"

She looks at him, then away. Folds her arms across her chest, letting the question sink in, her eyes on the ground. "I'm as happy as anyone else." She lifts her face and stares at him. "Why?"

Terry looks past her shoulder. Shakes his head. Shrugs. "No reason."

A speck of rain clips the tip of her nose. Another lands on the back of her hand.

"Let's go in before it starts to pour." She gets to her feet.

Terry's about to say more, but before he can get any words out, the back door swings open, revealing Heather. She offers them a side profile of her face in order to speak to someone that's standing behind her. "She's out here," she says, stepping aside to let Irene Baker pass.

Irene seems to have aged ten years since yesterday, Emily thinks. Paler than usual, her eyes red-rimmed and swollen, her belly so large she looks like she might fall forward.

"Irene," she says.

The woman comes closer, her two hands on the belly of her raincoat, as if it's the only way to keep the baby from suddenly dropping out.

"Don't *Irene* me," she says.

"What's the matter – "

"Stay out of this, Terry," Irene says. "This has got nothing to do with you."

Heather's still in the doorway, her fingers bracing its frame.

"Mind the cash," Terry tells her.

"There's no one in there," Heather says.

"Go."

She does, rolling her eyes in the process and slamming the door. Terry offers the pregnant woman his seat.

"Stay where you're to," Irene says to him, "this won't take long." She takes a few more steps so that she's within touching distance of Emily. "No layoff's, huh? 'Maybe it won't come to that,' you said. Filthy liar."

"That's enough," Terry says.

Irene turns to him. "It's fine for you. You got your precious little store. But what about us that depends on the plant, huh? What about *us?*" She looks again at Emily. "You knew all along that Myles didn't stand a chance, didn't you?"

Emily doesn't answer.

"Didn't you?"

"She's got nothing to do with any of that," Terry says.

"Except that she lives with the very one whose business it's *supposed* to be to look after men like my husband."

Emily points to her milk crate. "Won't you sit down, Irene?"

"Just answer my question?"

"Yes."

"Yes what?"

"Yes, I knew. Or had a pretty good idea, at least."

Irene's knees suddenly buckle. Terry is close enough behind her to catch her before she falls. Emily goes over to help, draping one of Irene's arms across her shoulders. They lower her gently onto the milk crate.

"What's wrong?" Emily asks.

The woman is clutching her stomach, her chin buried into the top of her chest.

"It's not coming, is it?" Terry says, his voice a whisper.

Irene lets out a long breath, then takes a few more. "Not today." She looks up at them. "I'm so thirsty."

"I'll get you some water," Terry says. He runs to the door, throwing it open, then disappears inside.

Emily rubs the pregnant woman's back – up and down, then in a circular motion.

"Stop it," Irene says.

"Sorry." Emily leaves a hand on the pregnant woman's shoulder.

No words between them now, just the sound of Irene's breaths – deep and steady for a while and then her holding it. Her holding it for a while and then deep and steady.

Not yet noon, but the clouds are making it feel like dusk. The rain's still pecking, about to unleash its downpour. She looks to the door, wondering what's taking Terry so long.

It's ages before she senses Irene's body relax. She takes her hand away as the woman sits up to full height.

"Feeling better?" Emily says.

Irene nods. Spits and then wipes her mouth on her sleeve. Massages her closed eyes. One more long breath before she whispers, "How will we live?"

Emily says nothing. *How will we live?* Out west without nearly enough money or resources or hardly knowing a soul other than Jackie and Stephen. And not even Stephen really, seeing as she's never met him. How long before they kick her and the children out, she wonders? A week? Two? And what was it Stephen had said: something about knowing people and finding her a sublet? Great, except how long – seeing as there's only $1,125 underneath the basement floor – will she able to pay the rent? She imagines Jackie and Stephen asking them to go finally. The three of them walking the streets of downtown Vancouver. Gripping one another's hands for fear of being swept away. Three lost faces in an ocean of them.

Terry's back. Rather than water, he's holding Fruit Punch Gatorade. "To replenish those electrolytes," he says, holding the bottle beside his face like he's in a commercial or something. He twists the cap en route to Irene. Hands it to her.

Irene takes a gulp, some of it dribbling down her chin. She wipes away the spillage, then the wetness beneath her eyes.

"Let me drive you to the clinic?" Terry says.

She shakes her head. Takes another sip before twisting the top back on the Gatorade. Holds out her arms like a child who longs to be picked up.

Terry goes over.

"Sit a minute longer," Emily says.

"I'm alright."

Terry helps her to her feet.

The rain's steadier now.

"Come inside," Terry says.

"No." Irene puts the hood of her raincoat over her head and draws the string. "A bit of rain won't hurt." She holds up the Gatorade. "How much?"

Terry sticks out his palm. "I won't hear of it."

The pregnant woman puts the drink in her coat pocket, her face strained with pain, and turns to Emily. "I wish you wouldn't have lied about it, that's all."

"I'm sorry," Emily says. "I was hoping for a miracle, I guess. That maybe the layoffs wouldn't happen after all."

Irene stays looking at her for a moment, then turns around and starts walking.

Emily and Terry watch until the woman disappears around the corner.

The rain suddenly comes – cold, hard enough to split your skin.

Terry runs for the door. Turns back once he gets there. "Come in!"

She stays where she is, staring off at where Irene had just gone, the woman's words still ringing in her ears. *How will we live?* Fear rises to the back of her throat. She swallows it back down. Uncertainty takes fear's place then, so she swallows that too. You'll never get away with it, she thinks. Kidnapping your own youngsters.

"You're getting drenched!" Terry shouts.

She ignores him, allowing Irene's words to float around in her mind still: *How will we live?* It occurs to her that that's *why* she's going in the first place. So that she *can* live. So that her children can too.

Terry's voice again. "Please come in!"

Finally she turns to him, but can barely see through the blinding rain. Still she doesn't go in, preferring instead to linger in the same spot, letting the drops pound against her head, her face, soaking her uniform. This kind of weather reminds her, sometimes, that she's alive.

4

SHE TURNS THE CORNER ONTO HER STREET. The hand in her pocket has a tight grip around the electric bill, while the other hangs at her side. No need for the hood of her jacket since the rain has stopped. A piece of blue sky is visible now through the clouds, and the strong wind of earlier has abated to a lackluster breeze that's verging on warm, almost pleasant.

She walks slowly, her eyes focused on the tips of her sneakers. Not looking, really, so much as thinking. Mostly about Friday. Going over everything in her mind: 7:00 – Wake, 7:05 – Wake kids, 7:07 – Get money from downstairs…

The first pangs of a headache now. *Lynette's giraffe,* it occurs to her. Can't leave without that. Lynette'll need that more than food. More than a bed.

She's surprised to see her father's Pontiac Bonneville in the driveway. In Kent's spot.

A knocking sound makes her look up. Her mother's there in the front window, one of her hands pulling apart the drapes while the other struggles to hold onto Lynette.

It's Lynette's little fist pounding the glass, excited eyes and a smile that's missing one of its front teeth.

Emily waves, then continues along the driveway and up the porch steps.

Near the door she stops, wondering if the reason for her parents' visit is because her mother has that 'feeling' again. The one she often gets whenever something big is happening in Emily's life: the tightening abdomen, the dreams, the cold sensation in her hands and feet, all of it culminating in the voice that her mother swears is not her own yet comes from somewhere inside her, the voice that had predicted Kent's marriage proposal the night before it happened and the boy Emily would have less than a year later. In junior high, her mother had spoken about the burst appendix before Emily had felt a single stab of pain.

She grips the knob of the door, but still doesn't go in, thinking how odd it is that, in all the years she and Kent have been together,

her mother had not once foreseen a single slap or whispered threat or hand gripping her daughter's neck and pinning her against the wall.

Her mother and Lynette are just inside the door to greet her when she finally walks in.

Lynette runs over.

Emily's too tired to lift her, so she crouches on her knees and gives her daughter a hug. "Mom," she says, her chin resting on Lynette's shoulder, "this is unexpected."

"I wish you wouldn't leave those two alone."

"It's only for half an hour." Emily lets Lynette go and then kicks off her sneakers. "Just until I get home from work. Less sometimes."

"I don't know why you do that job anyway."

"Mom – "

"It's not like you need the money – "

"Don't start –"

"The poor things were starving. Jeremy's hands were in the Fruit Loops."

"They're always in the Fruit Loops."

She comes into the kitchen. Stands in front of her mother.

"No kiss or what?" her mother says.

Emily takes a step closer and pecks the offered cheek. Gives a weak hug.

"My Lord, you're nothing but a skeleton underneath that raincoat."

Emily tries to push away, but her mother latches on.

"Didn't I say that you weren't to lose another pound?"

She manages to disentangle herself. "Don't exaggerate, Mom." Emily unzips her jacket and makes her way farther into the kitchen. There's a bucket of take-out chicken on the table, a container of coleslaw, two boxes of fries, and a huge mound of macaroni salad. Cokes set at every place. Paper plates and plastic knives and forks. "What's all this?"

Her mother comes closer. "With the layoffs and everything else going on, we figured that cooking would be the last thing you and Kent would want to do."

"How did you know?"

"It's all over the news."

"Is it?"

"Poor Kent."

Quiet for a moment, then her mother adds, "How's he holding up?"

"He's fine." She takes off her raincoat, drapes it across the back of a chair and then sits down.

Her mother gasps. "Just look at you!"

"That's enough, Mom."

Her mother starts plopping food on Emily's plate: two chicken breasts, two scoops of macaroni salad, a scoop of coleslaw, and way too many fries.

"Do you want my stomach to explode?"

"Eat it." Her mother turns to Lynette. "Call your brother and grandfather in from the garage will you, sweetheart?"

Lynette runs out.

Emily peels a piece of skin from a chicken breast and puts it in her mouth; her mother's eyes on her. She swallows despite its greasiness, its saltiness. She doesn't want to be thin either. Or make herself sick by not eating. What good is she to the children then? She'll need every bit of strength in Vancouver. There'll be jobs to look for, an apartment to rent, a school for the kids that's close by, welfare forms to fill out. That on top of all the emotional support her babies will need. Will she be able to keep them happy, she wonders? Content in a strange place without their father? What about herself? Will she be able to find happiness too?

"Don't count on Kent," Emily says. "He hasn't been home before eight in nearly a month." She puts some macaroni in her mouth.

"I wish your father was more like him."

She stops chewing. Looks up just in time to see her mother pick something invisible off her blouse.

"I just mean that he works so hard. Not like that thing *I* married. If there was a job for sleeping your father'd be employee of the century."

Emily looks away, managing to swallow what's in her mouth before pushing her plate aside.

Her mother slides the food back.

Emily glares at her. "I've had enough."

"You've barely touched it."

"I'm not hungry."

"Eat."

"I'm not a youngster."

"Eat."

"You *EAT!*"

Her mother stares at her for a long time, then hauls out a chair and sits down. Snatches a fry from Emily's plate and takes a bite. Chews. Swallows. Then says, "Is he behaving himself?"

Emily looks up from the tablecloth. "Who?"

"You know who?"

She pauses for a second, then says, "There's isn't a woman in this town that's not envious."

Her mother reaches for another fry, holding it out in front of her as if it were a fine cigar. "Better than McDonald's these chips are." She puts the whole thing in her mouth this time. Leans towards her daughter. Talks while she chews. "He hasn't laid a finger on you then?"

She shakes her head.

The older woman sucks the French fry grease from her fingers, then says, "All that men like Kent need is a strong woman." Another fry. Another licking of lips. "Look at your father sure, no one knows the kind of trouble I had with him in the beginning – the boozing and the coming home at all hours, the light bill going down his gullet. The grocery money –"

"Why are you telling me this?"

"Hmm?"

"Why are you telling me this?"

Emily's mother stops speaking for a moment. Looks towards the porch door, then turns back to her daughter. "But look at him now. Doesn't touch a drop, does he? Barely raises his voice, even when he's contrary at me for one thing or another. Still the laziest thing going, mind you, but at least now I know where he is come evening. And it's all because I refused to put up with his foolishness."

Foolishness. It's like that jug of cold water being thrown in her face all over again, except in slow motion, every ounce of her humiliation being drawn out, like wringing the last drop of water from a soaked dishcloth. *Foolishness.* It takes all of her willpower not to pick up the plate of food and send it flying across the room. Coleslaw and the grease from the chicken running down the walls and pieces of broken plate and macaroni bits scattered all over the hardwood floor. *Foolishness.*

"Leaving him that time was the best thing you could have done."

The few forkfuls that she's managed to swallow threaten to come back up. She tries breathing the sensation away.

"Put the fear of God in him, it did… the possibility of losing you, the youngsters. Sometimes that's all it takes."

She's too busy concentrating on her breathing to say anything.

"We've all got something. No one's perfect, God knows. Plus, there's Lynette and Jeremy to think about. They need their father – "

"Stop it."

"What?"

"Just stop!"

Emily's dad comes in then, one grandchild on each side of him.

"Pop likes the new bench press," Jeremy says.

"You didn't try lifting anything, did you, Felix?" her mother says to her father.

"Why shouldn't I?"

"He did a pull up and some arm curls," Jeremy practically shouts.

Her mother shakes her head. "And he's still walking?"

"There's plenty I can do yet my dear. Don't you worry."

Emily offers her cheek for her father to kiss. His moustache tickles. There's Tetley tea on his breath.

"He should charge admission," her father says, pointing behind him in the direction of the garage. Before sitting himself, he pulls out chairs for his grandchildren.

She's struck, suddenly, by how old her father looks. Had he always been so rounded at the shoulders, his hair so grey?

Her mother piles his plate, then serves Lynette and Jeremy, and finally herself.

Emily sips her Coke and watches them eat. *No one's perfect, God knows,* her mother had just said. *They need their father.*

Her Dad's just said something to her.

"What?"

"Chew what's in your mouth first, Felix," her mother says.

Felix does, then says, "I asked if he'll be home before the final crossing? We can't miss the last ferry."

She doesn't answer right away, still taken by the years, it seems, her father has aged in the weeks since she last saw him. She shakes her head. "I doubt it."

Her father nods then goes back to eating.

It's not so much his growing older, it occurs to her, as it is the time that's been slipping away almost without her realizing. Time that can never be gotten back.

She turns towards the window. Breathes deeply, letting it out slowly, thinking of all the days and weeks and months and years that have been wasted. Nearly thirty and it's as if she's never lived. Not really. In someone else's body it seems, someone other than herself waking up each morning, walking the children to school, checking groceries through, coming back home at the end of the day, and then lying beside him. *Leaving him was the best thing you could have done.*

She looks at them all again: Lynette's humming while she chews; Jeremy's reaching across the table for more chicken; her mother watching her; her father's face hung over his plate as if he's the only one in the room.

No one's perfect, God knows.

She'll start over on Friday, she thinks. A second chance to get right what she couldn't the first time.

* * *

HER DAD'S DOZING IN THE LA-Z-BOY. Jeremy and Lynette are on the floor in front of the widescreen television; Jeremy holding the remote and flicking through the stations while Lynette braids her own hair.

Her mother holds open a garbage bag while Emily throws in paper plates full of chicken bones, used napkins, and empty Coke cans.

Her mother looks at her. "You barely said a word during supper."

Emily throws in the last of the garbage. "You said enough for us both."

Her mother ties the bag, but is unsure what to do with it.

"Here." Emily takes it to the porch. She's just back in the kitchen when she hears the sound of his truck in the driveway.

Her mother turns. "Kent?"

Emily goes back into the porch and looks through the window at the top of the door. It's him. She looks at her watch: six o'clock. Wonders what him being home so early means. Whatever mood he's in will have to wait until her parents leave, she thinks. Always on his best behaviour when they're around. Loves her mother more than his own.

"Wake up, Felix!" her mother yells into the living room. "Kent's home."

Emily hears a snore cut short, then her father saying to himself but loud enough for them all to hear, "Wake the dead that one would."

Emily's still watching Kent. He turns off the ignition and sits there for a moment, hands on the wheel and face forward, lost in thought, like someone needing a few more seconds in order to summon the courage to face the world. Like Emily herself, lately.

Kent reaches over to the passenger side and grabs something sitting on the seat. Two brown paper bags, she sees as he steps out, and a bottle of something tucked underneath his arm, close to the pit. He presses the lock on the keychain before heading to the porch. Who does he think is going to break in?

He starts climbing the steps.

Jeremy's already waiting there, like a well-trained dog; Lynette too, except that she's more fixated on her hair. Her father's up now, running a hand over the back of his head where some hair is sticking up. Her mother smoothes her slacks, as if she's about to meet the premier or something.

Before Kent has a chance to open the door, Emily is there to do it for him.

"Hey, gorgeous," he says, coming in, the bags covering his face to just below the eyes. Above the eyebrow on his left are six neatly sewn stitches.

"You didn't bring food, did you?" She steps aside to give him room to enter.

"Why?"

"'Cause we brought your supper already," her mother says. She points her head in the direction of her husband. "Felix, take a bag why don't you."

"Chicken?" Kent says.

"And fries and coleslaw…"

"You must have been reading my mind, Shirley," Kent says.

Emily's father is there now. He takes one of the bags before noticing Kent's eye. "You walk into a pole or what?"

Kent laughs. "I wish."

Her mother rushes over, practically knocking Felix out of the way. "Your eye!" She says it like Kent's unaware of the gash himself. With her free hand, she appraises the damage, gently running two fingers along the freshly stitched wound like one would do on a piece of furniture to check for dust.

"A scratch is all." Kent wriggles out of his shoes. "People tend to get upset when their livelihoods are being threatened."

"Just take a look at this, Felix," her mother says.

"I just did."

"That's the thanks you get for all you've done?" Her mother lowers her hand. Takes a step back, then turns to Emily. "You report it?"

Kent laughs. "No need for that."

Shirley looks back at Kent. "Aren't you on their side?"

"It was crazy yesterday. I don't think even *they* knew who they were swinging at half the time," Kent says.

Emily goes over and takes the other bag from Kent, bringing it to the kitchen table. Puts it down and then stares across at them. When had her mother ever fussed over *her* like that?

Kent comes in, takes the bottle out from underneath his arm, and holds it up with the label towards Emily. "I got the Aussie kind."

Jeremy runs over to him. "Pop did a pull up."

"He did?" Kent says. "Wow."

"Feel, feel." Jeremy flexes his bicep until he turns red in the face.

"Almost as big as your old man," Kent says.

"Hi, Daddy." Lynette still holds a section of her hair.

"Hello, my love." He lifts her into his arms and carries her into the kitchen. He puts her down in one of the chairs.

"Are we celebrating something?" Emily asks. When was the last time he brought wine home?

He puts the bottle down on the table. Breathes out slowly, like someone would upon realizing that the bad news they'd expected is not so bad after all. "We're close to setting up a nice severance package. Where's the corkscrew?" He moves over to the counter and hauls open a drawer. Finds one.

Her dad asks, "How nice?"

"Nice enough to keep the heat and lights going." Kent comes back over. Picks up the bottle and inserts the spiraled blade. Twists the top like he's been opening wine all his life. Like there isn't anything he can't do. He pulls out the cork as easily as if it were a plug in the sink. "Nice enough to keep the deep freeze packed with meat," he says, looking up at his father-in-law, a smile across his face. He holds the tip of the bottle under his nose. Closes his eyes. Inhales deeply.

As if he knows anything about wine, she thinks.

He opens them suddenly. "Glasses. We need glasses."

Her mother makes to move toward the tumbler cupboard, but Kent stops her.

"The *good* ones, Shirley," he says, indicating the dining room cabinet with a quick point of his chin.

"I'll help you, Mom," Emily says.

It isn't really a dining room so much as an extension of the living room. There's no partition or change in the colour scheme or anything to indicate a separate living space, just a long oval table, its surface gleaming, in front of a floor-to-ceiling-window. For show, really. When was the last time anyone had sat there? The cabinet is flush against the wall. Taller than Kent. The sparkling glass allows an easy view of rows of cups and saucers, plates and bowls. Blindingly polished silverware. A shelf in the centre sports an immaculate row of whiskey glasses identical to the ones she'd given him three Christmases ago, and that he'd smashed in a fit of rage after she'd said something that he didn't like. Jeremy had stepped on a shard in his bare feet and needed it taken out at the clinic.

The wine glasses with the elegant stems are on the top, beside the flute glasses and the crystal.

"I need a chair," she says to her mother.

Shirley takes the one at the head of the dining table, positioning it behind her daughter. Emily grips the tiny brass knobs and pulls. The seldom-opened doors stick for a moment before giving way. Everything inside the cabinet vibrates.

"Careful," her mother says.

She stands on the chair. "I'll hand them down to you." She does so slowly, one after the other, both hands on each thread-thin stem, as if the glasses were ticking bombs.

She lets go of the fourth one before her mother has a chance to grab it. It breaks against the hardwood.

"Everything all right in there?" Kent says.

Her mother turns in the direction of the kitchen. "Just a broken wine glass."

Emily gets off the chair. "Why didn't you grab it?"

"It was nowhere near my hand."

Kent comes in with a broom and dustpan. "Excuse me, ladies."

They move aside, but watch him as he sweeps up all the pieces.

"Lately, she's always dropping something," he says to her mother. She feels like she's not even in the room.

"The other day it was a cup of coffee. A pan of french fries the day before that." He squeezes between them, back to the kitchen.

Emily gets back on the chair to try again for that fourth wine glass.

"Nothing but a waste of money," her mother says, finally.

Emily pauses to look down at her. "What?"

Her mother points up to where the good crystal jug is, its top made more visible now that the wine glasses in front have been removed. "You never use it."

She thinks of it in Kent's hands last night: the rising and falling of his chest as he held it in front of himself, the whites of his eyes in the dark, the smell of rain despite there not being any, and the damp sheets. Cold. So cold.

She hands down the last wine glass, then closes the cabinet doors. Slides the chair back in place before brushing past her mother without bothering to help her carry the glasses in.

* * *

IT'S NEARLY DARK WHEN HER PARENTS decide it's time to go. Her father, with Lynette in his arms, is the first to step out onto the front porch, then Kent, one hand in his pocket and his laces untied.

Emily's surprised to see Jeremy holding his grandmother's hand. He used to hold *her* hand like that. It occurs to her, since the top of his head goes past his grandmother's shoulder, that her little boy is not so little after all. How could she not have noticed until now? What else has she not noticed, she wonders? Before she started planning an escape, there had always been after-school chats: Jeremy sitting on the arm of the chesterfield and Lynette in her lap. Each of their accomplishments would be posted on the fridge back then – Jeremy's A in Physical Education or Lynette's drawing from Art class. When was the last time she'd posted anything? Or sat either of them down for a real talk? I haven't *really* been here, she realizes. Not lately. Not like I should be. *Used* to be.

"Fine evening," her mother says.

They've all stopped to linger on the porch.

"Like summer," Kent says. "Nearly."

The wind's warmer than it had been earlier. A clear sky now with a half-moon, the perfect night for stargazing. She can make out Venus, and the Little Dipper.

"Are you sure we can't convince you to stay?" Kent asks.

"You know Felix, Kent. Can fall asleep at a booth in a restaurant, but claims he can't sleep in a bed that isn't his own."

"I wish *you'd* sleep more so your tongue would stop flapping," Felix says.

"A flapping tongue," Jeremy repeats, laughing.

They walk down the porch stairs to the driveway.

At the car, her mother says, "You should bring the kids this weekend."

She doesn't speak. The roar of the Boeing 747 that she and the children will have taken by then is in her ears.

"Can we, Mommy?" Lynette says, from high up in her grandfather's arms.

"We'll see, sweetie."

Her father kisses Lynette before putting her down. Goes over and shakes Jeremy's free hand. Looks at his wife. "Let's go, unless you plan on swimming across."

Emily goes to him, hugs too hard. Doesn't want to let go.

"I'll see you soon, sure," her dad says.

"I know," she says, letting him go finally. She goes to her mother and kisses her coolly on the cheek.

Kent walks her father to the driver's side door. Shakes his hand; her dad won't look him in the eye. Kent comes back and hugs her mother. "Good to see you, Shirley." He opens the passenger side door for her.

"Convince that wife of yours to come this weekend," Shirley says, ducking her head and getting in.

Kent waits for her to swing her legs in before closing the door.

Her father says to Kent, "Let us know about the severance package offer."

Kent nods. "Will do."

"And be sure to keep that cut clean," her mother says.

"I got the best woman in the world to take care of that," he says, reaching out and taking Emily's hand.

They watch the car back out of the driveway.

"Be good youngsters!" Her mother shouts through her rolled-down window, just as the car pulls away.

Jeremy and Lynette run out into the street, waving.

His grip on her hand tightens. "Let's go in," he says.

5

HE'S PRESSING EACH OF HER WRISTS into the mattress above her head. His grip is so strong. She imagines her blood fighting to make its way through her too-thin veins, then clotting, bulging before exploding. Dark purple spreading out near the top of her skin.

He flips her over suddenly. Because he can. Because he's used to getting what he wants. Because she knows better than to fight. She turns her head, letting her right cheek sink into the pillow that smells of him: outdoors and gasoline. The moonlight, through an opening in the blinds, is casting their shadows on the opposite wall. It's like she's spying on two other people, the larger of them on top, going up and down with metronome-like rhythm. The bottom shadow perfectly still. So small it might not even be there.

Why does he never seem to be able to take any of his own weight? *Stop, you're crushing me!* It's like her life being snuffed out, little by little.

He bites her lower neck.

She doesn't cry out.

He's salivating. Droplets falling against her skin. Clumps of her hair in his hands. Deep breaths and strained moans. Grunts.

She's silent. Deadened now to the part of him inside her. Hadn't always been. In another life it seems to her now, she'd been louder than he: lifting herself to meet his thrusts, holding onto him like he was the last person on earth. Then lying with him afterwards. From that to this, she thinks. That. This.

He tenses – shudders, then goes still. The shadows on the wall, she notices, have gone still, too. He says her name. At least she thinks it's her name. Perhaps it was a moan that sounded like it.

"I can't breathe," she says.

He gets off, still pulsating, still stiff.

She rolls onto her back, filling her lungs as if for the first time. Slips beneath a sheet.

"Don't."

"What? "

"Cover up." He pulls the blanket off. "Let me look at you."

He does. Then says, "You didn't make a sound."

"Didn't I?"

He lays his palm on her stomach, just above her belly button. "Let's go somewhere."

"What?"

"Just you and me."

They haven't gone anywhere in ages.

"We'll leave the kids with your parents."

She pauses. Then says, "Where?"

"St. John's."

St. John's, she thinks. Kent's centre of the universe. There's so much more to see beyond the Narrows of St. John's harbour, she imagines. Perhaps one day, when the children are older, she'll get a chance to see it. Without *him*, though.

"We'll stay at the Battery and you can shop all weekend."

Without him. She lets the words drift inside her mind. Waking…*without him*, suppers…*without him*, holidays… *without him*, everything… *without him*. She turns to look out the window, unsure what to call the feeling in her belly.

"Wouldn't you like that?" he asks.

I'd rather die than go anywhere with you. She nods.

"When was the last time you bought yourself something?" he says.

"I buy plenty."

"Something fancy, I mean. A nice dress, or jewelry?"

She can't remember the last time she's worn a dress. And it's hard to get earrings in since she's allowed the holes to grow over. *A nice dress. Jewelry.* She imagines her hair unbound, and a tinge of eyeliner. Long nails instead of bitten ones, and smooth, unchapped lips. In her mind, she's being stared at. Desirable again. Sexy again. A woman again.

"How about Friday?" he says.

She nods again, absent-mindedly.

"With everything that's been going on, I could use a little break." He raises himself to one elbow. "It's settled then. We'll bring the kids to your mother's on Friday morning and spend the weekend in Town. Come back on Monday. Fuck it, Tuesday – we'll come back Tuesday. We deserve a little rest."

Her whole body is suddenly cold. Tingling. Either her heart has stopped or else it's beating so fast that it only appears to be. She longs for breath but can't draw any, wants to move but doesn't think she can. Friday? He really didn't say that, did he? Friday? As in the one coming? Not the one after? Or the one after that? *This Friday*! She's only imagined that he's said the word, she thinks. Of all the days and the weeks and the months how can he choose *this* Friday? *This goddamn Friday!*

"What's wrong?" he says.

She's still not able to speak.

"What?"

She shakes her head. It's all she's able to do.

"You don't want to go?"

She's thinking of the right words now, the right phrases that will convince him to stay – to pick another weekend.

"Say something – "

"No."

"No?"

"No, I don't want to go."

Silence.

"I try to plan something nice and you go and ruin it." He says it softly, his face so close that the heat from his breath warms her nose. "Selfish bitch."

Tell him you're sorry. Quick. Quick! "I'm – "

"You're going," he says, the hand that was placed lovingly on her belly earlier now clamped around her upper arm, "supposing I have to drag you."

Drag me. Wouldn't be the first time, she thinks. *Dragged* across the floor, *dragged* out of the car, *dragged* down the basement steps. *Dragged, dragged, dragged.* Sometimes she wonders what need she has for legs.

"Okay," she says.

"Okay, what?"

"I'll go."

His grip loosens, but he doesn't let go. "Terry can manage without you, I suspect. Not rocket science is it, checking in groceries?"

She has no control over anything, she realizes. What point then in this mind, in this body, when she's shackled to him? Led around like some pet. Move too far off course and that familiar yanking at the neck. No breath.

Let's go somewhere. Three little words. Friday's plan ruined.

He lets go of her arm. Lies again on his back. "It'll be fun."

"Yes," she says.

"We'll see some live music."

"Okay."

"Eat seafood."

"Yum."

* * *

HE'S ASLEEP IN MINUTES. She listens, then slides out of bed. Slips on her robe and leaves the room. For the first time in ages she doesn't stop at Jeremy or Lynette's door.

She sits down at the kitchen table. Nothing but blackness around her. No boiled milk tonight. She doesn't care about sleep now. If she ever does again. It feels like somebody reaching inside her suddenly and hauling something out. She's not expecting the sound she makes and tries her best to stifle it by burying her face into the sleeve of her robe, biting down hard on the thick cotton. She gets up and moves to the porch, pushing open the door and walking out onto the deck.

Still warm, the air. Spring. Time for new, but she feels so old. An ancient woman inside a withered body.

She sits in one of the deck chairs. Wipes her eyes and nose with her sleeve. Spits out over the railing. A dog barks. A man's voice tells it to shut up. The dog barks again.

Change the reservations, she thinks. Call the airline and pay the difference. Hardly enough money downstairs to do that, but what choice does she have?

Next Wednesday. They'll go next Wednesday. What's one more week?

She leans back over the railing again, feeling as if she might be sick. Coughs but nothing comes up.

She sits back.

The light in the kitchen goes on. Then the porch door opens and Kent is there with Lynette in his arms. Lynette wipes sleep from her eyes. Hair everywhere. Her stuffed giraffe in her other hand.

"I heard you coughing?" Kent says.

"A tickle in my throat."

"It's late, come back to bed."

She gets up, walks toward them. Kisses Lynette's flushed cheek. "Sorry to wake you, my darling," she says.

She follows Kent through the kitchen and down the hall to Lynette's room. Waits at the doorway for him to tuck her in. Kent rejoins her, taking hold of her hand. They walk in silence to their bedroom.

WEDNESDAY

THE WINDOW. GO TO IT, SHE THINKS. She rises, slides her feet into her slippers and goes over. Once there she suddenly becomes afraid. Of what, she wonders? Her hand is shaking as she inserts it into a slat of the blinds. A deep breath then before she peeks through. There's a car blocking their driveway, the engine running, exhaust coming from its muffler, but no headlights. Someone's behind the steering wheel, just sitting there in the dark. Who?

"Kent," she says, "come look."

He doesn't say anything.

"Come and look Kent," she says again.

When he still doesn't answer, she turns to him.

He's not there.

Dry mouth and a thick tongue now. Fast heart. "Kent?" She looks from left to right. "Kent?" Moves to the bed just to be sure. Pats down the comforter even though she knows he's no longer underneath.

A slamming door makes her jump back. A palm over her heart. The other over her mouth. "Kent?"

She goes back to the window. Sees him. He's running across the lawn in bare feet and boxer shorts. No shirt. There's something in his hand. The driver's side door pops open. It's the recently polished shoes she notices first, then the slacks, then the body: stubby torso, short arms, and thick neck. *Jesus.* Terry. It's Terry. She screams in a pitch that she's never screamed in before, but there's no sound, just the feeling of her jaw nearly unhinging, the muscles in her cheeks cramping. She tries to let go of the blinds but can't; tries to turn around but her body is frozen. Terry's out of the car now, standing beside the open door. The interior lights are on. She sees the two furry dice jangling from the rear-view mirror. Kent's not stopping; he's running faster if anything. Oh my God! It's a knife. He's running with a knife. Her sharpest one too. The one she uses to debone fish, to slice through cabbage and turnip. Kent's so close now. The knife raised above his head like a hunter. Why is Terry just standing there? *Raise your hands!* she'd shout if she could. *Defend yourself!* She presses both palms against the glass as the knife goes deep into Terry's chest. Him not making a sound, the force of the stab sending him backwards against the car, knocking the door shut. He falls. Kent bends over him and pulls out the knife, its blade darkened with blood, and then draws it back, thrusting it in again and again – into Terry's chest, face, legs. Terry as calm as anything the whole time. The children. They're there now, feet away, staring at their father. Finally her voice is back. She screams.

Kent's holding her by the upper arms, his face inches away from her own. He's shaking her. "Wake up. Wake up."

She's trembling.

"You're having a bad dream."

"Terry," she says, half in the waking world and half out.

Kent is still shaking her. "Who?"

"Leave him alone," she mutters.

"What? Leave who alone?"

She's drenched. Finally she's able to open her eyes. Looks right at him.

"You were whimpering," he says, letting go of her arms and sitting back.

"Was I?"

"And clawing at the sheets."

She breathes in and out. In and out. Is there any way to slow her heart? Completely awake now. A dream – no, a nightmare. The worst she's had in a long time. What else might she have said out loud that she's unaware of?

"What was it about?"

She sits up. Wipes the sweat from her forehead with the back of her hand. "What?"

"The dream."

"It's gone."

"As quick as that?"

"You know I rarely remember."

He's staring right at her – through her, almost.

Last night comes back to her then. Ruined. Everything ruined. St. John's this Friday instead of Vancouver. Just him and her. She imagines all of the acting she'll have to do to convince him that she's having the time of her life: holding hands while they walk the waterfront, touching wineglasses before each sip, wrinkled sheets and pillows askew because of all the fucking he'll feel entitled to.

"Terry from the grocery store?" he says finally.

"What?"

"Your dream. Was it about him?"

"I don't remember."

"You said his name."

"Did I?"

His eyes likely to burn holes through her skin.

"If I did, I don't remember."

He sits there looking at her for a long time. Then he says, "Well, it didn't sound like much fun."

All she can think about is that knife going in and out. Terry's blood all over the blade.

Kent's already dressed. Navy button-up shirt and matching dress pants. Hair gelled back, and the wound above his eye nearly already healed. After a moment, he reaches out and places his palm on her forehead. "Your fever from yesterday's broken."

It's true: she feels less hot, and the swollen throat is not so swollen anymore. Just a dull throbbing at her temples instead of those imaginary thumbs pressing into each. The fatigue's still hanging on though, enough to make her want to lie back down, pull the sheets over her head, and go back to sleep. Sometimes sleep is the only thing she looks forward to.

He moves closer and kisses her forehead. His lips, like the rest of him, are boiling. It's one reason she has to move to the edge of the bed each night. He's like a furnace.

He gets to his feet. "Can you make us hotel reservations today? I'll leave my Visa on the kitchen table."

Hotel reservations, she thinks, and the rest of the town out of work.

He moves to the door. Turns back once there. "And don't be stingy, okay. Nothing but the best for my Emily." He smiles. "You're not going to want to come back."

She listens to his walk down the hall, him opening and closing the front door, the truck's engine revving, crunching gravel, and those horn blasts. Always those horn blasts. Waking everyone on the street, no doubt.

She manages to get up. One hundred and ten pounds if she's lucky, but feeling more like two hundred. The pads of her feet are tender. Her right knee cracks with every step. She doesn't bother with her robe or slippers, just walks out in her nightgown to the kitchen.

She sees it lying there, his Visa with the mystery limit. Five thousand? Ten? Twenty-five? How would she know? *Take it*, she thinks. *Book*

new flights and leave this afternoon. Save the money in the sock for Vancouver.
She'll need that and more besides, she knows.

She picks the Visa up, runs her forefinger along the card number like a blind person reading Braille. Goes over to the phone. Picks it up. But he'll track the purchase and find her, she realizes. Easy as that. He isn't supposed to find her.

She flings the card across the kitchen. Slams the phone back onto its cradle. Steadies her faltering balance by placing her palms flat down on the countertop.

She's losing. Deflating almost. What little there is left inside her is being suctioned out like blood into the body of a needle. How much more can she take?

"Just one more week," she whispers to herself. She lets her head fall against her chest, then breathes out slowly. *One more.* But she can't wait another week, day, hour, minute, or goddamn second. The waiting is over. There's just *leaving* on her mind now. Body turned towards the west and her mind already forgetting.

She walks across the kitchen and picks the card up off the floor. *Make new reservations and he'll find me.* Probably be on Jackie's doorstep before the end of the week. No getting away then. Ever.

But Vancouver's a big place though. Isn't it? People must be able to disappear if they want to. Maybe she can too. Cut her hair and change her name. Become someone else. She hasn't been herself in a long time anyway.

She goes back over to the phone. Puts the receiver to her ear and punches in some numbers. *Make the reservation, then get lost. Anyone can in Vancouver.*

Just one ring before the call is picked up.

"Bell directory assistance," the female voice on the other end says. "For English, say English –"

"English," Emily says.

"For what city?"

She hesitates a moment, then says, "St. John's."

"Do you want a residential number?"

"No."

"For what name?"

"The Battery Hotel."

"One moment please."

Emily waits and then takes down the number.

2

SHE WIPES THE STEAM FROM THE MIRROR, then stands there looking at herself. The near-scalding water she'd used in the shower has turned her flesh pink, giving her face a healthy glow. She runs a comb through her hair and then afterwards runs a few fingers along her pronounced cheekbones. She imagines detailed ribs too, beneath the towel she's wrapped around herself. Amazing what stress can do, she thinks.

Her towel slips off, but she doesn't reach out to grab it, letting it fall to the floor. Not that long ago, she knows, her fuller breasts would have kept it in place.

The hotel room she's booked is facing the Narrows of St. John's harbour. Almost five hundred dollars for four nights. That's almost as much money as she makes in two weeks at the grocery store. Valedictorian of her high school graduation class to work for ten dollars an hour. She knows what they think – those still left, those who come back from time to time to visit aging parents. She sees it when she hands them their receipts, the way their eyes stay on her longer than necessary, as if searching for the right words to let her know that there's no shame in doing what she does. She can hear it in their voices. In Jackie's voice even. Her old teachers are the worst: downcast eyes and awkward small talk as they trip over her unfulfilled potential.

There's a scream suddenly. Then crying. Lynette.

She rewraps the towel around herself and pushes open the bathroom door. The bottoms of her feet are still wet and she nearly slips on the hardwood.

"Get off!" she hears Lynette say.

"What's going on in there?" She quickens her pace, nearly tears the handle off Lynette's bedroom door when she opens it.

Jeremy's on top of his sister, using his knees to pin Lynette's arms down. He's hauling on her hair.

"Mom!" Lynette screams.

"That's right, cry to Mommy you little bitch," Jeremy says.

She stands in the doorway for a moment, unable to move. "Get off your sister!" she screams. It's a voice unlike her own.

Jeremy barely has time to turn around before she's gripping him underneath each armpit, pulling him off as easily as if he were a stuffed toy. He falls onto his back. She gets on top of him. One hand holds her towel in place while the other, it's palm open, draws back and then comes down hard across his face, the sound of it filling the room. She hits him again on the same cheek before Jeremy can raise his hands to protect himself. A smack accompanies each word she says now: "*You're – never – to – hit – your – sister!*" Two land on the crown of his head, the others against the back of his hands. The last one, because of a sliver of space between Jeremy's pinkies, makes partial contact with the tip of his nose.

She sits looking down on him now, hardly able to catch her breath, beads of sweat in the space between her breasts.

So quiet. What happened to Lynette's crying?

She turns around, sees that her daughter has backed herself up against the closet door. Big eyes and a face wet with tears. Her giraffe is lying prostrate near to her toes.

"Who started it?"

Lynette doesn't answer.

Jeremy wiggles beneath her. It's him crying now, she realizes, his shoulders and lower belly bouncing, his hands still pressed against his face. Not making a sound though.

She's never hit her children, not before this. Nor has Kent. They'd decided long before Jeremy was born that a palm would never make contact with a cheek. That a belt would never be unbuckled.

She tries to pry Jeremy's fingers away from his face.

"Don't touch me!"

"Jeremy – "

"Don't!"

"Mommy's sorry." She feels her bottom lip quiver, a thickness at the back of her throat. *You've taught him, haven't you? Beaten him up in front of his little sister.*

She gets off of him, tries to stop him from running away, but he yanks himself free from her grip. "Come back!"

She listens to his steps down the hall. Then him fiddling in the porch. "You've got school!"

Before opening and then slamming the front door, he says, "I hate you!"

She stands up, the remnants of the slaps in her palms. She lays them on the moist towel, against each thigh. After a moment she turns to Lynette. "Why aren't you dressed?"

Lynette doesn't answer.

"Didn't I tell you to?"

Lynette nods.

"Hurry up then, we need to go and find him."

3

IT'S WET AND COLD. The sky has that: I-might-dump-some-snow-on-you look. The wind is like November wind, like it could crack your skin.

Lynette's walking beside her, her little fists clenched in spite of her mittens. Wearing her favourite toque with the fluffy tassel. Head pointed down towards her green sneakers with the multi-coloured laces.

At least one of them is dressed for the weather, Emily thinks. She wishes now that she'd put a sweater on underneath her windbreaker.

Her daughter, usually humming the latest pop song by now, is quiet. Hasn't so much as opened her mouth since Emily came charging into her bedroom earlier.

"Cold, baby?"

Lynette shakes her head.

"Hold my hand."

Lynette offers hers without looking up.

So far they've looked for Jeremy in the garage; the playground three streets over from their house; the beach where, three weeks ago, Kent had helped him erect a makeshift fort; and the shabbily built baseball diamond behind the Lightning Cove Museum, half of its backstop fencing hanging down, the third base missing altogether.

Emily looks at her watch: nine-thirty. Half an hour late for work already; the kids an hour late for school.

Where is he, she thinks? He's never just run off before. Freezing by now without his jacket still on its hanger in the closet. Nothing on his fatless frame but a *Simpson's* T-shirt and a pair of jeans.

She tugs on Lynette's hand. "Hold on, baby." Why didn't she think of this before? He's at school already. Of course. "This way," she says, pulling Lynette in the opposite direction.

She quickens her pace, Lynette having to speed-walk to keep up.

She wonders if she's left finger marks on his cheeks. Imagines Mrs. Pike, his homeroom teacher, looking at him above the frames of her black-rimmed glasses. "Who did that to you?" she asks. Then Jeremy saying, "Mom." A police cruiser waiting for her when she gets home. Child Services from Gander.

Crying without making a sound, she remembers, his fingers pressed to his face in spite of her trying to pry them off. *What kind of mother are you?*

He'll fight her now, she knows, to stay with his father once he learns the truth. She sees him refusing to get on the plane. Him looking for some way, once they're in Vancouver, to contact his father.

They pass the Royal Bank.

A tapping against the glass makes her turn. It's Sonya, the teller, her hand a collage of sparkly rings and polished nails inches long. A fat wrist with a fatter gold bangle. Lipstick and too much eyeliner for a face as round as hers. She's pointing at the wall clock behind her, then at Lynette, the fat underneath her arm jiggling.

Emily considers mouthing: *fuck you*, but instead says, "I know." She pulls Lynette harder than she means to in order to get out of Sonya's field of vision; Lynette's feet almost lose contact with the pavement.

"Too fast, Mommy."

"Sorry, sweetie." She looks back to be sure that Sonya isn't stealing a peek at them from the corner of the bank entrance, then turns back around. "I'm glad you're talking to me again."

They walk the length of Main Street without seeing another soul and then take a right onto Trinity. The smell of fish coming from Hanrahan's Seafood makes her dry heave; Anique's Antiques, a little farther along, has a big 'We're Closed' sign in the window. Odd for Wednesday, Emily thinks.

She hears the sound of an approaching vehicle going too fast for a residential street. Its front appears over the rise in the road ahead, glittering grill and bumper despite the heavy cloud cover, big front tires, and treads deep enough to fit your hand into.

She stops cold. It's Kent. Sitting so high in his seat that the top of his head is nearly touching the roof. Someone's sitting in the passenger side. Jeremy, she realizes. Jeremy. He must have run all the way to his father's work.

Not expecting Kent to honk his horn, she and Lynette jump with fright when he does. Her daughter's grip tightens.

He's not slowing down. Going faster, actually. The revving engine making a racket.

She waves her hand in the air, as if flagging a taxicab. I suppose he sees us, she thinks. The only two people out. "Come here," she says to Lynette, pulling her farther onto the road's shoulder.

The truck speeds past, flicking gravel into the air. They lower their heads so as not to get anything in their eyes.

The screeching of tires on pavement then. A black mark on the road; Emily sees it when she raises her head. Gears shifting now, the truck's rear-lights aglow. His arm draped over the seat, his head cocked back. Reversing. Again too fast. When he's positioned the truck so that the driver's side is facing her, he slams on the brakes. Lowers the power window. Rests his forearm on the window ledge, then juts his head out. Looks at her.

She goes to him, still holding Lynette's hand. Near the door, she stops, looks past him to get a better view of Jeremy. Despite the darkness of the cab's interior, she can still make out the red blotches on his face. "Thank God you found him."

"Found *me*, more like it," Kent says. "Right in the middle of a meeting too."

She doesn't say anything.

"Barged right in, he did." He pauses before saying, "Imagine the looks I got."

Jeremy's staring straight ahead like she's not even there. He looks older to her, somehow. More man than boy, suddenly.

"Jeremy," she says, "Mommy's sorry – "

"Your goddamn handprints are all over his face, Emily!"

"I didn't mean it – "

"I got enough to worry about at work."

In the silence, Lynette tries to slip her hand out from inside her mother's, but Emily holds on tighter. A car approaches from the other direction and slows down as it nears the truck. Young Alan Cross, she notices, the one Kent had said was taking his wife and getting the hell out of Lightning Cove. He's just about to stop, but Kent honks his horn and waves him on. Alan looks right at her, raises his hand in a wave as he passes.

They listen until the sound of his engine dies away.

"Get in," Kent says, finally.

"I'll walk them from here – "

"No."

"Why not?"

"Because they're not going to school today."

"But I want to," Lynette says.

"You heard me." Then, "Not with your brother's face the way it is." The last bit, Emily notices, is directed at herself.

Funny how he's never bothered hiding me indoors. "But I've got work. I'm already so late."

He sticks his head out farther. Lowers his voice like a late-night radio DJ. "Get in. Now."

There it is, she knows – that look. Calm almost but not quite. The lines in his often-wrinkled brow gone, those few in the corners of his eyes gone too. Lids slightly lowered over cold eyes. Dead eyes.

Kent opens his door. Pushes his seat forward so that Emily and Lynette can climb into the back. Puts the truck in gear and presses hard on the gas before Emily has a chance to fasten Lynette's seatbelt. She doesn't bother with her own.

He drives fast. Not talking. Staring back at her in the rear-view mirror.

So she doesn't have to meet his eyes, she turns to gaze out the window at the passing world: patchy lawns in front of paint-chipped bungalows; lopsided two-storey homes that seem on the verge of falling over; a grey, endless sea, and icebergs in the distance. She knows this world – *her* world, as well as she knows the bodies of her own babies, as well as she knows the smell that Kent leaves on his pillow, yet somehow it all seems strange. Like she doesn't belong. A foreigner.

He pulls into the driveway. Breaks too hard.

Lynette's seatbelt digs into her chest; Emily braces her palms against the back of Jeremy's seat.

He shuts off the engine, then goes to open his door.

"*You're* coming in?" she asks.

He stops. Looks back at her.

Those eyes. If not for them, she thinks, she might be able to cope. Maybe. "I thought you were in the middle of a meeting?"

He's still looking at her, not saying a thing.

"Go in you two," she says to Lynette and Jeremy.

Lynette starts to leave, but Jeremy pretends he hasn't heard her.

"We're *all* going in," Kent says, turning from her in order to look at Jeremy.

Jeremy undoes his seatbelt and goes; Lynette's already halfway to the porch.

Kent gets out. Slams his door with so much force that Emily can feel the inside of the truck shake. He takes a step back to where she's still sitting in the back seat. Raps the knuckle of his middle finger against the glass as casually as if he were knocking on the door of a buddy's place, then signals for her to get out by crooking his forefinger.

She doesn't move. Looks instead to the front door of the house. Even though her brother had pinned her down this morning, Lynette is holding it open for him. He walks past her. Lynette comes out, still holding the doorknob, wondering what's taking her and Kent so long, probably. Emily waves her inside.

He's knocking again, except that now he's using all four knuckles. Without thinking, she reaches up and locks the door. Then slides her bum to the centre of the backseat. *I'm safe as long as I don't go into the house.*

It's the sound of his laughing that makes her turn to face him. Big teeth. He raises his keychain, and dangles it teasingly in front of her, then presses the unlock button. Laughs again, before saying, "Come inside so we can talk."

She shakes her head. "Is that what you call it?"

"Come in, Emily – "

"No." She slides all the way over to the other side.

His knuckles hitting the window again. How has the glass not shattered? "Don't make me come in there."

Liar. You won't. A neighbour might see.

He walks around to her side.

She locks the door again.

He unlocks it again.

It starts to snow. Wet flakes.

He puts his face close to the window, his nose nearly touching, his eyes as big as Frisbee's. "Come in." He pauses for a second, then says, "Last chance."

She considers it. Then imagines what will be waiting for her if she does, and how long it will last. It's the just-before time she most dreads. *Just before* he grabs her or *just before* he slaps her face or *just before* he kicks her stomach. How strange that the anticipation should be worse than the act. But it is. Every time. At least once it's begun she knows that the ending is closer. It's all about getting to the end. To the point where he's an exhausted lump of remorse. On his knees with his hands resting on his thighs, down-turned mouth, pale face, watering eyes, and forever that rising and falling chest, like something inside him struggling to get out.

You won't. Not in front of the whole street.

She's surprised when he grabs the handle of the door and yanks it open. She manages to slide a little in the other direction before she feels him grip her upper arm. She makes no sound when he twists and pulls and then drags her out the open door. How can he be so strong?

He kicks the door shut, then pins her against the truck – his body like a bag of stones – nearly crushing her.

"All right." She struggles to breathe beneath him. "I'll come." He's holding her by the neck, yet she manages to say, "Someone will see –"

"Yeah…that you're a fucking bitch."

Lynette's staring through the window.

"She's watching, Kent. Please stop."

He lets go of her neck and grips her again around the bicep. Hauls her along the driveway towards the porch.

She digs her heels into the crunched rock. Although she wants it over, she still has trouble with it starting.

"I'm sorry," she says. She *is* too. For hurting Jeremy the way she did. Perhaps Kent's fists will be useful for once. Still, though, a part of her resists. Near the bottom of the porch stairs she says, "Don't, Kent. Please."

Lynette has moved away from the window now, probably on her way to the front door, Emily imagines.

He pulls her so hard that she trips on the bottom step, then falls forward onto her knees. The steps are wet now because of the snow.

"Get up."

It's like her shoulder is going to come out of its socket by the way he's tugging at it. "Okay, okay."

How easily he gets her back up. As if she's weightless. Pure air. Nothing.

A vehicle pulls in the driveway before they can take another step.

"Who is it?" Kent says.

There's a sensation of everything dropping inside her: heart, lungs, intestines, breath, blood – all of it, going right to the pads of her feet. It's a wonder she doesn't fall where she's standing.

It's Terry's car. What's he doing here? Her dream comes back to her: the furry dice, the idling engine. The knife going in and out. *Go away, Terry, for Jesus' sake.* What will Kent think, him showing up like this?

Kent's grip loosens, as Terry pulls in behind his truck.

"Who is it?" He asks again.

She's unable to answer, her mind going over what she'll need to do to prevent the second part of her nightmare from coming true.

Kent's truck is blocking their view now, so instead they listen. A car door opening, then the steady *ding ding ding* from inside until Terry closes it, boots on crunched gravel, lighter steps than Emily would have expected. He appears from behind the truck: an apron around his waist and a pen tucked behind his ear. He's looking right in their direction, yet seems surprised to see them, stopping suddenly, like a dog with no slackness left on its leash.

Kent lets her go.

"Terry," she says. "What are you doing here?"

Terry's about to say something, but he stops himself. Looks at Kent instead.

Kent stares back.

For a minute, it feels as though her legs won't be able to support her. She has to take hold of Kent's arm to steady herself, feeling its solidness through his coat. It dawns on her suddenly that, for as many times as she's wanted to get away, so too are the number of times that she's depended on him – needed him. Funny to need support from the very arm that, just moments ago, had wanted to knock her down.

Finally Kent says, "What can I do for you, Terry?"

Terry's hair is getting flattened because of the snow. He wipes his hands in his apron. Clears his throat. "Sorry for showing up unannounced. I tried calling, but there was no answer."

Neither Kent nor Emily says anything.

Her boss puts his hands into his pockets. His eyes go to Emily, then to the wet spots on the knees of her pants. "Did you fall?"

Silence for a moment.

She goes to speak, but Kent does before she can get the chance. "Jesus slippery steps. Caught her just in time."

Terry keeps staring. Doesn't say anything.

"Lay down some salt, later on," Kent says.

Terry nods, his eyes still locked on Emily's knees.

"What was it you wanted?" Kent says.

Emily clocks Terry as he lifts his gaze and zooms in on her neck. Kent's fingerprints all over it, she bets.

"Terry?" Kent says.

Terry's eyes snap back to her husband.

"What did you want, I said?"

Terry steps forward, then stops. Is about to say something, but Kent speaks first.

"Our oldest is sick, so she can't come in today if that's what you're wondering."

All her boss can do is nod.

"Guess you'll have to mind the till on your own this morning."

In the silence, Terry looks from Emily to Kent. From Kent to Emily. Then, at last, he says, "Nothing serious, I hope."

"What?" Kent says.

"Your youngster. Nothing serious, I hope."

Her husband shakes his head. "No, nothing serious."

After a moment, Kent walks down a few steps, then stops and looks right at Terry. "Gonna have a hard time getting back to work with you blocking me." He juts his chin towards the parked vehicles.

Terry's pocket must be full of coins considering the racket he's making. "Right. Well... I'll be on my way." He stays where he is for ages, then finally turns to go, looking back only once before getting into his car.

She stands there watching him leave, imagining herself taking the stairs two, three at time down to the driveway, then running along the crunched stone to his car and jumping in the passenger side and locking the door and screaming for him to drive. Terry stomping on the gas and Kent's figure growing smaller in the side mirror.

She shakes the thought away to find that her husband is glaring at her from his place on the stairs. Lifting her chin, she looks for Terry only to realize that he's already gone. Nothing left of him but the sound of his car engine fading away.

She looks back at Kent. Breathes deep. Lets it out. Plants her feet firmly beneath her, a slight bend in each knee. *Okay, you son of a bitch. I'm ready.*

He doesn't make his way towards her though. He turns away instead and continues down the steps towards his truck.

She watches him get in, turn the ignition, back out, then take off up the street. No honks this time.

Wet flakes against her face.

Safe.

For now.

4

SHE OPENS THE FRONT DOOR OF HER HOUSE. Heather is standing there. Messy hair and open, worn leather coat with a blue work shirt underneath, thick eyeliner and unzipped black boots. She's sucking Orange Crush through a straw.

Before she can speak, Heather says, "What the fuck..."

Emily wipes her eyes. It's like she's been asleep for one hundred years. Limbs like wood, one side of her face numb from where she'd been lying on it, her throat dry.

"Did Bell cancel your phone or something?"

"What?" She can't remember what day it is.

"How many times does a girl have to call?"

"I fell asleep..."

"Yeah."

"On the chesterfield –"

"Died, more like it."

"Didn't hear the phone, I guess." It occurs to her that she'd slept without dreams, without a sense of her own existence. The best kind of sleep. "What time is it?"

"Well, seeing as I'm supposed to be on break, I'd say around... twelve-thirty."

It's Wednesday. Wednesday. She remembers Kent's strong grip. Being dragged up the steps. Terry showing up just in time. "Terry called you in?"

Heather sucks on her straw again.

"I'm sorry, I would have come in if – "

"You could have – yeah, I know."

They're silent for a moment; Emily still trying to wake up; Heather jamming her tongue ring in and out of the space between her front teeth.

No wet snow now, but a dark sky still, the breeze less chilly than earlier.

"So how's the little one?" Heather says at last.

"Hmm?"

"Jeremy. You know, the reason you couldn't make it into work this morning – "

"Better. Well, not better *yet*, but getting there."

"That's good."

She notices Heather trying to look past her, into the kitchen.

"Who's minding the store?" Emily says.

"I don't know. Terry, I guess."

"You mean you just up and left?"

"Yeah. So?"

"Heather – "

"Why do you care?"

"I don't. I just feel bad, that's all."

Heather sucks the dregs from the bottom of her can, then says, "Not gonna invite me in, or what?"

Emily hesitates a minute before saying, "I wouldn't want you to catch what Jeremy has. Especially when you've got a show tonight. It *is* tonight, right?"

Heather nods. "Have to go straight there from work. I'll miss the setup. Probably the sound test, too."

It occurs to her that she has no idea where the children are. Didn't see them when she woke up, or before she fell asleep either. She wonders why neither one of them answered the phone when Heather called. "Well, I should be going. Lunch for the kids and everything." She starts closing the door, then stops. "I really am sorry, Heather." She goes to shut it all the way, but Heather stops it with her hand.

"Quit the bullshit, Emily."

"What?"

"You think I'm as stunned as that?"

"I have no idea what you're on about –"

"Don't you?"

"No."

"What was dear old hubby doing hauling you up the steps, then?"

"What?"

"Jesus, why do I always have to say everything twice? Terry said he saw Kent manhandle you."

She freezes, her mouth half hanging open.

"Did you hear me?"

She finds her voice finally. "He's a fucking liar!"

"Why would he make it up?"

"The stairs were wet and Kent was making sure I didn't fall."

"Trying to knock you down them, more like it."

She goes to slam the door in Heather's face, but again, the younger woman stops her.

"Mind your own business!" Emily says.

Heather doesn't move.

"Get away from the door! I don't have time for this."

"Make time! I'm done covering for you."

"Just go, Heather!"

"I won't!"

"*Heather –* "

"Just admit it why don't ya?"

"Admit what?"

"That your perfect hubby's at it again."

"What are you talking about?"

"You know."

"I don't."

"Let me in."

Emily squeezes herself in between the door's opening, blocking Heather's way.

"It all made sense this morning, suddenly," Heather says.

"What? What made sense, suddenly?"

"The weight you're losing. The way you look scared when there's nothing to be scared of."

Emily says nothing.

"And then Terry's driving up your street and what do you think he sees?"

Again she stays quiet.

"Only that bastard knocking you off your feet, that's all. Hauling you back up like you're no better than a dog."

Despite her long nap, she's weary, her hand barely able to keep hold of the doorknob, her knees nearly buckling. Her lungs are drawing breath still, although reluctantly, as if they're sick to death of the same old in and out. She's able to muster up two little words with what energy she has left. "I slipped."

Heather just stares, jams her tongue ring between her front teeth. She slides it out, then says, "He's beating you around again." It isn't a question.

It never stopped. Her ears are ringing, like someone has just slapped them. Every part of her tingles and, despite the cold, she's overheated, a tide of it runs up the entire length of her body. "I need you to leave now."

"I'm right though, aren't I?"

It occurs to her that a secret only remains one for so long before revealing itself. The unraveling is first. She's been unraveling for years, slowly in the beginning, then faster, like a tear gaining momentum as it trickles down the cheek.

"Who is it, Mommy?" says a voice behind her.

She turns around to see Lynette with an open colouring book in her hands, the page displaying a beautifully coloured meadow in front of a log cabin. Not so much as a smear outside the lines. There's a deer standing off to the side, which she hasn't gotten around to filling in yet. "It's Heather, from Mommy's work."

Lynette jams herself in beside Emily. Looks up at the young woman.

"Hi cutie," Heather says.

"Hi," Lynette says.

"That's awesome colouring."

"Say thank you, honey," Emily says.

"Thank you."

"Are you sick too?" Heather asks.

Before Lynette can answer, Emily says, "Where's your brother?"

"Playing PlayStation."

"Okay, go on now. Your mother is having a grown-up conversation."

Lynette turns to go.

"Bye," Heather says to her back.

"Bye," Lynette says without turning around.

Emily disappears for a second and then comes back with one arm in a heavy sweater. She comes out onto the porch. Closes the door.

"I guess I'm not going in," Heather says.

She slips in her other arm, then does up the buttons. Walks to where the deck chairs are and sits down. Extends her hand for Heather to do the same.

Heather comes over and sits across from her, torso leaning forward, widely parted legs, elbows on her knees, and her hands interlaced with the empty Crush can in between.

After a moment, Emily says, "Share a smoke?"

Heather puts the can down between her feet. Reaches inside her coat and hauls out a pack of Player's Light. Pulls one out of the pack and, cupping it to block the wind, flicks open her Zippo lighter and produces a flame. Leans her face into it, her cheeks indenting as she sucks.

Emily breathes in the smell of tobacco before holding out her own hand. Placing the cigarette between thin, dry lips, she inhales, holding the smoke in for a moment before blowing out. Light-headed immediately. She drags on it again, then hands it back. Looks across at the high school dropout who still lives at home with her mother, who can't add to save her life, who constantly has customers coming back to complain that she's overcharged them, and who'd prefer a *People Magazine* to a novel any day. Even Terry had been apprehensive about hiring her. "It'll just be a *job* to her," he'd said. "A job is just a job to *most* people," had been Emily's reply. Yet Heather's the one, before anybody else, to put it all together. Not even six months they've been working together. Before that, the most Emily had seen of her was in posters taped to light poles: Heather in the foreground, her bandmates behind her, *The High-Top Bay Girls* in unfocused lettering above their heads. *One Show Only!*

"Here," Heather says.

Emily takes the smoke. Drags twice more. Gives it back. "That's enough for me." She puts her hands in her sweater pockets as a shiver shoots through her.

Heather finishes the rest and then snuffs it out on the sole of her boot. Puts it in her pocket. Tilts her face towards the sky. "I could do this at work."

"Do what?"

"Sit here doing nothing."

"Don't you, usually?"

They share a laugh, then go quiet.

A car drives by, the child in the back seat staring right at them. A squirrel drops from a tree onto the deck railing, then leaps back into the same tree. The wind picks up for a second, then dies away.

Heather zips up her coat, tucks her chin underneath the collar for warmth before taking it out again. Looks across at her. "There was something else too."

Emily returns her co-worker's stare. Doesn't say anything.

"Besides looking scared, I mean." Heather crushes her empty pop can with the sole of her foot.

"What?" Emily says, both wanting and not wanting to know.

It seems like forever waiting for Heather to speak. Then finally she says,

"Sadness."

Emily's eyes are suddenly wet. She uses the collar of her sweater to wipe the tears away, then looks beyond the younger woman, at the sea. Not a boat to be seen. *Sadness.* All this time it hasn't had a name. It's been heavy limbs, sore feet and headaches, nausea and dizziness, it's been waking up and wanting to go back to sleep, drifting too far into the middle of the street, hearing hello and not saying it back, looking into a face but not seeing it. All these years to have this woman – girl, nearly – tell her what she hasn't been able to tell herself: Sadness.

She feels Heather shift even closer, so that their knees are almost touching.

"How long this time?"

She tries to attach a number, but can't. How long since she's been eating? Sleeping? "I don't know."

"The kids too?"

"No," Emily says. "Not the kids." *More than I can say for myself.*

Neither speaks for a while.

"There's places," Heather says. "Not here, there's fuck all here, but in Grand Falls, I mean. St. John's."

"You mean a shelter?"

"Yeah."

She shifts in her chair. "I did once. This place in Gander. Couple of years ago."

"And?"

She looks away. Breathes in the smell of salt water. Rubs her hands over her face. Looks back. "And...I went back to him."

A flock of seagulls passes over the house, their hungry squawks slicing open the morning's quiet like a scalpel through flesh.

"You're shaking," Heather says.

"What?"

"Your hands."

She looks down, remembering when she could thread a needle without wetting the thread's tip, when she could hold full cups of coffee without spilling a drop, when she could read to her children without needing them to hold the book so that she might see the words.

"Then leave again," Heather says. "Whatever it takes."

She pauses for a moment, then says, "Don't tell anyone, okay."

Heather nods.

Emily leans in close. "Promise."

"I promise."

No relief has come with sharing her secret, she realizes, not like she'd hoped. If anything, her worry has increased. In her mind, she'd imagined a discreet disappearance: she and her children walking along the gangway, then up the stairs to the top level of the ferry. The fog as thick as butter. No words between them. Suitcases at their feet. No one to wave goodbye to as the boat drifts away.

"It's easy to forget that you deserve better," Heather says.

"What?"

"Over time, I mean. It's easy to forget. Then suddenly you're used to it." She pauses. Then says, "Just like my mother got used to it."

It's quiet for ages.

"Not that long ago people used to think my mother and me were sisters," Heather says finally. "Can you imagine that? She wouldn't pass for my grandmother now. Lines around her mouth. Not from laughing, don't worry." Heather pauses to undo her jacket. "Jesus place, cold one minute then warm the next."

She notices too that the wind has grown milder.

"Then Dad dies and I think she'll be okay, you know. But it's too late, right."

After a moment, Heather gets to her feet. "Come tonight."

"What?" She stands too. "Where?"

"To the show."

"I don't know."

"*He* won't let you, I suppose."

"It's not that. I don't expect he'll even be home by then. The kids'll need a sitter and everything."

"Right. Well, if you change your mind, you know where we are. It won't be anything too heavy if that's what you're worried about. Rock/Celtic sort of thing, you know."

She nods.

For a while they just stand there looking at each other. Then Heather says, "I should get back. Can't leave that *one* customer waiting."

They both laugh.

Heather turns away and starts down the steps. Halfway down she turns back to Emily. "Let me know…if there's anything I can do. You don't have to be alone in this."

Something about the word 'alone' makes her look away. Steals her breath. Swells the back of her throat.

"You okay?"

She looks back at the younger woman. Nods. Then says, "Thanks."

5

"SORRY," SAYS THE MALE VOICE ON THE OTHER END, "it's all booked for tomorrow. Would you like me to try Saturday?"

"No."

"Sunday –"

"This weekend's no good."

"How about Monday?"

"No! I'm sorry, um…that won't work either." She sits on the edge of the bed. Then turns around to make sure that the bedroom door is still closed. Puts the cordless to her other ear. "How much did you say it was to change the flight to a day next week?"

"Like I already said, Miss, your booking was during a seat-sale, and everything next week is full price. You'll have to pay the difference."

"How much is the full price?"

She listens to his busy fingers atop the buttons of his computer.

"Three thousand two hundred and seventy dollars," he says.

"*What!*"

"Three thousand two hundred – "

"I heard you, I just don't believe it."

"It's eight-seventy-two per person."

"The kids too?"

"Yes. After fees and surcharges that's the total."

More than what she's saved at the grocery store, she thinks, letting herself fall backwards onto the bed. She imagines it splitting at the centre and sucking her in.

"Are you still there, Miss?"

"That's nearly double what I paid."

"If you'd called sooner then maybe – "

"It's just that I'm on a fixed budget."

He doesn't say anything, just breathes.

"Look, I'll have to call you back –"

The line suddenly goes dead.

She presses the 'off' button and just lies there staring at the ceiling fan. She doesn't have enough money, but what choice has Kent left her? Either she pays the difference or she doesn't go at all.

The phone's still in her hand when it rings. She nearly flings it across the room in fright. She presses 'talk' and, thinking it might be Air Canada calling back, says, "I'll pay the difference –" she stops herself. *Oh my God. It could just as easily be Kent on the other end.*

She waits.

"Hello?

She sits up.

"Emily?"

"Terry?"

"What did you just say?"

"What?"

"Something about paying – "

"I was talking to one of the youngsters."

"Oh."

Quiet now, just the sound of each other's breathing.

She remembers her dream: the knife going in and out, Kent standing over him, Lynette and Jeremy watching it all. Again she looks to the door. Keeps her eyes on it for a minute just to be sure that no one will come barreling in. That *Kent* won't come barreling in.

She looks at the alarm clock. 6:15 p.m. All evening she's been waiting for him to come back, to finish what he's started. There's nothing worse than waiting, she thinks. Nothing in the world.

"Can we talk?" Terry says.

"Aren't we?"

"No. Not over the phone. Can you come to the marina?"

"What? Now?"

"Can you?"

"I've got the youngsters."

"Bring them."

Again she looks over at the clock. Takes a few seconds before saying, "What's so important that it can't wait 'til tomorrow?"

He says nothing.

"This wouldn't have anything to do with earlier, would it?"

Terry doesn't answer.

"What did you say to Heather?"

He stays quiet.

"What did you say to Heather, I said?"

"Only what I saw."

"And what do you think you *saw*, Terry?"

His breathing in her ear, and then him saying, "Come to the marina, please. I'll drive you home afterwards."

"What do you think people will say, Terry? Me and you sipping coffee over there at the marina." *What would Kent think?*

"What? Two work associates can't have coffee?"

She looks over at the door. Gets up and walks over to the window. Stares out. No sign of his truck. She stays there, still feeling where Kent's hand had been at the top of her arm, his grip so tight. If she bothered pulling up her sleeve, she'd find finger marks.

Ten minutes to walk there, she figures. Another few to hear what Terry has to say. If she runs back, she can make it in six or seven minutes. 6:16 now, back by 6:45 the latest. Other than last night, when has he made it home before eight these past months? Plenty of time, she thinks. Plenty.

"Hello?"

"I'm here," she says.

"You're distracted."

She nearly laughs. *Distracted. How does forgetting what I'm doing right in the middle of doing it sound? Distracted.* Another word she can add to *sad*, she thinks. "Just tired." *So tired.*

Silence on the other end.

Then she says, "Ten minutes, Terry, that's all you get."

"Okay. Thank you. I'll just lock up here and drive on over."

"I won't wait, if you're not there," she says.

"I will be. Promise."

She presses the *off* button without saying goodbye. Turns away from the window and leaves the room. Walks down the hall and into the kitchen, putting the cordless phone back into its cradle. Goes to the living room. They're lying on their stomachs watching television.

"Gotta go out for a few minutes," she says.

Only Lynette bothers turning around. "Can I come?"

"Stay with your brother, I won't be long."

Lynette turns back around.

"Look out for your sister."

Jeremy doesn't answer.

She goes into the foyer, then slips her jacket off its hanger. Hauls on her boots. Before opening the door, she says, "Don't touch anything, Mommy'll be back soon." She steps onto the porch, the cold going right through her. 6:45, she thinks. The latest.

6

TERRY POURS IN A CREAMER AND THEN STIRS. Hers is black. She takes a sip. Looks over at Evelyn Ricketts sitting at a centre table with her fat, diabetic second husband, Perry, half-eaten slices of pie on their plates and large mugs of still-steaming hot chocolate in front of them. So much for his diabetic coma last year, she thinks.

Some teenagers she recognizes have pulled two tables together, sharing from three baskets of home-cut fries and sipping glasses of Pepsi. The few girls amongst them are getting more attention than the fries, having to endure pinched thighs and pulled bra straps.

She leans towards him. "So. Talk."

Terry stops himself in midsip. Puts the cup back down. "You don't waste any time, do you?"

She doesn't say anything.

"Why didn't you bring the little ones?"

"Because I didn't, that's why. Now, either say what you have to or I'm leaving."

"Okay." He pushes in his chair, then takes another sip of coffee. He looks at her. Picks at a callus on the palm of his right hand.

"Terry," she says. "*What?*"

He pulls a piece of hardened flesh away, holding it between his fingers, then says, "I'm worried about you." He lets the skin fall to the floor, then reaches for his mug.

"You shouldn't be," she says.

He takes another sip. "No?"

"No." After a moment, she says, "Is that it?"

He shakes his head.

"What else then?

"I don't know. Can't we just sit here?"

She leans forward, even closer than before, so that her jacket is almost dipping into her coffee. "No, we *can't* just sit here," she whispers, looking again at Evelyn, then at the teenagers before coming back to him. "We can't." She pushes out her chair and half stands –

"Don't go."

She shoots Evelyn another glance. Evelyn's looking right at her, smiling. Emily smiles back, then sits down again. Breathes deep, letting it out slowly. "The porch stairs were slippery and I fell okay. Kent was helping me up."

Terry stares at her, but doesn't say anything.

"A wild imagination you've got."

There's suddenly a roar of laughter amongst the teenagers; one of the boys is using a french fry as a moustache while another squirts a line of mustard across it. Evelyn and Perry exchange annoyed looks.

After the laughter subsides, Terry says, "You've never been inside my house, have you?"

"What?"

"You've seen it from the outside, I know, but I've never given you the grand tour, have I?"

She pauses for a second, then says, "No, I guess you haven't."

He downs the rest of his coffee. "I got one of those claw-footed bathtubs installed. Remember how you used to say how much you loved them?"

She nods, remembering having shown him a couple she'd admired from a magazine about a hundred years ago.

"Finally got around to renovating those two guest bedrooms too. You can see the water from the window of one."

She takes a long sip. Then another.

"A fully functioning fireplace too. Gets things nice and toasty. I'll just sit there staring at it. For hours, sometimes."

Evelyn and Perry are putting on their jackets, while Ivy, the young waitress and only daughter of Pat Gullage, the owner, pours the rest of their hot chocolates into take-out cups, then walks them to the door, holding it open for them.

"Too *much* room, if you ask me."

"What?" she says, turning back to him.

"The house. Too much room. Other than the living room and the bedroom, the rest of the place hardly gets used. And not even the bedroom really since I fall asleep on the chesterfield most nights."

She looks at her watch: 6:35. Should be on her way home by now. "Terry, I have to go."

"I know."

She tries to get Ivy's attention.

"It's on me," he says, motioning for her to lower her hand.

"Thanks."

She's in the process of doing up her jacket when he says, "What I'm trying to say is, if you and the youngsters...ever need a place..."

She stares at him.

"...for any reason, let me know." He lets another piece of skin fall on the floor beside his chair. Clears his throat. "That's all."

She thinks about touching his hand but doesn't. Stands up instead.

"Let me give you a lift," he says.

The knife going in and out. Kent standing over him. The children watching. "No."

"It's on the way."

"No," she says again. "I like the walk."

Terry nods. Then says, "Thanks for coming."

"Okay."

She's halfway out the door when he says, "I'll see you tomorrow then."

She turns around. Nods. Then leaves.

7

SHE STANDS THERE STARING AT KENT'S TRUCK. Home early for the second night in a row. She takes a few steps towards the porch but then stops. Thinks about going back the way she came, taking Terry up on his offer. *I got one of those claw-footed tubs installed. Remember how you used to say how much you loved them?* She loves them still.

A few more steps before she stops again. Imagines him throwing her across the floor, then loosening his belt and wrapping it around his fist as he comes toward her. She'll try to stand, but he'll knock her back down with the heel of his foot, then stand there looking down at her: wide stance and a slight bend in his knees, his chin slightly downward, his left hand hanging at his side, the other raised to just above his belly button. Eyes so large. When was the last time he blinked? Completely still. Their breaths in sync. He draws back his fist like he's pulling back an invisible arrow –

She shakes the thought away. Looks to the front window just in time to see tiny fingers part the curtains. Lynette.

More steps. More still. She stops at the bottom of the stairs. Remembers the humiliation of being on her knees earlier, her face near to his boots, then being yanked up like something not living – a sack of potatoes, a bucket of salt meat. Terry's face then, the same look she'd often seen in her own children: helplessness; frozen feet incapable of carrying them to a bedroom or a bathroom or any place; wide eyes in pale faces, like stage-frightened actors beneath the heat of too many lights.

The front door swings open, nearly making her faint with fright. She grabs the railing.

He steps out onto the porch. The laces of his boots are untied. He walks to the top of the stairs, then stops.

She sees herself running, along the driveway, up their street, the turn onto Trinity, past Hanrahan's Seafood and Anique's Antiques, faster, faster, faster, not even him in his truck able to catch her.

He stares down at her.

She looks up at him, then turns away. Looks up, turns away.

He crosses his arms in front of his chest. He's still in the clothes from this morning. "Strange you not being here when I got home."

"I was walking."

Silence.

"Strange you out walking, this time of the evening, the youngsters left by themselves."

"I was craving fresh air."

"Open a window. Come out on the porch."

More silence.

"Where'd you go?"

"Around the block."

"Where?"

"Along Trinity, where it connects to Main. Why?"

He takes a step down. Stops. Lays a palm on the rail. "The same way I came not ten minutes ago."

She's warm underneath her jacket, but she has a chill. "Why this talking first?" she says. "Always this *talking.*"

He doesn't say anything.

"I'm here," she says.

Kent steps back up onto the porch again. Moves to the door, opening it, his hand on the knob. "Come in."

She climbs the first three stairs, then stops. Winded, like an asthmatic. Too young to be this tired.

"Come on," he says.

Up some more before she stops again. Then finally all the way up. She stands at the other end of the porch staring at him. His face is calm, his body relaxed and leaning against the door frame, feet crossed at the ankles.

She goes toward him, the porch wood straining beneath her though she weighs less than ever, her own breath in her ears, and the pulse in her neck quickening. Stops right in front of him.

Instead of grabbing her like she expects, he steps aside in order to let her pass.

She grazes him as she goes in.

The door closes.

A lock is turned.

He's right behind her, the energy from his body pressing against her back. She stays standing a couple of feet inside the door. *Take off your boots and go in. Get it done with. The sooner it starts the sooner it will be over.*

Another moment before she finally kicks off her boots and unzips her jacket.

He's still behind her.

She goes to take off her coat, but he slips it off for her. Hangs it up. Lays a hand on the small of her back, leading her past the foyer and into the kitchen.

"Mommy," Lynette says, looking up from her colouring book, a red crayon in one of her hands.

Jeremy's got hockey cards strewn about the table. His glance at her and then away is hardly noticeable.

Kent guides her towards them, his hand still resting on her sitting bone. At the table, he pulls out his chair and lowers her onto it, then walks around and stands behind her.

She waits. Her hands in her lap. Her eyes on the children. "Go to your rooms," she says.

"They're okay there," he says.

Lynette's eyes linger in her direction for a moment before going back to the colouring book.

His supper. It's in the oven, covered in tinfoil. Three quarters of a meatloaf. She thinks about standing, but then changes her mind, her face slightly turned now towards the window. "Your supper," she says.

"Not yet."

Why this waiting? she thinks.

She flinches when he touches her shoulders. He lifts her hair in order to get his hands underneath, then massages deep into the muscles, the place where the shoulders connect to the neck, the place he's kissed ten thousand times. Although she tries not to, a moan releases itself from the back of her throat. She chews down on it just as another one comes.

He stops. His mouth is next to her ear. "I'm sorry about earlier," he whispers. He kisses the grown-over hole where pretty earrings had once hung. "Forgive me?"

She manages a nod before all of her – so tight a moment ago – goes slack. She has to squeeze her bottom teeth against her top ones just to keep her jaw from flopping open, grips the sides of her chair to keep from falling out of it. The breath she sucks in is so deep that she wonders if she's left any oxygen in the room. Heart beating slower, finally.

He walks around until he's facing her, wedges himself in between her thighs. Kneels down.

She turns from the window and looks at him. Despite having shaved this morning, there's already the shadow of a beard longing to break the surface of his skin. His neatly combed hair is now hanging in front of his forehead, a few strands reaching into his eyes. The cut she'd seen to the other night probably won't even leave a scar, she thinks. If he'll let her, she'll take out those stitches later.

"I almost forgot," he says.

"What?"

"Irene had her baby. Nearly nine pounds, Myles said."

"Finally."

"He was outside waiting for me after the meeting, a flask of Johnny Walker inside his jacket. 'Drink to my new son,' he said. He was relieved, I think, to hear that the crooks from St. John's had agreed on the severance package. Even got it in writing from Mr. Fisheries and Oceans himself."

"How's Irene?"

"Tired, Myles said. Worried, you know, about everything down at the plant, how they're supposed to manage with him out of work. Wants Myles to apply for a job in Fort McMurray." He rubs the top of her hands as if to warm them even though they're not cold, then says, "Myles gets homesick when he goes to Gander."

In the silence, Jeremy returns his hockey cards to their box; Lynette searches through her book for a colourless picture she might have missed, humming as she does. Kent looks down at her hands. Plays with her wedding band, pulling it in the direction of her fingernail, then back again. "Getting loose," he says.

She looks down at it, remembering that long ago blustery September when he'd knelt on her front stoop and offered it to her, how he'd had trouble sliding it on at first, how he'd hugged her too hard even though she hadn't said yes yet.

"Let's take a drive," he says.

"What?"

"Yay!" Lynette pushes out her chair.

"It's getting late," she says. "They need their baths."

"They can do that afterwards."

She pauses for a moment, then says, "Where?"

"Around the shore. Then afterwards we'll get french fries at the marina."

"Yay!" goes Lynette again.

Jeremy's eyes lighten a bit too at this suggestion.

"But they've just had their supper."

"A few fries won't kill them. Get your coats on youngsters."

She watches them run to the foyer, then fight to get into their coats, to shove on boots without tying the laces.

He's still between her thighs. "There's something else I was meaning to mention."

"What?" she says.

"It's about Friday."

She's unable to speak. Wonders if he's somehow figured out what her intention had been for that day. Has she left some clue behind? A floorboard not quite in place? A phone call that he might have been listening in on? *It's about Friday. Friday.* Funny how it was just a day of the week not that long ago. "What about it?" she says, finding herself sitting a little more erect, her bum perched on the chair's edge.

He leans in closer, his nose almost touching the space between her breasts.

What if it's all been an act, she thinks – his gentleness? What if his intention all along has been to get her out of the house? Some place secluded. Outside of town. Could really let her have it then. With the kids, though? No way he'd bring them along.

"Can't do it."

She looks down at him. Holding her breath. "Can't do what?"

"Let's go!" Lynette shouts from the foyer.

"In a minute," Kent tells her. "Your mom and I are talking."

"Tie up those laces," Emily says.

Jeremy's tucked his pant bottoms into his boots. He's wearing a blue windbreaker, his hand on the knob of the door, watching them.

"This Friday," Kent says, his nose grazing her chin now. "I know I said we'd leave then, but – "

"What?" she says. If not for gripping the edges of the seat, she'd be on the floor by now.

"I can't. There's a big meeting called for Friday morning that I can't miss. Severance package stuff. And Mr. Fisheries and Oceans is supposed to have a say about the future of the plant too."

A fluttering in her chest. "That's too bad, I was looking forward it."

"We'll still go, don't you worry. Saturday. And instead of coming back on Wednesday, we'll stay for the whole week. How about that?"

"I'd love it."

"Thought you would. Call your mom tomorrow, so she knows to expect the kids."

"I will." She lays her hands on his shoulders. How close she'd come to changing the flight, she thinks. If Terry hadn't called it might have been too late. "If we're taking a drive, let me get my sweater."

She goes to stand up, but he keeps her there. Wraps his arms around her, one side of his face pressed against her chest. After a moment, he says, "I'm sorry about this morning."

"I know."

"It's just when I saw Jeremy's face – "

"I know." She wonders if he's ever bothered looking at hers afterwards. "I didn't mean to hit him."

He lets go and helps her to her feet. "How could you have, right?"

Halfway to her bedroom, her vision blurs. She wipes the corners of her eyes and finds them soaked with tears. She pushes open her bedroom door, then flicks the light switch. In the middle drawer of her dresser she finds her favourite beige sweater, its length going past her bum, its collar perfect for keeping the wind out of her ears. She walks to the long mirror and watches herself as she buttons up.

"Hurry up, Mom!" Lynette shouts from down the hall.

"Just a minute!" she says.

She turns back to the mirror. Quickly pushes the final two buttons through their designated holes. Stands there for a moment. Breathes in and out, in and out. It's back on again, the plan. Tomorrow will be her last day of work. At the end of her shift, she'll grab her pay and be gone. She'll toss a goodbye over her shoulder at Terry so he'll have no reason to suspect anything, no reason to think that she's planning what she is. No reason to think that they'll never see each other again.

She'll ask Sonya for all of her money this time, not just the regular sixty dollars. "A special weekend together," she'll tell the nosey teller when she asks.

"Emily!" It's Kent's voice this time.

"Coming!"

Two days, she thinks. Not even. Two sleeps, although she knows there'll be little of that now. *Just get through Thursday.* She feels her throat tighten. Her heart races. The next breath she takes she holds, releasing it slowly, feeling herself relax a little. Just a little. *Thursday. Just get through Thursday.*

"Emily! Come on!" goes Kent again.

She turns from the mirror and heads towards the door, switching off the light as she goes.

THURSDAY

SHE'S AWAKE WHEN HIS ALARM GOES OFF. He's pressed against her. Slightly hard penis between the top of her ass and her tailbone; one of his thighs inserted between her two, the heat of the tooclose limbs making their skin slippery with sweat; chest hairs tickling her back; his chin resting on top of her head. One of his arms is wrapped around her ribcage, its hand cupping her right breast. Usually, during the night, their bodies will drift apart, so that by morning each of them is one roll away from landing on the floor. Not this day, though. She'd woken with him intertwined like this nearly three hours ago. She'd disentangle herself only to have him latch on again and again.

She pushes her bum against him. "Your alarm, Kent."

He mumbles something but doesn't turn over to switch it off.

"Time for work." She goes to shut the alarm off herself, but he won't let her. She feels all of him harden, muscles flexing, skin on skin. "Kent!"

"No," he says, far from asleep now. "Don't make me."

"It'll wake the youngsters."

"But I'm so comfortable, and you're so beautiful."

"Please."

He finally lets her go. Stretches out an arm and turns off the alarm. Grabs her again before she has a chance to move. "Just a minute longer." He sniffs her hair, then the base of her neck. "I love your smell."

Three and a half hours she'd managed last night, she figures. Asleep before her down pillows could take the weight of her head. Then waking in a panic some time later with the feeling that she'd forgotten something cramping her belly. No sleep then, just a perpetual going over of the plan for Friday. Then nearly screaming upon realizing that that is tomorrow. *Tomorrow.* Forming the word with her mouth but making no sound. *Tomorrow. Tomorrow.* Kent's limbs like snakes, wrapped here and stuffed there. One side of his burning face against her own.

He kneads her bum, one cheek then the other.

She hates loving it, the muscles reluctantly giving themselves over to his touch. Releasing their toxins.

"Odd that you're up," he says.

"Maybe if you'd stopped mauling me, I'd go back to sleep."

"If you could see what *I* do, you'd be mauling too." He laughs, then gets on top, burying his face in the nape of her neck.

"Stop," she says, "that tickles."

He burrows deeper, then flutters his tongue tip against her throat like a sex-starved teenager.

"Stop!" she manages, before laughter comes, the quality of which surprises her: higher-pitched than usual, younger-sounding, a girl's laugh. She twists to the left, then right, but can't budge him. She grabs his hair. Pulls. For a moment the licking stops, but then it starts again, even faster than before, all of him shaking because he's laughing too. She can't breathe. Might pee herself if he doesn't stop. She reaches down and takes hold of his balls.

He stops.

She squeezes.

"Okay," he says, lifting his head, "you win." He's red from laughing.

She doesn't let go.

"I said you win."

She's still holding on, imagines squashing till something pops.

"Ouch. That's starting to hurt."

She lets go.

"What's funny?"

"Nothing," she says, pushing him off.

He crawls over her to get to the window on her side of the bed. She watches him twist the rod that opens the blind. What morning light there is filters in, displaying his firm hamstrings and behind, calves and shoulders, chest and still-flat stomach.

He stares out. "Looks chilly."

"It's not raining, is it?"

"No, but there's wind."

Wind's nothing new in Lightning Cove. Wind and more wind. Wind with sun and fog and rain and snow. Wind needs to be the centre of attention here almost as much as Kent does.

He turns to her, his now-flaccid cock coming to face her before he does, the shaft long and narrow, its foreskinned tip like pouting lips.

He stretches, pointing his fingertips towards the ceiling, arching his back.Yawns before bringing his arms back to their sides. He sits near her on the edge of the bed. Runs a hand through her hair. "Gotta go to Gander this morning."

Me too. Tomorrow. "You do?"

"Meetings. I'll try not to be too late."

She nods.

Instead of heading to the shower, he continues stroking her hair. After a while, he says, "You don't feel neglected, do you?"

"What?" she asks, despite having heard him clearly.

"With me working so much. You don't feel neglected, do you?"

She doesn't answer.

He stops smoothing her hair. "You know it's all for us, right? You, me, the kids."

Still she says nothing.

"It's why I do anything."

She sits up. Rests her back against the headboard, the sheets covering her breasts and nipped underneath her armpits.

He shifts closer. "Perhaps I don't tell you enough."

She's looking at the wall now, just above his shoulder. Finally, she says, "Tell me what?"

He takes her chin into his hand as if he's about to kiss her. "That I appreciate everything you do. For me, for the kids."

She wants him gone – in the shower or in the kitchen or out the front door or in his truck or in whatever meeting he's supposed to be in, anywhere but here beside her, anywhere where he can't make her feel as though she might not want to go through with it.

"You look sad," he says.

"Do I?"

"Yes."

"I'm not."

"Okay."

He pulls her towards him. "Hug me."

She does. And then she's first to pull away, her hands pressed to his chest. *Get out of my sight!* "Go on or you'll be late."

"See?" he says, smiling. "See how you take care of me?"

She watches him grab his bathrobe from the hook behind the door. He puts it on with his back to her.

"I'll make you coffee," she says.

"No, go back to sleep."

"I want to."

He smiles again. "Not too strong, though, okay."

"Okay."

* * *

SHE SITS AT THE KITCHEN TABLE LISTENING to the coffee percolate, her chin resting on cupped hands, and the chair cold against her backside. Enough wind outside to blow the house down.

She's facing the window. It's because she's leaving that she looks more closely, taking everything in as if for the first time: swaying trees and overloaded clotheslines; the sea unfurling its bullying waves onto the landwash below; the ferry making its first crossing of the morning. The tip of the sun far out on the bay, almost but not quite hidden behind a veil of mist. She tries to brand the picture in her mind, breathing it down into the pads of her feet, holding it there.

A door opens down the hall. She turns to see Jeremy in his Spiderman pajamas, heading for the bathroom, his hair stuck up. He tries the door, but it's locked.

"Your father's in there," she says softly, so as not to wake Lynette.

He twists the handle again, crosses his legs and then bends forward at the waist.

"Use the one downstairs."

He turns to look at her. Shakes his head.

"I'll go with you."

For a moment she thinks he might wait it out up here, but then he approaches her, his feet slapping against the hardwood.

She leads him to the door of the basement at the far end of the foyer. He's right behind her. Like she's done hundreds of times, she pulls and lifts simultaneously to get the door open, then waits at the top of the stairs, staring down into the dark, dampness filling her nostrils. The chain for the light dangles near the bottom of the stairs so they'll have to walk down into blackness.

Jeremy looks afraid when she turns around, on the verge of changing his mind, she thinks. He's bouncing at the knees.

"Come on then," she says.

The first stair is even colder than the kitchen floor. The second one groans when she allows it to take her weight. By the third, she realizes that Jeremy is not behind her. She turns around to see him still standing at the threshold, his hands bracing the door's frame.

"Don't be afraid," she says, "I'm here." It occurs to her how futile those words are. She's *always* been here, and yet Jeremy's still been afraid, he and Lynette both. What has she ever really done to protect him, she wonders? Sure she's sent him to his room, but could he not still hear the yelling and banging and twisting of bodies? Sometimes, she thinks, it's worse not being able to see.

"Hold my hand," she says, extending hers to him.

He hesitates before taking it, his grip so tight that, for a moment, she doesn't know if she can bear it. She waits for him to take the steps down to her. Side by side now, he nearly as tall as she is, nothing but the whites of his eyes in the murk.

"We'll go down together," she tells him. To guide them, she places her free hand on the railing, her fingertips gliding downward and keeping pace with their footfalls.

His palm is sweating. Does whenever he's nervous or excited or… afraid too, she guesses.

Step six, seven, and eight. Straining wood and musty air. Their steps in sync, their shoulders nearly touching. Nine, ten, and eleven. There's a final step, but it's better to pull the chain for the light from here, not so much of a stretch upwards. She waits for him to do it. He pulls so hard that she thinks the chain has come away in his hand. It's still intact though when she looks.

They're awash in light now, so blinding they have to shield their eyes.

"That wasn't so bad, was it?" she says.

He lets go of her hand and runs toward the bathroom.

She watches him flick the light switch and then go inside, slamming the door. Listens to him lifting the seat, then his steady stream.

Finally she takes the last step down and stands for a moment at the bottom of the stairs, the floor as cold as an ice rink, goosebumps on her arms and legs.

Even though the majority of Kent's tools are in the garage, he still keeps a mini-workstation here, pressed against the wall, not far from the washer and dryer. There's a wooden table with a toolbox on top; glue gun and handsaw hanging from brass hooks, an open ratchet set near an assortment of screwdrivers and wrenches; a tan work belt, not a loop or a pocket empty, as if he'd just taken it off that second; and a map of Newfoundland attached to the wall, multi-coloured thumbtacks marking each cove or town he's visited over the years for either work or pleasure.

She walks towards the table, surprised to hear her son still peeing. Once there, she looks underneath, lifts the tarp that's covering everything and sees what she wants behind a never-used humidifier: suitcases. More than any family needs as far as she's concerned, but that's Kent – never content with just enough. She rummages through to find the two she'll need for tomorrow, so that she doesn't waste time looking. Lightheaded for a second. *Tomorrow.* It doesn't seem real somehow. Can you wait too long for something, she wonders, so that you doubt it will *ever* come? But she's here though, right? *Tomorrow.* It can't *not* happen now. All waiting comes to an end eventually.

"What are you doing?"

His voice startles her so much that she nearly falls in amongst the suitcases. She crawls out bum first, then turns around, sitting back on her haunches, looking up at him.

He's in boxers and an undershirt, hair combed back and freshly shaven, a mug of coffee in his right hand, its wisps of steam swirling.

"What?" she says.

"What were you looking for?"

She looks around like she's lost something. "Where's Jeremy?"

"He's upstairs, where else?"

"He was peeing."

"Now he's done. He's upstairs."

How could she not have heard him flush the toilet, push open the door, then walk back up the steps?

"Well?" Kent says.

She stares down at his feet, knows that he's in the vicinity of the loose floorboard, perhaps right on top of it. Nothing but thin wood separating his toes from the plane tickets and the old Adidas sock stuffed with twenties and tens and fives. Although she's positive that she'd fitted the board firmly back in place the last time, a part of her wonders now if perhaps a corner or an edge might be sticking up just enough for a bottom of a foot, with all its nerve endings, to take notice.

"Emily – "

"Suitcases."

"What?"

"For our St. John's trip."

He takes a few steps closer.

"I can't decide which two," she says.

He helps her up. "What odds."

They stand there for a moment.

"Do you want me to bring them up for you?" Kent says.

She shakes her head. "Enjoy your coffee before work."

He pulls her towards him. "Have one with me."

"Okay."

They walk across the floor. At the bottom of the stairs, she asks, "How is it, by the way? The coffee?"

"Honestly?"

"Yes."

"Bit strong."

He takes her hand and then – not needing to stand on the first step to reach the chain – turns off the light. They walk up the stairs, Emily a half step behind him.

2

SHE KISSES LYNETTE'S CHEEK AND THEN watches her little girl walk toward the main entrance of the school. At the doors, Lynette waves.

Emily waves back.

Jeremy's one of a circle of boys playing Hacky Sack in the courtyard. They're using the tops and backs of feet, knees, chests, even their foreheads to keep the little pouch in the air.

She stands there watching for a minute, her sweater buttoned to the top, her arms wrapped around herself to keep out the wind. Though she's constantly tucking her hair behind her ears, it keeps fluttering out to dance in front of her eyes.

The first bell goes and kids start scattering, but Jeremy stays where he is, taunting those who walk away. Another boy beside him, after the second bell, makes to move, but Jeremy grabs him by the shoulder and shouts something that Emily can't make out. Whatever it is, it's enough to make the smaller boy stay longer.

She wonders if he's even aware of her presence. If he cares at all that she stands watching every morning before going off to work. Slipping away from her, he is. Each day bringing more distance between them, an ever-widening gully that she worries might be impassable some day. She knows that he blames *her* when Kent gets mad. It's the look he gives her afterwards when he sees his daddy in the rocking chair, or sitting at the kitchen table with his face in his hands, shoulders bouncing. No matter that she's the one on the floor, the one cut and bruised. Torn clothes and hair out of its ponytail. Skin beneath her nails and the taste of his sweat on her tongue. "You've made him cry," Jeremy will say.

The few boys left in the schoolyard – Jeremy included – walk reluctantly towards the main entrance after the third bell, each of them already dreaming of recess, Emily thinks.

She watches until the last of them goes in then turns around, tucking her chin into the top of her sweater in preparation for the walk to work headlong into the wind. She manages only a few steps before a car pulls up to the curb, its tires screeching as it comes to a stop. A child pops out – Rodney, Myles and Irene's boy. Jeremy's age but half his size. He runs past her without saying hello, his school bag unzipped and his shirt hanging outside his trousers. His hair stuck up, and a half-eaten slice of toast in his hand, blueberry jam on top, she thinks.

Myles sees her through the passenger side window.

Emily waves, walks towards the car.

Myles gets out, flicks his cigarette into the air, then comes around the car's front to meet her. "How am I supposed to know what time it starts," he says. "I'm usually at work by now." He lifts the bill of his Toronto Maple Leafs cap in order to kiss her cheek without poking out her eye.

His facial hair is coarse against her skin.

She wonders if worry carries an odour, and if so, could that be what she smells on his clothes, on his breath. "Congratulations on your new baby."

His eyes are red-rimmed from lack of sleep. Or from too much of it. He readjusts his hat, looks past her. "Thanks for the flowers."

"Flowers?"

"Yeah. Irene loved the vase. Going to put it in the centre of the kitchen table when she comes home, she says. Thank Kent too, will ya?"

"Of course," she says, wondering why her husband would not have mentioned he'd sent flowers.

Myles slips his hands into his jean pockets and then stares down at his work boots. "She's better at this stuff, anyhow."

"What's that?"

"Getting the young one to school. That sort of thing."

"How is she?"

"Done nothing but sleep since she had him."

"It's tiring work."

He nods, staring off into the distance.

"What's his name?"

"The jury's still out on that one," he says, his gaze going back to her. "She likes Daniel, but I'd prefer Carl... after my ol' man, you know."

"I like Daniel," she says.

"Most do."

Another school bell.

"Irene told me that she came to see you the other day."

Emily nods.

"She shouldn't have."

"It's okay."

"It's not your fault what's going on. Kent's neither. He's been relentless against that government crowd since all this started." He pauses before saying, "It's a shame what happened to him the other night. Youngsters they were, a few too many in them. We put them in their place pretty quick."

The wind grows stronger.

Exhaust spews from his still-idling car.

The "Ode to Newfoundland," the school's morning anthem, plays in the background, faint children's voices singing along. She imagines Lynette with her hand on her heart, singing louder than the rest of her classmates; Jeremy just mouthing the words, poking his finger into the back of the boy in front of him.

"Has Kent heard anything else? About whether or not they're going to keep the plant going? Not that it matters to me."

It feels like a first date suddenly, stuck facing each other with nothing in common, nothing to say. "No, he hasn't. I'm sorry."

"It's okay. I'm not the only one, right?"

In the silence she tries looking at her watch without him noticing. Then she says, "I hear you might be going to Fort McMurray?"

"The *missus* would like me to."

"Lots of work there, no?"

"Oh yes, there's work."

She imagines him in a crowded bunkhouse, prostrate on a bed that, despite his being exhausted, he can't find any comfort in, a picture of his family on the night table beside the lamp. A world away from all that he's accustomed to.

That will be her, it occurs to her, tomorrow night. Lying beneath bed sheets that smell nothing of home. Lynette and Jeremy's deep breathing coming from either side of her.

She realizes that Myles is staring right at her. "Did you say something?"

"Never mind." He pulls the bill of his cap down even farther.

"Sorry if I seem distracted."

He cocks his head. "A lot to be distracted about."

"I suppose."

"What with the whole place on the verge of becoming a ghost town and everything."

"It won't come to that."

"Don't be so sure. It's happened before, and in places a lot better off than this one here."

She looks at her watch again, making more of a show of it this time. "I should be getting to work."

"Let me drive you."

"That's all right."

"I don't mind."

"I like the walk."

"You sure?"

"Positive."

"Okay, then." He bends down to kiss her cheek again.

She thinks now that the aroma of worry smells a lot like rum.

"Say hello from me to that husband of yours."

Out of politeness, she waits for him to get back in his car. She starts walking when he puts the car in gear.

"Be careful the gale doesn't blow you away," he says through his rolled-down window.

"I will," she says, raising a palm.

She watches him drive to the end of Trinity Street and then make a left onto Glover, disappearing from view.

3

TERRY LEANS ACROSS HIS DESK and slips the envelope into her hand.

She folds it and goes to put it in her pocket.

"Look at it," he says.

"Why?"

"Just look."

She opens it and peers inside. Glances at him. "It's more than usual."

He sits back, a proud look on his face. "Consider it a token of my appreciation."

"You didn't have to."

"Didn't I? You're long overdue, I'd say."

"Thank you."

"You're welcome."

There's another piece of paper in her pocket, she realizes, upon shoving in the cheque. She pulls it out and nearly loses her breath. It's the old electric bill, her travel itinerary written on the back, the confirmation number of her flight in bold across the top. How could she have forgotten that she'd put it there?

"Something wrong?" Terry asks.

She shakes her head and puts the bill back in her pocket, thinking how easily it might have been discovered. Jeremy going through her pockets for loose change every other day though she tells him not to. Easiest thing in the world for it to fall onto her bedroom floor as she's changing into something more comfortable. Kent reaching down to pick it up on his way to the closet. Reservations for three. No return date.

"Want a coffee?" Terry points to the fresh pot on the other side of the room.

She shakes her head. "Had some already this morning."

The office is cleaner, she thinks, dusted and papers stacked. An air freshener's hanging somewhere. Terry's got his shirt buttoned up too far, practically cutting off the circulation in his neck. How many times has she told him to unclasp a few, let his chest hairs breathe? He smells different. Whatever cologne it is, he's splashed too much on.

"Shouldn't you be opening up?" she says.

"In a second."

She stands. "I'm going to get my till ready – "

"Hang on," he says. "Sit a minute longer."

She sits down. Unclips her nametag and then reattaches it a little farther to the left, below her breast. Pushes up the hair tie that's keeping her ponytail in place.

"Heather won't be coming in," he says finally.

Probably one too many drinks at her show last night, Emily thinks. "Is she sick?"

Terry shakes his head.

"Her mother okay?"

"No, it's nothing like that."

She leans forward. "What then?"

He half stands in order to press the lever that raises his seat, then sits back down, looking at her, not looking at her.

"What, Terry?"

"I had to let her go. I'm sorry, I know how much you two liked each other." Terry looks away. Fiddles with the pens and pencils in the white mug.

"Why would you do that?" Emily says.

Terry doesn't answer.

"What'd she do?"

"What *didn't* she do more like it."

"Does this have anything to do with her coming over to my house yesterday?"

"No, although she shouldn't have left the store without telling me. I'm down in my office filling out an order and she just walks out. What a state things were in by the time I came back up. Sonya Cooke screaming at me that Heather had overcharged her forty dollars, and Mike Rowe's two boys in the back stuffing caramels inside their jackets."

"But it's your fault she left in the first place."

"How's it my fault?"

"Because of what you told her, that's what. She came to check on me. Make sure everything was all right."

He pauses for a second, then says, "That was good of her, I know."

"So why'd you fire her then?"

"Because of what happened later on."

"And what was that?"

"Just her waltzing back in like she didn't have a care in the world, that's what. She snatches a pack of Crunchets off the rack then – and not the small pack either, the big pack. Rips them open and starts eating them right in front of me, brazen enough to lick the cheese off her fingers and everything."

"She'll pay you for them. Take it off her cheque."

"Then when I ask her to come to my office for a little chat, she says that I can say whatever I have to upstairs. That's when I noticed her eyes, bloodshot and practically seared shut. Stoned right out of it, she was."

"Oh, come on."

"I'm telling you, Emily, she was. The whole time I'm talking to her, she's smiling, chewing with her mouth full, Crunchet bits caught between her teeth. 'No odds,' she says to me then, 'I'm leaving anyway.'"

"Leaving?"

"'Moving to St. John's with the band,' she said. 'There's more to this *chicky* than bagging groceries,' she says to me over her shoulder as she's walking out. 'Look for me on *Much*.'" He pauses. "What's *Much*?"

She doesn't answer.

"Anyway, you can talk to her yourself. She's coming in later to pick up her final cheque."

She looks away, then rests her forehead in her hand. Rubs her eyes. Who else will she drag into this mess before Friday? Heather out of a job on account of her, she and her mother destined to eat Spaghetti-O's straight out of the can.

"I'll need you to pick up the slack until I find someone else."

She nods.

"Can I count on you for Friday then?"

"Won't be here."

"What?"

"Nothing. Friday's fine."

"I'd appreciate it." He smiles, then says, "No complaints from me, seeing more of you."

A long silence then.

Neither of them seems sure where to set their eyes.

Using the armrests, Emily gets to her feet. Stands there looking down at him. "Opening up or what?"

He goes to stand too, but then changes his mind. "I'll be right up."

"Okay." She turns and leaves, passing through the storage area en route to the stairs. Stops at the bottom of them. Always climbing stairs, she thinks. She grips the handrail and trudges up like someone twice her age.

4

AS SHE WAITS TO GO UP TO THE TELLER, Emily takes the old electric bill out of her pocket and transplants it to the bottom of her purse beneath a hair-infested brush and a pack of Juicy Fruit. She takes her hand out only to shove it back in again. *It's there, see. Safely at the bottom of your purse.* She zips up and then shoves the bag into the hollow of her armpit.

Muriel, the only other teller besides Sonya, calls the next person in line.

Emily's next. She considers turning around and telling young Peter Dawe to go on ahead of her so that she doesn't have to cash her cheque with Sonya. Not that Muriel, with her wrinkled, smelling-of-sour-milk skin, and a finger always partway in either ear is much better. But Muriel at least has a limit to how much gossip she likes to either hear or spread. And if you catch her on a good day, Muriel will hardly talk at all. Just punch her computer keys with bony, almost transparent fingers, her face, despite thick glasses, so far forward that it looks like she might kiss the screen.

Someone's tapping her shoulder.

It's Peter. "She's ready for you."

"Come on up, my love," Sonya says, waving her hand.

Comforted by the fact that, after today, she'll never have to see the teller again, she goes up to the counter.

"How are you, my love?"

"Good," Emily says, reaching inside her purse and pulling out the cheque. "You?"

"The best kind."

"Good."

Sonya's makeup is inches thick. "How's the darlings?"

"The darlings are fine," Emily says.

"And that handsome husband of yours, how's he?"

"Handsomer."

"Not possible." Sonya leans forward a little. "I believe you've gotten tinier."

Emily looks down at herself, then back at Sonya. "I don't think so."

"Yes, you have. Melting away is what you are. Not sick are you?"

Emily shakes her head, then hauls back the sleeve of her sweater revealing her Timex. She taps the top of it. "I'm on my break."

Sonya goes back to sitting upright in her chair. Starts hitting the computer keys with the tips of her glue-on nails. "The usual?"

"No," Emily says, herself the one leaning closer now. She notices the remnants of a bagel or toast trapped in the lipstick on Sonya's top lip. "I'd like it all."

Sonya's fingertips freeze on the keys. She looks up. "Hmm?"

"I'd like it all, I said."

Sonya's mouth slightly parted now. "Nothing in the account then?"

Emily takes in the bulging eyes on the other side of the counter, then shakes her head.

"That's a change for you, isn't it?"

She doesn't say anything, just stares back until Sonya's fingers go back to work on the keys. "In denominations of twenties, tens, and fives, please."

Sonya flips the cheque over and stamps it harder than Emily feels is necessary. "Give me a minute," she says.

Emily watches her struggle to lift her bulky buttocks off the chair, then waddle to the back, her slacks too tight and showing the outline of her massive underwear.

Next to her, Emily hears Muriel call Peter up and then ask him about the university he's attending in Halifax. "Sure, you're all grown up," Muriel says.

"You haven't aged a bit," Peter replies, kissing the older woman on the cheek.

Muriel laughs like a teenager, then says, "The charmer, just like your father."

Something stirring in Emily's belly causes her to clutch the handle of her purse and shift closer to the counter. She shuts her eyes for a moment, then opens them.

Muriel and Peter are still engaged in small talk despite the people waiting in line. Peter holding a blue bankbook in his delicate-looking hand. A hand that, she thinks, has grown accustomed to flipping through the pages of a book, and hitting the buttons of a computer. A hand so unlike her own calloused and dry one, its skin cracking from counting old money, lifting packages out of boxes, pricing cans of soup, and tearing receipts from a till.

She turns away. Lets go of her purse only to latch onto it again, afraid of letting go for some reason.

Across the room, Sonya is holding out her palm as Phonse Avery, the bank manager, places crisp bills there. After every few he has to lick his thumb and forefinger. His belly hangs over his belt, and the bottom button of his dress shirt is undone, which no one has bothered mentioning to him.

"Criminology," says Peter.

There's a pause before Muriel replies, "Well, it sounds important."

Emily loosens her grip on her handbag, then takes a deep breath. Remembers a time when she herself, like Peter, was filled with excitement about the future: studying at a university, meeting new people, traveling perhaps. Tired muscles around her mouth, back then, from all that smiling.

Sonya rises to her tiptoes and whispers something in Phonse's ear. They both look at her, Phonse waving, his hairy belly button visible at the opening in his shirt. She tilts her head to him, then watches Sonya walk toward her, bills that look ironed in her hand.

It occurs to her that the girl she once was is gone forever, replaced by this older, more cautious version. A woman perpetually glancing over her shoulder although no one's there, who weighs less but treads heavier, who sometimes has trouble lifting her eyes from the floor.

"Sorry for the wait, my love," Sonya says, lowering herself back onto her chair like a person recovering from a herniated disc. The chair strains under the weight of her. She starts counting out the money, her knuckles rapping against the counter with each laid bill. "Five hundred and thirty-four dollars and eighty-three cents."

Emily takes the change first, putting it in her coat pocket. Picks up the bills.

"Big plans, my love?" Sonya asks.

She stops in the middle of unzipping her handbag. Stares into the teller's eyes. "Did I say I had any?"

Sonya shakes her head, then says, "I just assumed that with – "

"St. John's – "

"What?"

"St. John's, if you must know. We're leaving on Saturday."

"That'll be nice, won't it?"

She resumes unzipping, then hauls out her wallet and shoves the money inside. Puts it back in her handbag.

She should be out the door by now, she knows, walking back to finish her last shift, but she can't seem to pry herself away from the counter.

"Is there something else, my love?" Sonya says.

Sixty dollars a week, she thinks, so that when the time came, Kent wouldn't see a large withdrawal on his bank statement. He's provided everything: the bills paid, the mortgage, the groceries, clothes for the kids, for herself. She's wanted for nothing.

"Emily," Sonya says, "was there something else?"

But she's raised his children, hasn't she? Taken care of the home, cooked and cleaned, and worked herself now this past year.

"Others are waiting, my love," Sonya says.

"Say hello to your mom and dad," Muriel says to Peter.

Peter says, "I will."

"Next," Muriel says, her pinky so far in her ear you can barely see it.

He'll be in Gander for half the night, won't he? And by the time he goes to the bank himself, she'll be gone, right? What's a little extra for all that she's put up with? If anyone's entitled, she is.

"Emily –"

"There *is* something."

"All right."

"I'd like to make a withdrawal from our joint account."

"How much, my love?"

She says nothing.

"How much?" Sonya asks again.

Emily feels herself trembling. When she speaks it doesn't sound like her voice. "Half of what's in the account."

Sonya freezes for a moment, then leans so far forward that her breasts plop atop the computer console. "What?"

"Half, I said."

Blotchy patches break out along Sonya's upper chest and neck. Eyes opened so wide that the balls themselves look like they might pop out onto the counter. "Half?"

"That's right."

Sonya's face contorts with longing, like a child lying awake on Christmas Eve. When she's able to speak again, she says, "Swipe your client card."

Emily does.

"Punch in your –"

131

"PIN, yes I know how to do it," Emily says.

She watches the teller get up again and walk to the back on wobblier knees, fanning her doughy, flushed cheeks with the withdrawal slip.

5

THE WIND'S SO STRONG SHE CAN barely catch her breath.
She tucks her chin downward toward her chest and leans into it, as if
walking through water, her handbag pressed against her, underneath
crossed arms, her fingertips pushed into the groove of each under-
arm. The handbag's the only thing, she thinks, anchoring her to the
street. It's a fatter bag now, she knows, So many bills inside that she
had to ask Sonya to wrap the bundle in elastic bands, then place it in
a large manila envelope. Sonya's eyes on her as she walked out.
Through the window too, probably, though Emily had refused to turn
around and look.

She steps over a Coke can that the wind blows into her path, then
narrowly avoids getting hit by a piece of flying cardboard. She'd walk
faster if the wind would allow it.

She wonders if there will be room under the basement floor to accommodate the extra money, and if not, where she should hide it.
Everything's been set into motion by making the withdrawal, she
knows. Out of her control now. A plane nose-diving towards earth.

Cry, laugh, scream – it's like they all want to come out of her at
once. Tingling in her belly and in the tips of her fingers and toes. Rac-
ing heart, deeper breath, her limbs looser, her mind focusing on what
lies ahead. One shot. That's all she'll get. One. Friday. Tomorrow. *My
God, tomorrow*. It's here.

Someone's shouting her name. She lifts her head and sees
Heather, waving to her just outside the main doors of Hodder's Grocery and Convenience.

They walk towards each other, meeting in the middle of the street.
Emily's not expecting the hug that Heather gives.

They part.

"What have you got in there?" Heather shouts, her voice nearly
drowned out by the wind.

Emily looks down at her handbag. "Wouldn't you like to know?"

"What?"

"I said, wouldn't you like to know?" She presses her bag against
her chest like a youngster carrying schoolbooks.

Heather smiles.

They stand looking at each other for a moment, like people who've shared something, revealed parts of themselves.

"I'm sorry." Emily says. "About your job and everything."

The wind blows open Heather's jacket. She grabs the fluttering coat and zips it up. "Don't be. It would have happened sooner or later."

The top of a garbage can goes sliding across the street, getting trapped beneath the back wheels of a parked truck. A pair of underwear, probably from someone's clothesline, sails past, just above their heads, white boxers with blue stripes. A pair of pantyhose goes whipping past too, wrapping itself around the railing of a front porch.

The younger woman says, "Fuckin' wind, eh?"

"Yeah."

A car horn blares behind them. Heather takes Emily's wrist, pulling her to the shoulder of the road. After the car passes, Heather says, "Come to the marina for a farewell coffee."

"I can't."

"Come on."

"Break's over."

"It's dead in there; Terry's dusting the Kraft Dinner for something to do!" She grabs hold of Emily's wrist again. "Come on, half a cup."

She looks down the road towards the front window of Hodder's Grocery and Convenience, half expecting to see Terry behind it, clipboard in his hand and pencil behind his ear, pants too tight and shiny shoes. His eyes always searching for her, she knows. Always for her. That's why she can't *not* go back for the rest of her shift despite having the money in her purse. Despite her mind being gone already. Because of him. Terry.

"Okay. Half a cup." Emily says.

"Let's go then before we blow away."

* * *

PAT GULLAGE, THE OWNER OF THE MARINA, stands over them, a pot of freshly brewed coffee in his hand.

"Just half for me," Emily says. She starts unbuttoning her sweater.

"Fill them to the rim, Pat."

"Heather –"

"To the rim, Pat." She shoots Emily a sly smile. "Dusting boxes of Kraft Dinner, remember."

Emily shows the younger woman the palm of her hand, its fingers splayed. "Five minutes."

Pat pours. "It's a system up from Florida."

"Hmm?" Heather says.

"The wind."

"Oh."

"One hundred and forty kilometres by this evening, the weather man said."

"Jesus," Heather says.

"Gonna bring some rain too."

Emily feels a chill pass through her. She's never taken the weather into account before, the possibility of it hindering her escape. She looks up at Pat. "How long's it supposed to last, do you know?"

"Tomorrow morning, they're saying."

If the weather can turn against her, what else can, she wonders? She imagines a fire in the galley of the ferry, a sleepy driver at the wheel of their taxi, their plane falling from the sky.

Heather pours some cream into her coffee. "You sure keep track of the weather."

Pat lifts his head, stares across the room at Anique, from Anique's Antiques, his only other customer. She's sitting at a table near the window, a pot of tea and a half-eaten slice of toast in front of her, staring out at the sea, her tremor making it look as if she's stuck saying 'No.'

He looks back at them. "Lots of time on my hands."

Emily sips her coffee.

Heather rips open three sugar packets and drops them in.

"Worse now with the layoffs," Pat says. "Who wants to spend ten dollars on Flipper Pie when they can't afford to heat their house?"

Neither woman says anything.

"I give this place 'til Christmas."

What odds, Emily thinks. She's been gone for ages anyway. In Lightning Cove physically, but elsewhere in her mind.

No one speaks for a moment.

She wonders if Pat's just going to stand there refilling their cups all afternoon.

"And me and Joan with the young one wanting to go to university too," Pat says, finally, his eyes once again scanning the empty room. "I should have seen it coming."

A middle-aged couple that Emily's never seen before walks in front of the window.

Pat zooms in on the out-of-towners as they stop outside the door. The woman holds onto her hat to keep it from blowing away, leaning against the glass to peer inside. The wind blows her partner's trench coat tightly against his longish limbs as he reviews the menu, his own hat in his hand, and not a hair on his head for the gale to blow asunder. He bends over to say something to her; she's much shorter. She nods, then loops her arm through his. They walk away.

Emily takes a sip of her coffee, unable to look Pat in the face.

Heather adds another sugar packet.

"I'd give you those on the house, but…"

"Wouldn't hear of it, Pat," Heather says. She reaches inside her leather jacket for some change but doesn't have any. She looks across at Emily.

Emily finds a toonie and some quarters in her pocket and hands them over to Pat.

From the other side of the room Anique raises a shaky hand. "Pat," she says, her voice weary.

Emily waves to the old woman. "Hello, Anique. How are you today?"

Anique leans forward. Concentrated eyes through thick spectacles. "Who's that then?"

"It's Emily."

"Who?"

"Emily."

"Oh."

"How are you today?"

"What?"

"How are you today?"

"Oh. Very good."

"Not at the shop?"

Anique just stares at her, then leans back and peers out the window. "Looks like rain." Then, "Pat!"

"Coming." He goes to move, but stops himself. "Top up, ladies?"

Emily covers her mug. Shakes her head.

"Not if I got to pay for it," Heather says.

He laughs. Comes over and fills her cup. "I'm not that far gone, my dear." He moves toward Anique, then says over his shoulder, "Not yet."

They watch him and Anique for a while. Then Heather says, "Good thing I'm going, I'd say."

Emily takes another sip. Puts the cup down but keeps her fingers wrapped around the handle. "I can talk to Terry, you know. Get your job back."

Heather leans forward. "Don't you dare. I was one shift away from setting fire to the place anyway."

They both laugh. Then Emily says, "You never said anything about leaving."

"Not gonna pack groceries all my life."

"Terry said you were going to St. John's."

Heather nods. Runs her index finger around the circumference of her mug. "Toronto...eventually."

"To do what?"

"Music, what else?" She takes a sip of her coffee. "By the way, you missed one hell of a show last night. Standing room only."

"Sorry."

"Yeah well, you can catch me on *MuchMusic* one of these days."

Emily laughs.

"What's funny?"

"*MuchMusic*."

"What?"

"You told Terry to watch for you on *Much*."

"Yeah. So?"

"He had no idea what you were talking about."

Heather laughs herself now. "Someone should tell him that there's more to watch on TV besides *Land and Sea*."

In the silence, Emily looks beyond the younger woman, through the window. Sees a boat in the harbour, crest-tipped waves sending its bow crashing downwards and then up again. Waves are hammering the dock, some of the water coming over the sides. The boats tied to the wharf undulate like modern dancers.

She looks back at Heather. "What about your mom?"

"Why do you think I'm leaving in the first place? Can't make it 'big' in Lightning Cove now, can I?"

For a while it's quiet. Then Emily says, "When?"

"Week from tomorrow."

"Friday?"

Heather nods.

Across the room, Pat pulls out Anique's chair and then helps the old woman to her feet. Hands over her walking stick. They walk slowly to the cash.

"Take care," Emily says as they pass by.

"Who's that then?" Anique asks.

"It's Emily."

"Oh."

"Take care."

"You too."

Pat guides Anique to the entrance and then holds the door open as she passes through. He slams it shut after she's gone and disappears into the kitchen.

Emily finishes what's in her cup, then starts buttoning up her sweater.

"That's five minutes already?" Heather says.

She grabs her handbag hanging on the back of the chair. "It's been longer."

Anique passes by the window, her pink shawl fluttering, and her walking stick fighting to free itself from her hand. She's able to hang onto it though, able too to keep her methodic pace through the wind. When she's gone, Heather says, "Eighty-two her next birthday."

Emily pauses for a second, then says, "Always by herself. Must get lonely."

Heather turns back to the window. "I think she's happy just to wake up."

Emily thinks about that. Waking up happy. Had there ever been a time? The closest she'd come, she thinks, was just after Lynette was born. Kent – or so she'd thought back then – had gone through a reformation of sorts. Hadn't so much as raised his voice in anger, let alone his fist in months. She'd slept soundly, and woke full of energy. Managed a laugh from time to time too. Perhaps her mother had been right after all about marriages needing time to work. Time for the rough edges to smooth themselves out. How surprising it was then when he'd leaned across the supper table one evening and smacked her across the mouth with the back of his hand. Blood trickled from the cut on her lip. Her happiness too. Drip, drip, drip, down her chin and onto her slacks.

"Emily?"

She snaps back into the moment. "Hmm?"

"Here, I said."

She looks down and sees a slip of paper by her hands. Her eyes go back to Heather's. "What's this?"

"It's a phone number of a social worker in Grand Falls."

She picks the paper up, bringing it close to her face. "Evelyn Sharpe."

"She specializes in cases like yours."

For a moment longer Emily stares at the name, then she folds the paper and puts it into her pocket. "Thanks."

"If Mom had only listened to a quarter of what she said…" Heather looks away, then, after a moment, turns again to Emily. "Promise me you'll call."

Before she can, Pat comes back out with a full pot of coffee. He raises it in the air. "More, ladies? She's fresh."

"None for me, Pat," Emily says. "Gotta get back to work."

Heather raises her empty cup like a beggar. "To the rim, Pat."

Pat goes over and refills Heather's mug, then goes back to the kitchen.

Emily gets to her feet. "Terry'll have my head."

Heather smiles. "I wouldn't worry too much about Terry. You can do no wrong in his eyes."

Emily picks up her handbag.

"The way that man looks at you."

"What? How does he look at me?"

"Like a heartsick schoolboy, that's how."

Emily feels the heat in her face. "Don't be foolish."

"You'd have to be blind not to notice. Always with his hands in his pockets whenever you're around. More than loose change he's playing with, I bet."

"Heather!" She can't help but laugh.

Heather does too.

After they stop, Emily says, "Well, if I don't see you, good luck with your music."

Heather stands up too. "Sure I'm not going 'til next week. I'll see you again."

Emily nods and walks around the table and gives her ex-co-worker a hug. "Thanks for everything."

"You're welcome." Heather sits back down. "I'll just relax here for a bit, work on this new song I've been writing."

"Oh. What's it about?"

"Nothing much. Smokin' up and eating Crunchets and· telling your boss to stick it up his arse."

Emily smiles.

Heather smiles too.

Emily turns and heads for the door. Yells, "Thank you, Pat," towards the kitchen.

"You're welcome, love," Pat shouts back.

She struggles against the wind in order to pull open the door. The air's moist now, almost raining but not, like a cold sweat. She leans into the wind, wrapping her arms around herself, her purse underneath. Waves to Heather as she walks past the window.

Heather waves back.

6

7:00 a.m. – WAKE

7:05 – Wake kids.

7:07 – Get suitcases from downstairs.

7:10 – Fruit Loops for Jeremy, Honeycombs for Lynette.

7:20 – No showers. Just wash faces. Everyone gets dressed.

7:30 – Pack. Basics. Don't forget Lynette's <u>GIRAFFE</u> !!!

7:50 – Get coats and bo –

"Where did you say the leak was?"

She straightens up with a start, drops her pen. "Jesus!"

"Didn't mean to frighten you," Terry says.

She balls the paper up and puts it in her pocket. Looks at him. "Your feet touch the floor when you walk?"

"Didn't realize you were in the middle of something. Sorry." He's holding a yellow bucket and a mop.

She bends over and picks up the pen. Less than two thousand people in Lightning Cove, she thinks, yet there's hardly a moment when someone isn't looking over her shoulder or standing right behind her.

She steps out from behind her cash, slips past him. "Follow me."

She takes a left and then a right towards the produce: a few bundles of spotted bananas, four or five bags of apples, some spoiled tomatoes, and several mutant cabbages.

So much for the rain that Pat had said would not be starting until after midnight, she thinks. All afternoon she's had to listen to it hammering the windows and roof.

She looks at her watch: twenty minutes until the end of her shift, until the end of the grocery store for good. No more uniform with the logo of a grocery cart on the breast pocket, and no more name tag with EMILY in block letters.

"It's right here," she says finally, pointing to a huge puddle on the floor.

Terry looks up towards the ceiling. "Gonna cost a fortune to get that fixed."

For the first time she thinks she sees worry on his face, in the corners of his eyes. The town's been falling apart for months, layoffs every week, the few young ones moving away with their young families, and the whole time Terry's never said a word. Not a thing about his business needing the plant as much as the plant's workers do. Who do you pack groceries for when no one's left?

Terry lays down the bucket. Begins moping up the water.

Emily starts to head back to her cash.

"Wait," Terry says.

She stops. Turns around.

He lays the mop aside and slides the bucket underneath the leak and then goes over to where she is, stopping right in front of her. Jams his hands into his pockets.

Heather's words from earlier come back to her: *More than loose change he's playing with, I bet.* She lifts her gaze from his belt buckle. "What is it?"

The sound of coins between his fingers then, and keys too, mixing with the raindrops. He clears his throat and says, "The other day..."

She goes to speak, but he lifts his palm as if to silence her, as if to say: *Please let me finish.*

She doesn't say what she was going to.

"If you tell me it was nothing...what I saw, then I have to believe you," Terry says.

She keeps still. Her eyes on him.

"It's just that..." He stops fumbling about in his pockets and looks at her. "...well...*I* didn't know that, did I?" He looks up at the ceiling, as if his next words, like the leak, might materialize through the hole in the roof. At last, he focuses on her. "I mean, as far as I was concerned, he *was* hurting you." He breathes deep and lets it out. Shakes his head. "And what did I do?"

For a moment, because of his silence, she thinks he's expecting her to answer, but before she can come up with something, he says, "I walked away, is what." He looks towards the front window, then back at her again. "During the whole drive back to the store I'm telling myself to turn back around, you know, go right up to that son of a bitch and tell him to take his Jesus hands off you. Or, at the very least, I could have called Roy Driscol. Had him take the police cruiser on over. But I didn't do anything. Not a goddamned thing."

He looks like a youngster all of a sudden, she thinks, a youngster who's wandered away from his parents and is now lost. She goes to reach out to him, offer comfort, but then changes her mind.

"A coward is what I am."

"No," she says.

They're silent for ages then.

Rain hammers the roof.

The steady drip, drip, drip into the bucket.

Finally Emily speaks. "Okay, say you did one of those things: got in Kent's face or called Roy. What then? After you'd gone, I mean? And after Roy had written up his report and then wrinkled it up in his fist on his way back to the car because he thinks the sun shines out of Kent's ass, what then? I'd still be left, wouldn't I? And Kent'd be even more pissed, wouldn't he? And what do you think would happen?"

Terry lifts his gaze from the floor and looks at her. "So it's true then?"

"No, I'm not saying that. But if it were, I mean." Her dream from the other night comes back to her again: the knife going in and out. She pushes the thought away. Moves a little closer to Terry. Then says, "Perhaps sometimes... walking away *is* helping."

He doesn't say anything.

"But it wasn't what you thought it was, Terry. *Honest.* So there's no need to feel bad, okay?"

Although he nods, she doesn't think her words have offered him any comfort.

He'll miss her the most, she thinks. She imagines him looking for her in one of the aisles and then suddenly remembering she's gone. Up and left without telling anyone. Him driving home in the dark to that empty house, falling asleep in front of the television, the volume blasting from his surround sound. Waking up in the middle of the night, the cushion under his chin soaked with saliva, not bothering to find the stairs in the dark, or to sleep for once in his own bed.

He's just said something.

"What?"

"No, nothing."

"Tell me."

He takes a hand out of a pocket in order to scratch the back of his neck, then runs that same hand over his head, as if searching for stuck-up hairs even though there aren't any. "I said...I'm fond of you, that's all."

How many packages of Wine Gums had he slipped into her pocket over the course of her working here, she wonders? How many surprise cans of Ginger Ale and bags of ketchup chips? How about that finger-and-a-half of whiskey they'd share in his office at the end of every month? A reward for all their hard work, he'd always say. She'd obliged him because she knew there was no one else for him to share a drink with. That, and perhaps, despite her own family, she was lonely too.

"I'm fond of you too, Terry," she says.

It's his simplicity that's always drawn her to him, his matter-of-fact approach to living, taking things as they come and resisting the urge to look too far ahead. His predictability too. She knows that the man she sees when she pushes open the door in the morning is the same one she says goodbye to at suppertime, and still the same one when she walks in the next day. She knows, for instance, that when he smiles he's happy to have her near, and that his hand on her shoulder means that he appreciates her. There are times too when they'll graze each other as they pass on the stairs or in one of the aisles, and she'll know he's watching out for her somehow. He's been her comfort food, her extra glass of wine, her few minutes longer in the bath.

"Are you okay?" he says.

"Hmm?"

"You look sad."

She shakes her head.

Another silence. Then Terry says, "Should get back to that leak, I suppose." He starts to go, but Emily's voice stops him.

"Hang on a minute."

He turns around.

She walks up to him and stops so close she can feel his breath on her face. Cinnamon. She reaches out and undoes the top button of his shirt. "There," she says, "That's so much better."

Terry rolls his neck to one side and then the other. "It *is* easier to breathe."

They both laugh.

After they stop, Emily says, "Thank you, Terry."

He needs a moment before saying, "What did I do?"

She shrugs, and says, "I don't know," then hugs him.

He hugs back. Not too tight though. Terry gives her room to breathe.

7

SHE'S RUNNING, RAINWATER SPLASHING with each footfall. Despite Terry having loaned her his umbrella, she's soaked. It's because the wind keeps blowing the umbrella inside out. Her handbag is pressed against her ribcage, its strap digging into the groove of her neck, in the space between her breasts.

There's a car pulling out of the half-flooded parking lot of the Royal Bank, water up past its tires. Farther along, she notices an uprooted tree in the playground, its trunk lying across a broken teeter-totter. There are deep puddles beneath the swings. A gust of wind nearly blows the umbrella from her hand. She struggles to hang on as cool rain pelts her eyelids, the top of her head. She thinks of Jeremy and Lynette walking together in the likes of this. She should have left work early and gone and picked them up. She looks at her watch: 4:30. Should have been home half an hour ago.

She turns onto Trinity Street. Hanrahan's Seafood has taken the sign displaying the special on trout and shrimp out of its window. Anique's Antiques has a 'Going out of business, everything must go' notice on the front door.

At the end of Trinity, she turns right, continuing along the slow rise. Chest and thighs burning, gasping for breath. She slows to a fast walk. Thinks of tomorrow morning. The three of them lugging their suitcases. She doubts she'll even notice the burning then.

She'll call the airline when she gets in, she thinks, make sure the flight's on schedule for tomorrow. She'll ask them about the storm too, if it's supposed to move out by early morning as Pat had said.

At the top of the street she starts running again. Wind and rain and sneaker soles against the pavement in her ears. Her bangs in her eyes.

Lynette's staring through the curtains and waving when she turns into the driveway. She waves back.

At the top of the porch she closes the umbrella. Goes to reach for the handle of the door, but Lynette is pulling it open before she gets the chance. "Hello, baby." She steps inside.

"You're soaked, Mom."

"I know, sweetheart." She shakes the wetness from Terry's umbrella, then holds it out to Lynette. "Take this for Mommy."

Lynette takes it, leaning it against the coat closet.

Emily shuts the door. Runs her hand through her hair. Lifts the strap of her handbag over her head. Starts unbuttoning her sweater. "Where's your brother?"

"Watching TV."

She kicks off her sneakers. "Did you get caught in the rain?"

Lynette shakes her head. "We got a ride."

"From who?"

"Clancy's dad."

"Myles, you mean?"

Lynette nods.

"I'm so glad, Mommy was worried that you and your brother were going to get drenched." With her purse in one hand and the collar of her sweater in the other, Emily moves to the basement door. "I need to hang this up downstairs." She uses her shoulder to push open the door and starts walking down the steps. Nearly halfway down she realizes that Lynette is following her. "Go back up, sweetheart, Mommy'll be there in a second."

"I want to come."

"Go back up, I said."

Lynette does, closing the door behind her.

Emily continues down. On the second-last step, she stops and pulls the chain for the light, then goes to the far corner of the room, to the makeshift clothesline that she and Kent had put up some years before, each end of the rope looped and knotted through hooks that they'd screwed into the walls. That Kent had screwed into the walls, really. She'd just stood there and watched, directing him on the appropriate height since it was she who would be using it the most.

She throws the sweater on the line, not bothering with clothespins, then moves to the washer and dryer. Laying the purse down, she gets on all fours and starts running her hands along the floor. Eyes downward, then on the stairs. On the floor, then on the stairs again. *He's in Gander. Won't be home for hours yet. Hours.*

She finds the one, sliding her pinky underneath and pulling upward. Puts the panel aside before taking out the plane tickets and the Adidas sock. Hardly any room left in there for what's in her purse, she knows. Unzipping her handbag, she reaches inside for the manila envelope. Hauls it out, and slips her hand in.

The wad is too thick to grip with one hand, so she uses two. She sits back on her haunches then, just staring at it. More money then she's ever seen let alone held. How much did Sonya say was there? Eight thousand? Twelve? Fifteen? She has no idea. In fact she can barely remember the bank teller counting out the bills, or bounding the money with elastic bands, or sliding the envelope across the counter. She tries to recall the look on Sonya's face. Shifty eyes. No, she was smiling. Or was it more of a frown? Or had her lips been pursed so tightly together that they'd gone white? White with the gossip she could barely contain a second longer. Won't be long before the whole town knows, Emily thinks. Before Kent knows –

The basement door opens suddenly.

She drops the money, then scrambles to pick it back up. Turns towards the stairs, swears that she can see his boots, his way of taking the steps two at a time.

Not *his* boots though. Big Bird slippers, she realizes. Lynette. Just Lynette. *Gander. That's where he is. Won't be back until late.*

Lynette takes a few steps down, then stops. "Mommy?"

"What, baby?"

"Are you coming up?"

"In a minute."

"Jeremy's hungry."

"I'll be up in a minute. Now close the *door!*"

Lynette's slippers turning and then tramping back up.

She stays where she is, her eyes on the stairs. A moment later they're *still* on the stairs.

Finally she looks away. Picks up the money and jams it into the hiding place. The Adidas sock's next, then the three plane tickets, pressing everything down with her palms. All of it fits. She picks up the panel of hardwood, puts it back in place. She makes a fist and brings it down hard against the spot. From the other side of the room, she looks to see that it's flush with the others. Pretty good, she thinks. Not so much money that it eases her worry, yet enough to give them a fighting chance, buy them some time.

She goes back over to the clothesline. Takes off her pants, shirt, and socks, hanging them beside her sweater. Stands there in her underwear and bra then, the floor cold under her feet, her arms wrapped around herself for warmth.

So long she's waited. How many times had she imagined this very moment? Hours away from freedom. Imagining, yet never really believing it would come. How strange then to be here now and feel as if everything is moving too fast.

Breathe, just breathe. No choice now but hang on tight and focus on the end. Everything does, eventually. End.

She goes back over and presses the heel of her foot against the spot, just to be sure, and then picks up her purse. Goes up the stairs.

Lynette's at the kitchen table, drawing. Pencil crayons scattered.

Jeremy's against the counter, his hand in a box of Fruit Loops. "Mom!" he says, looking away because his mother is practically naked.

"You came out of this body, don't forget," she says, walking past them and into the hall. "I'll put fish sticks on in a minute."

"Can we have french fries too?" Jeremy says.

"Okay." She pushes open her bedroom door.

"Deep fried?" he shouts.

"Baked!" she shouts back.

She unfastens her bra and slips out of her panties, throwing both in the clothes hamper. She finds a new mismatched pair at the bottom of her drawer: white, with a tiny hole at the crotch, and a lacey red bra. Puts them on. Nice to be in dry underclothes after having spent too long in soaked ones. Over them she steps into her favourite jeans, the ones with the holes in the knees, and her grey fleece. Doesn't bother with socks, just slides into her slippers.

She goes into the bathroom and towel dries her hair, thinking how old the face that's staring back from the mirror is. Is it too late to get back all that's been lost, she wonders? To scavenge the scattered pieces of herself?

After she puts frozen fish sticks and french fries in the oven, she sits with the children. Lynette has flipped the paper over so she can draw on the other side. Jeremy is still eating Fruit Loops by the counter.

"Put those away," she says.

"But I'm starving."

"I said put them away, you'll ruin your supper."

He does so, reluctantly, not bothering to close the box. Then heads for the hallway.

"Where're you going?"

"To my room." He keeps walking.

"Come here," she says.

"Why?"

"Come here."

"I want to play PlayStation."

"Come here."

He stops. "What!"

"Sit down with us."

"Why?"

"Sit down with us."

He comes back, hauls out Kent's chair at the other end of the table and sits. Puts his elbows on the table and rests his chin in cupped hands. Barely a trace on his face now from when she hit him. Like his father when it comes to healing.

"What?" he says.

"Nothing." She pauses. "We never sit together."

Lynette slides her paper across.

"Who's that, Baby?"

"You."

"Wow, it's good." She looks closer. "But my hair's not red, is it?"

"Couldn't find the brown pencil crayon."

"Oh. Well, it suits me, doesn't it, red hair?"

Lynette nods. Takes the picture back. "It isn't finished."

Already there's a faint smell of baking fish.

Rain pattering off the roof.

She looks at Jeremy. He sees her watching but looks away, his face turned toward the window.

His profile so much like Kent's, she thinks. Same shape of chin and nose, same eyes with their long lashes. A carbon copy of her husband is what he is. Dad's boy. Slipping farther and farther away from *her*, but Dad's boy still. Always Dad's boy.

"Mom's sorry," she says finally.

He turns to look at her.

"You know that, right?"

He shrugs his shoulders, makes a grunting sound.

"It's just that when I saw you on top of your sister…" She stops herself from going on. What good in telling him that he had reminded her of Kent? That, instead of Lynette underneath him, she had seen herself.

He looks away again.

"You should never hit. Not your sister, not anyone."

Lynette stops drawing, looks at her brother, then her mother.

"And I should never hit either. Not you, not anyone."

It's quiet for a moment.

"How about we say that we both made a mistake? Okay?"

Jeremy looks at her, then nods. "Okay."

"Can you tell your sister, you're sorry?"

He looks over at her. "Sorry, Lynette."

"That's okay," Lynette says. She flips over her paper, to the drawing she was working on when Emily had first walked in. Raises it in the air towards Jeremy. "This one's you."

Jeremy laughs. "I got horns."

"I'll draw a new one."

They all sit in silence for a while as Lynette takes a clean sheet of paper and starts working on her brother's portrait, a less devilish version.

Emily says, "Go play PlayStation if you want."

Jeremy disappears so quickly she wonders if he was sitting with them at all.

Lynette colours while the wind moans between the spaces, while the rain drums against the house, while grey day slowly fades into greyer night.

Tomorrow, she thinks. *One sleep. No, no sleep. No sleep now.* Hopefully she'll be ready when the time comes. Ready to do what needs to be done.

"Go wash your hands before supper," she says to Lynette.

"I'm almost finished."

"You can finish after."

Emily listens to her daughter's steps in the hall, the opening and then closing of her bedroom door.

She sits back, slipping her hands into her fleece pockets, feeling suddenly lonely. Strange considering the many nights she's spent by herself at this very table, a cross-stitch in hand and warm milk in her favourite mug, the little ones in bed and Kent still at work. The radio playing lightly, the country station. Faith Hill and Carrie Underwood she'll turn up. Move her chair closer and sing along if she knows the lyrics, helping her forget for a time.

Everything seems bigger, somehow – the kitchen, the chair beneath her, the distance to the hallway, the bathroom, to her own bedroom. Maybe it's not so much that things have gotten bigger as it is that *she's* gotten smaller. Hardly noticeable now when she walks down the road with her youngsters, or checks someone's milk and eggs through. Sometimes it's like she needs to tilt her head back to see above the dashboard when Kent is driving them somewhere.

She gets a fork from the cutlery drawer and walks to the stove, opening it, her face turned away from the heat. When she reaches in, she brushes the edge of the pan and burns her pinky. She pulls her hand out, throwing the fork on the counter en route to the faucet. Lets water run over her smoldering finger, wishing that a little cold water could relieve everything as quickly: each foul mood, each threatening word, each slap across the face.

She turns the water off but has to turn it back on again because the pain returns. The finger's red now all along its length right up to the nail. A fluid-filled blister will appear later on this evening, she bets. Jeremy will want to pop it with a sewing needle. Lynette will watch between the spaces in her own fingers pressed against her eyes.

Emily holds the finger underneath the tap again, the pain instantly fading. Keeps it there as she goes over everything in her head. As long as they're at the ferry terminal by eight everything will be fine. She reminds herself that she'll have to get a taxi from Gander to pick them up when the ferry docks. She'll call before she leaves the house. Plenty of time, as long as the taxi's waiting, to catch the flight. No doubt Donny Boyle will ask where they're going with the suitcases and why Kent isn't with them. She'll smile and tell him St. John's. That Kent will join them on Saturday, after his fish plant business. She'll tell him to hand over the tickets then, so that the three of them can walk along the gangway and up to the canteen before the line-up starts. She'll say thanks when he wishes them a good trip.

The phone rings. She turns off the water and then grabs a drying towel hanging inside the door beneath the sink. The burning is back by the time she presses the 'talk' button.

"Hello."

"Mrs. Gyles?"

"Yes." She moves the phone away, then blows on her finger. Puts the receiver back to her ear.

"...here in Gander."

"Sorry, what?"

"This is Mrs. Butler and I'm a nurse at the James Paton hospital here in Gander."

"Hospital did you say?" It's her father. A heart attack, or one of those brain aneurysms. On a slab in the morgue. The top of her feels heavy suddenly, almost too much for her legs to support. The countertop helps keep her upright.

"Are you still there?"

Despite the lack of breath, she's able to say, "What's happened?"

"There's been an accident."

It's even worse, she thinks. Her dad mangled behind the wheel of his car. Mom too. Need to identify the bodies.

She can't speak.

"Your husband…"

Although she keeps the phone pressed against her ear, she can't hear anything the woman is saying. She's become blind and deaf, incapable of deciphering words.

"Mrs. Gyles?"

She doesn't say anything.

"Mrs. Gyles?" the nurse says again. "Did you hear what I just said?"

She forces herself back into the moment – in the kitchen with her hands pressed against the countertop, her head tilted towards her shoulder, the cordless phone trapped in between. "No."

"No?"

"Tell me again."

"I said your husband fell asleep behind the wheel…"

He can't be hurt, she thinks. Bruised maybe, cut too, but not hurt. Not really.

"…veered off the highway and down an embankment…"

She sees his eyes close in sleep, his head slump forward, his beautiful truck, his pride and joy, plunging over the bank and into the dark woods. Him waking long enough to be knocked unconscious, his body falling this way and that way because he's not bothered wearing his seatbelt.

"…glass from the windshield embedded in his forehead…"

Did he think of them, she wonders, in his brief moment of waking before the world turned black?

"…broken collar bone…"

Or was there nothing? Just the tumbling truck and the sound of crunched metal and snapping branches and him inside, alone. All alone.

"…overnight for observation…"

Quiet then. The headlights still on and his crushed chest fighting to rise and fall. Rain on the windshield, and only one wiper working.

"…released in the morning –"

"What?"

"I said, he'll be released in the morning. He's very lucky. It could have been a lot worse."

She manages to walk herself over to the table and sit down. *Overnight for observation*, the woman had just said. *Released in the morning.* It occurs to her that the one thing she's been trying so hard to run away from now lies beneath white sheets at the Gander hospital. Bare chest, probably, his arms outside the blankets pressed to his sides, new wounds on his forehead to keep the nearly healed one above his eye company, and a broken collar bone. It's like he's left without bothering to close the door, left it swinging on its hinges in the wind. Nothing to prevent her now from walking right through it.

"He asked for you," the nurse says.

"Did he?"

"Yes. He'll call, I'm sure, once he wakes up."

"I won't let the phone out of my hand."

"Can you come? He shouldn't be driving."

"I'll take the first ferry out of Lightning Cove tomorrow morning," she says. *I'd intended to anyway.*

"He's going to be fine."

"Okay."

"In the best hands here, he is."

"I'm sure. Thank you."

She presses the 'off' button before the nurse has a chance to say goodbye and brings a few fingers to her forehead, trying to massage the tension away.

How often has she wished for this very thing? Kent striking a moose on a foggy night or traveling too far over the median into an oncoming transport truck or spilling his Tim Horton's coffee and wrapping himself around a tree. A light pole. How comforting, for a time, those thoughts had been. So why then hasn't she run into the children's rooms and covered them in kisses, or poured herself a glass from the half-full bottle of cabernet sauvignon sitting on the counter, or run out on the porch and screamed at the top of her lungs, a scream of joy for being so close to what she's wanted since forever?

She tries summoning happiness. Imagines it as a liquid in the body of a needle, the tip being inserted into her vein. But happiness doesn't come. Not a drop of it. Instead what she feels is relief. That it wasn't her father. Her mother. That Kent was not badly hurt.

Lynette's there suddenly. Or perhaps she's been there all along.

"What, sweetie?"

"Something's burning."

It's takes a moment for her to remember there's food in the oven. "The fish sticks!" she says, rushing over to the stove.

A cloud of smoke billows out when she lowers the door. "It's burned, I've burned your supper." She grabs oven mitts and hauls out the pan. The fire alarm goes off as she lays the pan on one of the elements. "Ruined," she says, "ruined."

She slips off one of the mitts and walks to the fire alarm near the threshold of the hallway, close to where Lynette is. Stands beneath it, waving the mitt back and forth.

The commotion brings Jeremy out of his room. He stands behind his sister.

The alarm stops. She stays there looking up at it, expecting it to start again. It doesn't.

"How come you're crying?" Lynette says to her.

"Hmm?"

"You're crying."

She wipes at her eyes, surprised to feel wetness there. "The smoke, sweetie."

She walks back to the stove. Looks down at the shriveled, blackened fish sticks, the fries that look like charred bacon.

"What are we going eat now?" Jeremy says.

She turns around, the oven mitt still in her hand. Forces a smile. "How does take-out sound?"

FRIDAY

IN HER SLUMBER, SHE REACHES OUT TO HIM, then opens her eyes and remembers.

She's on top of the sheets, still in her clothes from yesterday. A miracle, she thinks, that some sleep has come. She turns towards the clock. 3:30. She'd been listening to the rain before drifting off, she remembers, her fingers interlaced underneath her head like a sunbather.

It occurs to her that she can't hear it anymore – the rain. Nor the wind.

On her feet now and moving to the window. Once there she parts the blinds and peers out. The street running past her house is slick-looking underneath the glow of the streetlight. A thin sheen of ice from the falling temperature and all that rain, she figures. Still cold despite it being May. A lot more nights like this still before the warm weather settles in. A lot of being fooled into thinking that the day's heat will carry on into the evening, that an open window at midday can remain so after dark, and that the sweater you wore earlier will suffice during your after-supper walk.

How strange not to see Kent's truck in the driveway. Usually it's so close to the porch steps that there's barely space enough to walk around it. Never enough space, she thinks. Always a situation to slither past, or a pair of eyes to avoid staring into. How funny to have the whole Atlantic Ocean just outside her window and yet feel as if everything is closing in around her.

She goes back over and sits on the edge of the bed. Rubs her thighs. Takes a big breath. *You can do this*, she thinks. *You can.* She turns on the lamp sitting on the night table, then waits for her eyes to adjust. Gets up and walks to the partially open door, slipping past it and out into the hallway, crunching up her face at each creak in the floor, not wanting to wake the children.

In the kitchen, she makes her way to the stove and then switches on the light above it. More breaths now. *You can do this. You can.*

There's enough ground coffee from yesterday to make a small pot. She does, then sits at the table while it brews. Places her face into her hands, then massages her temples, her eyelids.

157

That's when she notices it – the blinking red light coming from the answering machine. Must have rung while she was asleep. Strange that, as light as she's been sleeping lately, it wouldn't have wakened her.

She gets up and goes to it. Presses the 'message' button.

She waits. Listens.

"Hi there."

She spins around, positive that he's standing right behind her.

"Sorry for calling so late. (A tired laugh.) Must be this stuff they're pumping into me." (He pauses.)

She listens to his breathing.

"I'm fine. Been hurt worse shoveling the driveway." (Another laugh, then a silence.)

She thinks he's switched the phone to his other ear.

"Umm…I won't lie and say that I wasn't scared though…for a minute. (Coughing, then clearing his throat.) Can you believe it, me scared? Well, I was. (He pauses again.) I saw your face."

She swallows hard.

"Before the truck went off the road, I mean."

Now she switches the phone to her other ear, waiting for him to continue.

"You were smiling. (Yawn.) Sorry, I'm so tired."

She can relate to that.

"You seemed younger, somehow, like when we were first dating."

In the silence, she senses him wanting to say more about that, about being younger. He doesn't. Instead he says, "Tell the youngsters that daddy loves them."

Nothing then for a long time. But he's still on the line. She waits. And waits some more.

He sucks in a lot of air all at once and she knows he's crying. It's so foreign a sound coming from him that she fights an urge to throw the machine against the wall.

The message suddenly ends.

She stays where she is looking at the machine as if it might come to life.

The coffee percolator beeps.

She thinks about listening to the message again – *I won't lie and say that I wasn't scared* – but decides against it. *I saw your face. You were smiling.*

She walks past the kitchen and into the foyer, to the door leading to the basement. She twists the knob, lifts, then pushes, her nose at

158

once overcome with mustiness. It's the smell of her life, she thinks, this basement. Kent's unwashed hockey gear and wood glue, homemade quilts and Javex, old newspapers and stacked boxes.

Down she goes, one foot in front of the other, a hand on the rail to guide her. Near the bottom she pulls the chain, then stands there underneath the light feeling removed from herself, as if she's watching it all from outside and above her body.

She steps down finally, moving towards Kent's workstation, feeling as though she's treading water. She reaches underneath, removing the tarp that's covering everything, tossing it aside. She hauls out the two suitcases she'd eyed yesterday. First the smaller blue one – for Jeremy – then the larger green one for her and Lynette. She lays them on either side of her, knowing how difficult it will be to stuff their lives into two pieces of luggage, then carry those lives aboard a plane and try to transplant them someplace else. Each folded shirt a reminder of what was left behind.

She grips the handles and straightens her legs, not bothering to put the tarp back. She goes for the money now.

On her knees, she feels around for the loose panel. She finds it but has trouble lifting the edge. It was much easier when she had strong and polished nails instead of these bitten-to-the-quick ones, the skin around them either chewed or scratched off. She gets an index finger underneath at last, lifting and then pulling it away like a scab. Takes out the bundle she'd gotten at the bank first, transferring it to Jeremy's suitcase, then the airline tickets and the stuffed sock. Zips the suitcase closed and then fits the floorboard back in place.

Sadness presses down on her as she gets to her feet and heads for the stairs. On the second step she stops, wondering if what she's feeling might have something to do with the end of routine. No more weekly deposits beneath the floor, no more constant planning and writing out of lists, no more having to go over everything in her mind. It occurs to her as she pulls the light chain that there had been comfort in repetition, in structure, in knowing what to expect. But now – by taking the stashed money and hauling out the suitcases – she's starting down an unfamiliar path.

In the kitchen, she loses her breath when she sees Kent sitting at the table. Wait. No. It's Jeremy. Just Jeremy. Her boy's not the first that she's mistaken for Kent. Once, she'd walked into Hodder's Grocery and Convenience and could have sworn that the man holding the clipboard was her husband. Another time, at the marina, the man pouring her coffee was Kent too. She'd even see him in women. Heather. Her own mother. Sometimes he's everywhere – on her walks with the children, in her sleep, in each person she makes eye contact with. He's like a part of her, an organ in her body, an appendix about to burst.

She stops beside him and rests a hand on his shoulder, his forehead glistening with sweat. "What're you doing up, baby?"

He doesn't answer.

She pulls out a chair and sits alongside him.

His eyes are wide, unblinking, transfixed on the flower-patterned tablecloth.

Quietly, so as not to wake him, she says, "You're still asleep, my love."

Still he says nothing. Doesn't move.

"Let me take you back to bed."

She starts to get to her feet when she hears him say, "Where's Dad?"

She freezes. Sits back down. Looks again into his eyes. "Are you asleep, Jeremy?" she asks, unsure of it herself now. "Jeremy?"

He's quiet for a second, then says, "He won't let you."

"What?"

"He won't."

She has the strangest feeling of being watched – someone staring through the window at her, or waiting just outside the door, their hands around the knob. She looks behind herself, then towards the hall. Settles on her boy again. "Who won't let me?"

He doesn't answer.

She leans closer. "Who?"

Suddenly he wakes. Looks up at her with disoriented eyes, like he has no idea where he is. It's like he's about to cry.

Emily holds him before he can. Says, "You were talking in your sleep, my love."

He pushes her away, then says, "I want some juice."

"You're thirsty?"

He nods. "I want some juice."

She gets up and goes to the cupboard and takes down a tumbler, laying it on the counter. Grabs the fruit punch out of the fridge. Realizes that the hand holding the container is shaking so badly she can barely pour. A little misses the glass.

She goes to bring it over to him, but sees that he's standing right behind her, in the middle of big yawn. She hands him the glass.

He hardly takes any before handing it back.

"I thought you wanted juice?" she says.

"I'm tired," he says.

She lays the tumbler on the counter, leads him through the kitchen and back to his bedroom. After tucking him in, she goes to leave but then she stops herself and sits on the edge of his bed in the dark. Runs a hand through his hair. "Are you still awake?"

He pushes her hand away as if it were an extra blanket that he was trying to get out from under. "I'm tired."

"Jeremy?" she says. "Who won't let me?"

"What?"

He's slipping back into sleep, his legs already starting to twitch.

"You said that someone wouldn't let me. Who?"

Silence.

"Jeremy?"

Deep breathing then, young and unobstructed, his mouth hanging open. She pulls the blankets up to just below his chin, wondering if, somehow, her boy has figured out her plans for later on this morning. *He couldn't possibly know. No one does.*

She doesn't consider herself superstitious or even slightly religious. When was the last time she'd walked into the foyer of St. Paul's or cracked open the Bible in the drawer beside her bed? Still though, there are times when she thinks there's a higher power at work, someone watching over things, keeping His/Her hands out of it, but taking stock all the same, delivering messages through peoples' dreams, revealing pieces of the future. Although she's never experienced this herself, hadn't her mother dreamed of her grandfather's death the night before it happened? Saw her husband's swollen prostate before the cancer had a chance to spread? Perhaps Jeremy has inherited a bit of her mother's gift, she thinks.

He won't let you. He meaning Kent, she knows. And what he won't let her do is go.

Instead of going back to the kitchen, she decides to check on Lynette, Jeremy's words in her ears the whole way. *He won't let you.* He was sleepwalking, for heaven's sake, has been every couple of months since he was five or six. How many times has he said or done something strange? Hadn't he, one time, gone to the basement in the middle of the night and tried fitting himself in the dryer? Another time she'd woken to find him eating mayonnaise right from the bottle with his fingers.

Lynette's on her side, her giraffe pressed against her face, when Emily inches open the door.

It's the timing of it, she thinks, that of all the nights, Jeremy would pick this one, the eve of her leaving. *He won't let you.*

She goes over to Lynette's bed, feeling the years of living in her legs, in her insides. Although she hadn't intended to, and knowing all the things she's yet to do before the ferry in the morning, she slips in beside her youngest, relishing in the mattress taking her weight, little though it is.

She turns on her side so that her face is pointed towards Lynette's. Noses almost touching, her daughter's sweet breath on her lips and lifting the few hairs off her forehead with each exhale.

Can you believe it? Me scared? Well, I was, she hears him saying. And, *I saw your face, you were smiling.* She pictures him lying awake in his hospital room, his collarbone already fusing together, the cuts on his forehead scabbing over and shrinking. A little battered, exhausted too from all this fish plant business, yet every part of him wanting to pull the sheets off and put his feet on the floor. A man who can't be tied down for long. Full of life. Good to everyone. Almost.

She breathes in her daughter's scent knowing that she hates him, and, inexplicably, loves him too, a little. It's not enough though. She knows this now. Not enough so long as she's scared of him.

Her eyes get heavy. She'll close them for ten minutes, she thinks, then rise and pack her things. It occurs to her that she still hasn't arranged to have a taxi waiting after the ferry docks. She makes a mental note to do it first thing, soon as she gets up. Call the airline too and make sure the flight's on schedule. Perhaps put a call in to Jackie. Why not? No reason she can't now. Now that Kent's gone.

She drapes an arm across her daughter's tiny torso. Stares into the beautiful, sleeping face. After a moment, she tries shutting her own eyes, but all she sees behind the lids is Jeremy. "But where's Dad?" she imagines him saying. "I won't go without Dad." She sees herself grabbing him and forcing him out the door, but he's way too strong.

She flips over onto her back. Breathes. Breathes again. She'll lie to him if she has to. Whatever it takes to get him on that plane.

2

SHE OPENS HER EYES. Sucks in too much air and starts coughing. Brings her hand to her neck, expecting his to still be there. She sits up. Tries to recall her dream. Kent had been sitting astride her on the bed, bearing all of his weight down, his hands around her neck. Or had they been over her mouth? Threatening her, wasn't he? Something to do with the children. What was it? The more she tries to remember, the more it starts to crumble away until nothing's left.

She looks down and notices that all the sheets have been kicked off the bed.

Lynette's facing away from her, mangled hair and pajama top half way up her back. A ray of sunlight, through a space in the blinds, illuminates her daughter's smooth and unblemished skin. Like soapstone that skin.

The coughing has stopped, but now her stomach's bubbling. Something she should be doing, she thinks.

It's when she brings a fingertip to the corner of an eye to remove the crusty sleep that something electrical seizes her – a panic shooting through her whole system at once, stopping her heart, yanking the breath from her lungs, stiffening each muscle, each tendon.

It seems like forever before she can move again. She looks at her watch. 7:15. "Oh my God," she says breathlessly, "Oh my God." She doesn't quite know what wrenches her from the bed and plants her on her feet, certainly not her own power, rather something outside herself, some external, unseen force.

"Get dressed," she says, "We're late!"

Lynette wakes. Sits up. Disoriented eyes. "What's wrong, Mommy?"

"Get dressed, baby, okay?"

Lynette doesn't move.

"Now, sweetheart."

Lynette swings her legs out, then stands up, heads for her dresser.

"Hurry."

"All right."

On her way to Jeremy's room she tries to calm herself. Only 7:15. Would have had to wait until at least seven if Kent were here. Fifteen

163

minutes. Only fifteen. Lots of time to get ready yet. Well, not lots, but enough. Still enough.

She stops at Jeremy's room, then nearly takes the door off its hinges opening it.

Jeremy lifts his head, eyes still closed from lingering sleep.

She goes to his bed and tears the sheets away. "You need to get up, my love."

He's not wearing his pajama pants and does his best to cover himself. "What are you doing?"

"Right now. We're leaving in twenty minutes."

"But school's not 'til –"

"No school today. We have to catch the ferry."

"What –"

"Get dressed."

She runs out into the hall, back to her own room, then stops. Changes direction and sprints towards the kitchen. *Breathe, just breathe. Lots of time. Loads of it.*

The suitcases are where she'd dropped them last night; Jeremy's still upright, hers and Lynette's on its side. She grabs them and takes off back through the kitchen, and down the hall to Jeremy's room. Opens his door.

He's managed to haul on an undershirt and underwear but no pants yet. "Can't you knock?"

Emily tosses the suitcase on the floor beside him. "Fill this."

"What?"

"Your clothes, your hockey cards if you want. Hurry." She whips around and heads out into the hall again, not bothering to answer him when he asks where they're going.

Lynette's zipping up the back of her jean skirt when Emily stops by her door. She pokes her head in. "No."

"What?"

She thinks she sees worry in her daughter's eyes. "You need long pants."

"Why?"

"Do as I say, sweetie."

She runs down the hall, the green suitcase in her right hand and flopping against her outer thigh. Sends it flying on the bed when she enters her bedroom. Goes over and unzips the lid and is about to go over to her dresser when she suddenly realizes that she's forgotten to take the money and the tickets out of the blue suitcase.

Out in the hall again now, her feet barely touching the hardwood.

Jeremy's door is closed when she reaches his room. The knob catches when she tries turning it. Locked. She knocks. "Open up, Jeremy."

"I'm dressing."

They don't have the luxury of time, she knows. Each revolution of the second hand past the twelve brings them one minute closer to missing the boat, their ride to Gander, and the plane. The Jesus plane. "I need to get in there," she says, pounding on the door so hard it's a wonder she doesn't shatter every bone in her hand. "Open up!"

Footsteps approaching from the other side of the door then. Him fiddling with the lock. The door opens a crack.

She pushes herself in. Sees all of the money on his bed, the bills pulled out of their sock, and the three tickets opened and facing up. She rushes over. "Does this belong to you?"

"Are we going on a plane?"

The bundle, still bound by its elastics, she takes first, then the plane tickets, shoving both into the pockets of her pants. Starts gathering the loose bills then, not bothering to put them back in the sock. "You have to learn to mind your own business."

"I was just looking," Jeremy says. "How much is there?"

"Never mind. I told you to pack some clothes."

"I was about to," he says.

She thinks that, jumbled in her hand like this, it's like she's robbed a bank or something. "Every dollar better be here." She moves towards the door.

"Where are we going?"

"You'll see" she says, her back to him.

"Where's Dad?"

She freezes, amazed that he's waited this long to ask.

"I didn't hear him leave this morning," Jeremy says.

Whatever it takes to get him on that plane. "Dad spent the night in Gander. With work."

"Where are we going?" he asks again.

Before turning around, she tries relaxing the muscles in and around her face, to regulate her breathing. "You'll see, I said." She faces him now, trying her best to lift the corners of her trembling mouth.

Jeremy takes a step forward. "Is he coming with us?"

"We'll meet up with him later," she says, surprised at how easily the lie comes.

"When?"

"Later. Now get that stuff packed. We're leaving in fifteen minutes."

She goes back to her bedroom. Stuffs the money and the plane tickets into her purse and then starts packing, gabbing handfuls from hauled open drawers. Hopefully in Vancouver later this evening, a decent pair of jeans will be there to put on, a blouse or two, and a turtleneck maybe.

Shoes, she thinks. Need some of those – a job interview, or, if it ever comes to it, the welfare office. She runs to her closet and takes two pairs from the rack, one red, another brown, and throws them atop the mess.

Dipping her hands into the pile of clothing now, she finds a pair of jeans and a hooded sweater, bra and panties, and a thick pair of black socks. She changes in front of the mirror, yesterday's clothes a crumpled mess near her feet.

7:23. Fifteen minutes from here to the ferry. Less if they hurry.

She bends over and pulls on her socks, then runs over and zips up the suitcase. Slings her handbag over her head so that its strap lies between her breasts. Runs back to her daughter's room.

Lynette's fastening the last buckle of her jean jumpsuit when Emily comes in.

"That's better," she says, laying the suitcase beside the dresser. Unzips it and starts tossing Lynette's clothes inside. She goes to the closet and randomly yanks dresses and sweaters off hangers, a long coat and scarf.

She piles everything on top of her own unfolded clothes, then tries pushing it all down, one palm over the other, like she's trying to restart a heart. It won't close.

"Sit on top," she says to Lynette.

Lynette comes over. Kneels instead of sits.

She manages to get the zipper partway closed before the metal piece gives way in her hand. "Jesus," she says, "I just broke it." Then to Lynette, "Get off."

Lynette's too slow.

"Get off!"

Lynette gets to her feet awkwardly, tears welling in her eyes.

"I didn't mean to yell, honey." She opens the suitcase and dumps everything out. "Wait here."

Emily runs back to the basement and grabs another suitcase. Smaller than the first, but it'll have to do. She's on her way back to the stairs when everything suddenly tightens in her stomach. She makes it to the bathroom just as the rush of vomit comes. Coughing and spitting then, a few dry heaves, her arms wrapped around the toilet as if it were the last solid thing on earth. The smell like overcooked meat.

7:28.

She wipes her mouth, flushes, then goes upstairs.

Lynette helps her transfer the clothes into the new suitcase.

"Jeremy!" Emily shouts.

No answer.

"Jeremy!"

His voice faint, as if muffled under quilts. "What?"

"Are you ready?"

"What?"

"Are you ready?"

No answer.

Emily does the suitcase up and gets to her feet. "Let's go." She moves to the door.

"Wait," Lynette says.

"What?"

"My giraffe."

"Get it. Quick."

Lynette lifts it from the bed, holding it in her arms like something alive, like something she'll need to burp.

Emily leaves the room and rushes down the hall – Lynette right behind her – and stops at Jeremy's door. She knocks.

No answer.

She knocks again. Tries the handle. He's locked it again. "Jeremy!"

Still no answer.

Calm down, she tells herself, calm down. *Breathe.* "Honey, open up."

Nothing for ages. Then at last his voice, sounding close, as if he's positioned himself right against the door, his lips close enough to kiss it. "Dad's coming?"

Breathe. Okay, Let it out…slowly. You expected this, right? Knew he wouldn't come willingly. "I told you already, honey" she says, trying to keep her voice steady. "Didn't I?"

Another pause from the other side of the door.

She waits, repressing the urge to kick the Jesus door down and drag him out kicking and screaming.

Finally, he says, "Where's his stuff?

"His stuff?"

"His suitcase and that?"

Past 7:30. Less than half an hour to make it to the ferry. "His stuff is…he already has his stuff, silly. Took it with him to Gander now, didn't he?" *Please come out, Jeremy. I'm doing this for you, you know. For your sister. For all of us.*

"I don't want to go," he says.

Without intending to, she slams the door with her fist, sending waves of pain along her wrist and upper arm and into her shoulder.

Lynette jumps back in fright.

Emily turns to her. "I'm sorry, baby, I didn't mean to scare you. We're just running out of time, that's all."

"I want to talk to Dad," Jeremy says.

She turns back to the door. "Dad's in Gander."

"On the phone. I want to talk to him on the phone."

When did her hands go up to her face, she wonders? She imagines leaving without him, then him trying to track her down years later, the mother that had abandoned him. Her opening a door somewhere and him standing on the front stoop. A carbon copy of the man she married all those years ago. Neither of them having anything to say.

Lynette's voice brings her back. "I need to pee, Mommy."

"You'll pee on the boat – "

"Why can't I talk to him?" Jeremy says.

Lynette takes a step towards the bathroom. "I really need to go."

"ENOUGH!"

Lynette stops.

No sound at all from Jeremy's side of the door.

Her ears are ringing from the sound of her own scream. Trembling she is, and her heart beating so fast it might stop. She collects herself, then says to Lynette. "Alright, go pee. Quick."

Lynette doesn't move.

"Quick, I said."

Her daughter goes.

Emily turns back to the door. Steals a peek at her watch. Wonders then if this is how it's all supposed to end? All her planning to get no farther than the outside of her son's bedroom door. Kent showing up some time later to see Lynette and her seated in the hallway, their legs crossed at their ankles. "What's going on here, then?" she can hear him saying.

At last, she speaks. "Stay then if you want."

Jeremy says nothing.

"But your father won't be happy when he has to come all the way back here and get you."

Still nothing.

"You'll be grounded 'til you're twenty."

Quiet on the other side of the door.

The sound of the toilet flushing. Then Lynette walking down the hall and standing beside her.

"Come on," Emily says to her.

They get past the hallway and a few feet into the kitchen when she hears his door open. Then his voice. "Wait for me."

A breath escapes her. She nearly falls.

His steps on the hardwood, then he appears in a *Simpson's* T-shirt and jeans, his suitcase – looking too tiny to hold clothes enough to fit him – dangling from his big hand.

"Come on then," she says, pointing towards the foyer.

Jeremy and Lynette brush past her.

"Hats and mittens too," she tells them. "It'll be chilly on the boat." She follows them, then lays her own suitcase down and puts on her boots. Takes the long coat off its hanger, slipping her arms through, not bothering to do it up. Her handbag's underneath for safety, pressed against her side. Her whole life's in there.

Jeremy puts on his Montreal Canadiens' toque. "When are we coming back?"

We're not. Ever. "Next week."

She bends down and helps Lynette zip up her jacket.

The phone rings.

Lynette makes a move for it.

"Leave it," she says.

Jeremy comes forward. "What if it's Dad?"

"I said, leave it."

She picks up the suitcase and hurries to the door, throwing it open like the foyer were on fire, then stands there with her back against it as Jeremy and Lynette pass through. She hears his recorded voice on the machine: *Hello there, you've reached the Gyles's residence. Sorry we missed your call. Please leave a message and one of us will do our best to get back to you. Have a great day.*

The machine beeps.

"Hi there. Me calling…"

Although he's halfway down the steps already, Jeremy hears his father's voice. He drops his suitcase, then turns around. "That's Dad." He twists himself in Lynette's direction; she's already halfway along the driveway. "Hey Lynette, it's Dad."

"…thought I would have heard from you by now."

Jeremy starts back up the steps, but Emily thrusts out her palm to stop him. "Stay!" she says.

"But it's Dad." Jeremy keeps coming.

She stands in front of the door, blocking his way. "We'll miss the boat."

"Let me answer it."

"…I miss you guys…"

She pushes him so hard that he nearly flies off the porch, then reaches back inside for her suitcase. Picks it up. Stops though when she hears Kent say,

"…it's finished. They're shutting her down. Three months, but I allow it'll be sooner."

She wills herself to close the door, but still can't for some reason. 7:45. What's she waiting for?

"…could really use that vacation now. I can't wait. Hope you're looking forward to it. Just wanted to let you know that I'm –"

She slams the door so hard that the whole house shakes, then rushes along the porch and down the steps.

They're watching her from the end of the driveway. Bits of orange in the early morning sky behind them. Lynette, one hand in her coat pocket despite wearing mittens, and her giraffe in the other; Jeremy with his hat pulled down so far that it's a wonder he can even see. Lost-looking, she thinks. Orphans watching another young couple drive away. Damaging them if she stays, damaging them if she goes. But she can't leave them behind, she knows. Needs them like she needs water, food…air.

"Didn't have to push me down the stairs," Jeremy says. "I only wanted to talk to him."

"You can talk to him later. All you want."

7:50.

"We'll make it if we run," she says.

It's not until she's near the end of their street that she looks back. Both of them are at her heels. Jeremy's suitcase flopping at his side. He's holding his sister's hand. Lynette's strangling her giraffe.

3

A MAN IN THE DISTANCE GUIDES THE LAST VEHICLE ALONG THE GANGWAY. Another man standing on the wharf is untying the temporary knots that have moored the ferry to the dock.

"Wait!" she shouts, knowing that from this distance no one will hear.

"I'm tired, Mommy," Lynette says. She's lagging now, Jeremy having to pull her along.

"Just a little bit farther," she says, her eyes focused on the boat, as if the slightest turn of her head will cause it to disappear.

Her thighs are burning. Her arm too, from holding the suitcase. Her chest feels like it might catch fire. There's a pain in her lower back. She imagines the bottom discs rubbing together, eroding like stones on a beach.

"It's leaving," Jeremy says, barely breathing hard.

"We'll make it," she says, not quite believing it herself.

The man doing the untying throws the last of the ropes to another man on deck, then gives a 'thumbs-up' to the control room on the upper level.

"Wait for us!" she screams, flapping her free arm now like a castaway.

Churning water near the stern now. The ear-splitting departure horn.

She trips on a lace that's come undone. Face first into the pavement. The back of her hand coming up just before impact. Suitcase flying across the street. She feels everything shift inside of her on impact, the air being zapped from her lungs, her fingers protecting her face.

Almost immediately she is back on her feet, straining for breath.

"Are you all right, Mommy?" Lynette says. She and Jeremy have stopped beside her.

Jeremy lets go of his sister and points at his mother's hand. "It's bleeding."

She looks, skin like raw meat, flecks of it hanging off. No pain though. She glances sideways at the suitcase. Still intact. Back to her children now. "Go, I'll catch up!"

They don't move.

"GO!"

They start running again.

She goes over and picks up the suitcase. Feels a warm ooziness spreading along the palm of her hand, into the fingers and towards the nails. Somehow it's dulling the pain.

Running again now, although it hardly feels like it. More like flying. No sensation of feet hitting the asphalt, or of body resisting. Light now where, just moments ago, she'd been heavy.

She's gaining on them.

Lynette being dragged again, but still managing to look back, charting her mother's progress. She's the one calling now, the one ushering her forward. "Hurry, Mommy. Hurry!"

"I'm coming!"

The gangway is lifting. "No!" She screams.

They're one hundred feet away. Less. Eighty feet. Seventy-five. Yet they're pulling up the gangway. No point once that starts. But can't they see them running? The man coiling the heavy ropes, his face outward, seemingly looking in their direction? How about the one on the wharf? *Turn around and you'll see us. Why won't you?*

She's beside the children now, the three of them running. Running towards freedom, she thinks, away from Kent, although the youngsters don't know it. They're hurrying because they think they'll see their father at the end of the journey.

Forty feet. Won't make it. Gangway almost up. "Wait!"

"Wait!" Lynette says.

Even Jeremy says it.

The man standing on the dock finally turns around. It's Donny Boyle.

"Please wait!" she says.

He squints in her direction. "Emily?"

She finally makes it to where Donny is. Stops. "Yes, it's me," she says, fighting tears.

"You just missed her."

"No."

"Look at your hand why don't yah." He takes a step closer.

Lynette starts to say something but Emily cuts her off, "We need to get on this boat."

"It'll be back in a couple of hours, sure."

In a couple of hours, she thinks, *Kent* could very well be on board. *Overnight for observation*, the nurse from the Gander hospital had said last night. *Released in the morning.* Who's to say that he hasn't already been discharged? On his way to meet the ferry himself, probably.

"No, Donny," she says. "We can't wait."

Donny casts a glance at the now completely-up gangway, then looks back at her, his hand smoothing the four or five days' growth on his chin. "That hand's a mess."

"It's fine."

"I can't stop her now, my dear."

She takes him by the arm and drags him away from the children. Lynette starts to follow. "Stay with your brother," she says.

Lynette steps back with Jeremy.

Once she's far enough away, she whispers, "You have to. You have to stop her."

"I'd like to, but –"

"Kent's dying," she says.

It's like Donny's swallowed his tongue. "What?"

"He was in a car accident last night and they don't know if he'll live."

Quiet for a second.

"Jesus, Emily...I'm so sorry – "

"Don't be *sorry.*" She grabs the collar of his jacket with her good hand. "Just get us on board. *Please.*"

He pries her fingers off and then runs back to the ferry. Shouts to the man on deck who, a few moments ago, had been coiling the rope. "Emergency, Doug!"

Amidst the swirling engine and another blast of the ship's horn, Donny's words get lost.

"What?" Doug says after the sound of the horn subsides.

"Emergency, I said! Hold for three more passengers!"

"But the gangway's up!"

"Then lower it for Christ's sake! It's an emergency, I said!"

Doug disappears up the stairs to the second level while Emily walks back to rejoin her children.

Donny shoots her a look: squinted eyes below scraggly red brows, lower lip trapped beneath coffee-stained teeth, square jaw pulled taut because of those same teeth.

She imagines the boat inching away from shore, a plane lifting off without them, then going back to *that* house, every room echoing the sounds of their near escape.

Donny turns back to the boat – his hands on his hips.

She stands there holding her wrist, the first pinpricks of pain start-ing to flutter in the hand. Still nothing though, she thinks, compared to the thought of *not* getting on board. Might as well have a broken neck or have all the air snuffed out of her lungs or have her heart stop right where she's standing. No point in any of it if she can't get on.

"It's leaving, Mommy," Lynette says.

Jeremy says, "It *is*, Mom."

She's so positive of it too that she feels her whole body falter, as if she might crumble into pieces. Condemned and on the cusp of dem-olition – that's how she feels, the heavy ball about to smash into her centre.

She doesn't even notice Donny waving at her. Can't hear his shouts either.

Lynette's tugging at her coat, she thinks.

What's Jeremy saying?

It's the lowering of the gangway that brings her back. All this time she'd thought it was the ferry moving away.

Donny's beside her now. "Didn't hear me calling?"

She turns to him.

"It's not gonna wait all morning," he says.

She's got her arms around him now even though she doesn't re-member having gone to him.

"You're welcome," he says, gently extricating himself. "Come on."

He takes up the suitcase and heads towards the ferry.

They follow him, Emily just behind, and the youngsters at her heels, the gangway extending towards them like an unfurled carpet. Passage into another life.

Donny steps aside and hands over the suitcase as they pass. "All the best."

"Thank you," she says, not looking back.

Jeremy and Lynette are waiting for her on the other end of the gangway, the sun now high in the sky behind them. Not a cloud.

She forges ahead, sensing her old life fall away with each step, a new one just beginning. Scared, yes, but excited too. Not about to make the same mistakes.

Only a few minutes after eight but already the sun is warm against her face. The lightest of breezes. The perfect day for leaving.

She stops in front of them. Looks at their faces for a moment. Al-ready she can see the beginnings of definition around Jeremy's cheek-bones and jawline, like his dad. The thick hair that Kent had had in high school too. He'll be even bigger she thinks, taller, broader across the shoulders, bigger hands and feet.

There's more of her mother in Lynette than herself. Nose wider than her own, skin smoother, that elegant neck, and fuller lips. Emily's eyes though, deep green with flecks of grey. Cat's eyes, she's been told. Greener than July grass, Kent had said to her once.

They walk up the steel steps to the upper level and then to the stern. Lay down their suitcases, their hands holding onto the railing, faces outward towards the wharf, the marina, St. Paul's, the parish hall, the dying fish plant, the playground, the makeshift soccer field where an ownerless border collie runs free. She tries to imagine the place cleared out, boarded-up windows and empty streets, no boats in the harbour and no ATV engines roaring in the night, no dirt-marked children running in the road and no plant whistle to tell the stinking workers to go home for the day. No more Lightning Cove. No more for *her* anyway, one way or the other.

"We're moving, Mommy," Lynette says.

"Yes we are. Do you like the boat ride?"

Lynette nods.

Silence for a while. Then Jeremy says, "We'll see Dad soon, right?"

She doesn't look at him, preferring instead to focus on the re-ceding land, everything that she's leaving. Another moment before she says, "Soon, baby. Soon."

4

FROM THE STERN OF THE BOAT, LIGHTNING COVE is indistinguishable in the distance, a thin line on the horizon. Irrelevant almost. Easy to stuff in a box and forget.

Jeremy and Lynette are on either side of her, sipping hot chocolates. Whipped cream on the corners of Jeremy's mouth; a cute moustache over Lynette's.

She's working on her Styrofoam cup of coffee. At least that's what the girl behind the canteen counter had called it. She isn't so sure. Thick like syrup, coffee grinds on her tongue, a yet to be named colour that's blacker than black.

It's harder to move the fingers of her hand now. Her pinky, the one she'd burned last night, despite its blister, is the only one she can bend. She holds the wrist across her chest as if in an invisible sling. Thinks she can see it swelling, throbbing, stabbing pain like hundreds of needle pricks. How will she be able to sit on a plane for four or five hours like this? Something for the smarting, she thinks – extra strength Tylenol or Advil. Morphine.

"Watch out for your sister," she says. "Mom has to go inside for a minute."

She walks along the deck, throwing her coffee into the garbage en route, then pulls open the heavy door.

Apart from a few people playing cards at a table near the back, and an old man lying across three chairs, the lounge is empty.

She continues across the room to the small canteen adjacent the women's washroom. Stands in front of the counter while the chubby cashier piles a handful of ketchup chips into her mouth, and then holds up a red-stained finger as if to say, "Give me a second so I can swallow these."

Emily waits. Then waits some more while the girl sucks some Pineapple Crush through a straw.

"Sorry about that," the cashier says, smiling, pieces of soggy chips trapped in her front teeth, "but I'm starved. Left the house without so much as a Pop Tart this morning." She licks her fingers one at a time, then says, "Another coffee?"

Emily shakes her head.

The cashier leans forward, resting her elbows on the counter. "You don't remember me, do ya?"

Emily takes a half step back. Studies the face.

"I've been away for a long time, that's probably why. And I'm heavier too. Used to be a rake like yourself."

"Melissa?"

"In the flesh."

"You're all grown up."

"The spitting image of Mom, everyone says. You know my mom, Sonya, I suppose. Works at the Royal Bank."

Emily nods, wondering how she could have overlooked the resemblance. The same thick fingers and heaving bosom, the same lips and puffy cheeks.

"Yeah, well I'm back living with her now. Couldn't stand my father's boyfriend, you know. Control freak. Treated me like hired help or something."

"Oh."

"It's too bad really, I loved Victoria."

Emily edges closer to the counter. "Victoria?"

"Yeah." She takes another sip of her pop.

"As in Victoria, BC?"

"Yeah."

"What's it like?"

"A lot better than this shit hole, let me tell yah. Big trees and it hardly ever snows. More to do besides smoke and drink like everyone around here. No one's into your business either." She looks down at Emily's hand as if discovering it for the first time. "You just do that?"

"What?"

"Your hand?"

"Just before I boarded actually."

"It looks like someone scrubbed it with sandpaper."

"Gross isn't it?"

"It hurt?"

Emily nods.

"It looks like it does." Then, "Do you think it's broken?"

"Don't know. You wouldn't happen to have some Tylenol back there would yah?"

"Sorry, nothing but hotdogs and ketchup chips behind here."

"Okay," Emily says, starting to walk away. "Thanks anyway."

"Wait," Melissa says, bending down and grabbing her purse. "I've got something a lot better than that." She plops the purse down on the counter. "Make you forget you even got a hand this stuff will."

Emily just looks at her.

The girl smiles a beet-red tooth grin. "Don't worry, it's nothing illegal." She rummages in her purse. "Smile the whole night on this stuff, you will. Wake up the same way. Here." She pulls out a prescription bottle. Holds it beside her face as if she were doing a Trident commercial. Hardly likely with all that ketchup on her teeth.

Emily comes closer. "What is it?"

"Morphine's slutty girlfriend. The pharmacist calls it codeine."

"That's a prescription."

"So?"

"I can't take that."

"Why not? Mom does, whenever she can't sleep. I'm constantly having to refill the bottle."

Emily imagines Sonya sitting on the edge of her bed, a glass of Johnny Walker Red in one hand and a palm-full of her daughter's pills in the other. Mascara tears blackening each cheek. Probably still hurt by her husband's leaving.

"What'll they do to me?"

"Help with the pain. At least until you can get it seen to." She pushes down, then twists off the cap. Holds the bottle out to Emily.

Emily holds out her palm.

"I'll give you four."

"Isn't that a lot?"

"Not at all. Take two now and then another two in twelve hours."

Emily looks at the pills in her hand. Looks up at Melissa. "What do you take them for?"

"Irritable bowel."

"Oh."

"I can eat a whole pack of bacon if I take a couple of these beforehand." Melissa goes to the sink and pours some water into a Styrofoam cup. Hands it to Emily.

"Thank you." She pops two in her mouth and takes a sip of water. Hands the cup back and slips the other two pills into her pocket.

Melissa throws the rest of the water down the sink, then drops the cup into the garbage. Goes back to Emily. "Where you headed anyway?"

"Gander."

"Then where?"

She pauses, then says, "What makes you think I'm going any farther?"

Melissa grabs a few more chips. Chews with her mouth open. "I don't know." Washes them down with a sip of Crush.

Emily doesn't say where she's going.

Melissa holds out the bag.

Emily shakes her head. "I should get back to the youngsters."

"Okay."

"Thanks so much."

"You're welcome."

She starts to walk away.

"See you on the way back, probably," Melissa says.

Emily lifts her good hand in a wave, but doesn't turn around. "Probably."

* * *

SHE SLIPS HER BAD HAND INTO HER SWEATER POCKET, her fingers on fire from the pain, eyes watering. How long before the codeine kicks in, she wonders?

She retraces her steps through the seating area. The card players are laughing and sipping coffees and rapping their knuckles against the table with each laid ace or queen. Heavy parkas for weather so mild. Unfamiliar to her. Tourists, she bets. Mainlanders. Americans.

The old man lying down has turned onto his side now, his back to her, butt sticking out. Because the three chairs he's taking up are not enough to accommodate his whole length, his feet and ankles hang over.

She freezes in midstride. Holds her breath. Although she can't see for herself, she imagines the colour draining from her face. "Jesus," she whispers. "No ride to Gander." *Goddamn it.* In all the panic earlier it had completely slipped her mind to call ahead and have a taxi waiting.

8:35. Flight's at eleven. Over an hour to get to Gander from where the boat lets them off. Longer if the road's bad. So bloody careless. Even if she calls now they'll have to wait an hour. Maybe more. They'll miss their flight.

She scans the room. Looks once more at the group playing cards, thinking that they must be heading Gander way. Where else? She moves towards them, then stops. How, especially if they're all traveling in the same vehicle, will they be able to fit three more people? Not to mention their suitcases.

Melissa's brewing more coffee when Emily turns to her. She'll ask to use the cashier's cell phone and call that cab. That's if there's any reception in the middle of the bay. No. There's no time. They won't make it. She imagines clawing at her hair or screaming or banging her fists against the windows. Lashing out at her stupidity, her complete heedlessness at having gotten them this far only to have it all fall apart because she forgot to make a phone call. A Jesus phone call.

She wonders how long it will take to walk to the highway? Start hitching then. What vehicles will be on the road so early? Mostly transport trucks, she figures. Burly men in ball caps listening to the country station and trying to break into the police frequency on their CBs in order to know where the highway patrol might be lurking.

She'll have Lynette stand in front, and Jeremy a few steps behind his sister. She'll stand at the back. Who'll dare pass a sweet-faced thing like Lynette? A face like hers would probably get them a ride right to the airport's terminal.

Someone's calling her name. A voice too deep to be one of the children. Or Melissa. She turns and is shocked to see that the old man lying across the three chairs is not so old after all. "Myles?" she says. "That you?"

"Hope so." He rubs the corners of his eyes, then does his best to flatten his stuck-up hair.

Perhaps it was the way he'd had his chin tucked towards his chest that made him look three times his age. That and the dark bags she now notices beneath his eyes. She'd only seen him the other day, but she swears his face looks more shrunken, the skin around his cheekbones tighter.

She looks once more through the window at her two children, wondering how she'll explain this to Myles.

She moves to him. "What are you doing here?"

"Same as you, I suspect." He sits up, resting his palms on his knees. Pumps up his chest and arches his back. Lets his breath out slowly.

How tired he looks. More than her even, she thinks. "Where are you headed?"

"The James Paton." He rubs his eyes again, then coughs a cigarette cough, the thick sludge in his chest moving upward towards the back of his throat. He swallows it back down.

Kent's in the James Paton.

She takes another step nearer.

"It's Irene."

She goes all the way to him.

He slides over.

She sits. "What's happened?"

"Some complication or other."

His breath is stale. She tries not to breathe through her nose. "What kind of complication?"

"I was all ready to take her home yesterday, then she got these pains. Like someone was cutting her open without anesthetic, she said. She was screeching. The baby screeching and she screeching." He puts his face into his palms for a second. Takes his hands away. "Afterbirth it was. Stupid fuckers left a whole wad of it inside her."

"No."

"Yes they did. I half thought there was another baby in there." He laughs but there's no happiness in it.

"When will they discharge her?"

"Sunday. If she's doing all right, maybe tomorrow."

"Thank God it's nothing serious."

He nods, his face on the floor.

"Where's your boy?" she asks.

"School. He can't afford to be missing any as bad as he's doing. I should throw that goddamn Xbox out the window. Like someone addicted that boy is." He lifts his eyes from the floor and looks at her. "Your boy got one?"

"Hmm?"

"Xbox?"

She shakes her head. "PlayStation. He's not too bad though. Would rather be lifting weights in the garage."

"That's good. Healthy at least, weights."

She looks once again at her children. Then back at Myles. A ride to Gander fallen right in her lap.

"Where are *you* going?" he asks.

He'll know something's up when he sees the suitcases. That and the fact that neither Lynette nor Jeremy are in school.

"Gander too," she says. "The airport."

"Oh. Where to?"

"St. John's."

"The big city. Without the hubby?"

"He's meeting us later."

181

"Us?"

She points to the window behind him.

He turns around. "The whole family, eh? That's nice." He pauses. "I don't remember the last time me and Irene went anywhere."

"Thing is, we need a ride."

"A ride?"

"To the airport."

"You don't have one?"

She shakes her head.

"It's your lucky day then, isn't it?"

"So you will?"

"Of course. Although I'm surprised that Kent hadn't figured that out in advance, him being so organized and all. Mr. Union and everything." Although he says this with a smile, she thinks there's bitterness there, a tinge of resentment.

"What time's the flight?"

She looks at her watch: 8:42. "Eleven."

"Have you there in plenty of time," he says.

"Thank you so much."

"Nothing to it, my dear. A bit of company never hurt anybody."

She stands up. I'll let the children know. She turns and walks away but his voice stops her. "No word yet on the plant then? Kent's said nothing?"

It's finished. Three months, tops. She turns back to him. Shakes her head. "Not a thing."

She continues towards the door, realizing that the pain in her hand is almost gone. A light throbbing now. She'd kept it in her pocket the whole time so Myles wouldn't ask questions. So he wouldn't insist on taking her to have it looked at. She can just imagine Kent and Irene and herself all in the same hospital.

Melissa was right about the codeine though: *Make you forget you got a hand.*

* * *

SHE WALKS ALONG THE DECK TOWARDS THEM, pausing momentarily to look in the other direction. Nothing of Lightning Cove. Vanished. Had it ever existed?

The sun is higher, but small amidst so much blueness – a birthmark on a desert of flawless skin.

She'll have to tell them eventually. Perhaps at the airport. After take-off. That would be better – after take-off. No place to run. Who's she kidding? There's no place more suitable than another, no hour that's more appropriate. He's their dad and they have a right to know. Sooner rather than later. Allowing time to pass makes the things we have to say harder.

The smell of saltwater and gasoline. A breeze she knows will be warmer on land against her face. The rocking of the boat so gentle she wonders if it's rocking at all.

She thinks of Vancouver. Of the pictures she'd browsed on the Internet in the one-room library back in Lightning Cove. Mountains that make the ones here look like bruises. Buildings tall enough to reach the clouds. She imagines herself and the kids taking an elevator all the way to the top of one, then looking out over the strange city, at the ocean that's like the ocean here yet somehow different. *Big trees and it hardly ever snows.* Lots of rain, though. That's something else the Internet had said. Used to that though, living here in Lightning Cove. Never been bothered by the rain, she thinks.

She resumes her path towards them, empty hot chocolate cups at their feet.

Jeremy turns to her before she makes it all the way. "Me and Lynette saw a baby whale."

"You did?" She rushes over and dangles her head over the railing. "Where?"

"Gone now," Jeremy says.

Lynette says, "Swimming with its mother."

"Was it?"

Lynette manages to take her eyes off the water for a second and looks at her mother. "Just ahead of the boat."

"Wow." She stands in between them, a little light-headed, her body numb from fatigue, from codeine. Lays her good hand on Jeremy's shoulder. After a moment she looks towards the bow of the boat, at the approaching shore, their new life getting closer. Fifteen minutes maybe. Ten.

She wonders what Kent will think when he realizes they're not coming for him. And how long afterwards before he puts it together that they've gone. *She said you were going to meet her in St. John's,* she can hear Myles saying. *"He's meeting us later,"* that's exactly what she said. But Myles won't know where she is any more than Kent will, any more than her parents when Kent asks. *She was supposed to come in on Saturday,*

Terry will say, gripping his clipboard so tightly that his knuckles turn white. *Well, she couldn't have just disappeared,* Kent'll say to whoever will listen. But that is exactly what she'll have done.

"The mother's fin came out of the water," Lynette says.

"Did it?"

"Then they dove deep," Jeremy adds.

Even though she's certain they've gone, she scans the water's surface, thinking that she'll try to see more from now on. Not be inside her head so much. Look forward to the days instead of wishing them away.

She lets a minute or two pass before saying, "We're going on a plane today."

"We are?" Lynette says.

She nods. Then, "Who wants the window seat?"

Lynette jumps on the spot, her hand that's holding the giraffe in the air. "Me, me, me!"

She looks at Jeremy.

His eyes are on the sea, not so much downward as they are pointed towards the horizon.

She says to him, "For someone who loves planes you don't seem very excited."

He won't look at her.

How much his face is like his father's, she thinks: big, barely blinking eyes, tight lips, and hollows of cheeks inward as if he were chewing on their insides. He's right beside her but not too. Close enough to touch, yet miles away.

"Jeremy?"

Finally he looks at her, coming back a little.

"What's wrong?"

More like himself again now.

"Tell me."

She senses him wanting to speak; yet he's incapable of forming the words somehow. "What is it, Jeremy? *What?*"

When she hears what she does next, it isn't his voice but Lynette's. "Are you leaving Dad?"

Now it's *she* unable to find the words, more numb than the bloodied hand in her pocket.

In her mind, she'd envisioned the three of them on Jackie's chesterfield in Vancouver, light coming through a part in the curtains, and mountains, snowcapped, in the distance. Lynette lying crossways with her tiny legs over her mother's lap, and Jeremy drinking a Dr. Pepper with his hockey cards askew on the coffee table. Neither of them mentioning their father.

Nothing is ever like you think it'll be.

"Who told you that?" she says.

Lynette nudges a finger in her brother's shoulder. "He did."

She steps closer to him, so that their bodies are almost touching. "Did you, Jeremy?"

No answer.

"Did you?"

He nods, half of him looking like he wants to cry, the other half like he wants to smack her across the mouth.

The words come out before she realizes she's said them. "Would you come with me if I were?"

Without hesitation, Lynette says, "I would."

Jeremy takes his time before answering, his face once again in profile to hers, staring out at where Lightning Cove used to be.

It's an unfair question, she knows. A child wants to be with both parents. She wishes she could take the words back.

"I'd go with Dad," Jeremy says then, his voice so quiet.

She'd expected as much, but yet she's shaken. And why, despite the calm water, does she feel unsteady on her feet? Could it be that, by taking him away, she's doing him more harm than good? Torn. That's what she is. Shoulders being ripped from their sockets, the connection between the two lobes of her brain severing, a deep fissure along the centre of her. *Torn*. Between wanting him with her and leaving him behind.

"Look at me," she says.

He won't.

"Jeremy, look at me."

He does.

"You too, Lynette."

Lynette turns to her.

She couches down even though Jeremy is nearly as tall as she is. Looks over at Lynette. "Come here beside your brother."

Lynette comes close, the top of her shoulder against Jeremy's ribs.

She looks at them, her eyes going from one to the other and then back again. There's the smell of spring in their clothes, in their hair, the slightest of red – from being outside all this time – on their cheeks.

She holds out her good hand to them like the captain of a football team would. Lynette is the first to cover it with her own. Emily looks at Jeremy, waiting. Finally he lays his hand on top. She starts to speak, but can't. Breathes in and tries again. "I would never hurt either of you."

Neither Lynette nor Jeremy says anything.

"You know that right?"

She thinks they nod but isn't sure.

There's more she needs to say, she knows, but she can't. Not yet. Not while they still have so much farther to go.

"How much does Mommy love you?" she says.

Lynette stretches out her arms as if she were about to hug a giant ball.

"Wow, that's a lot," Emily says.

She looks at Jeremy.

"*Mom*," he says.

"Too old are you? To tell your mom you love her?"

He stretches out his arms like his sister and then quickly drops them again.

The ship's horn again now.

She stands up.

The ferry pulling into dock.

"Let's go to the front," Jeremy says to his sister.

"Don't run. I'll come and get you in a minute." She stands there watching them for what seems like a long time.

A hand on her shoulder. She turns.

It's Myles.

"Oh, it's you."

He adjusts his Toronto Maple Leafs cap. "I'm going down to the car. You can come, or I can meet you on shore."

"On shore," she says.

"Good enough. See you down there."

"Okay."

He goes, barely life enough to lift his feet off the ground.

She thinks of Kent. Those perfect fingers that, so often, had grazed the side of her cheek or had run down the length of her spine or had tucked a length of hair behind her ear. Or curled into a fist. Yes, that too. Canceling out everything that came before. Him reaching out to her then, picking her up off the floor like a child, carrying her in his arms to the chesterfield, or to the kitchen table. Sitting beside her or across from her, shoulders slumped. Chin lowered too. Watery eyes on her, then not. Him saying, "You make me so angry." Then, after a moment, "Why do you?"

A year of savings inside her suitcase. The money from the joint account too. A new beginning, she hopes.

The gangway is lowering.

She makes her way to the bow, sees her babies' backs in the foreground, them waving to someone on the dock below.

She continues forward. "Come on you two," she says.

Neither of them turns around, unable to hear her, she figures, under the sound of churning engines and the lowering gangway and the shouts of the men on the lower deck and the scattered boat horn.

She goes closer. Says again, "Come on you two." Then, "We can't leave Myles waiting."

It's Jeremy who turns just as she gets to within reaching distance of him, his face like a four-year-old at a birthday party: eyes nearly popping, the largest smile displaying big teeth, all his faith in her miraculously restored.

He points behind him. "Down there," he says, "he's down there."

"What?" she says. "Who? Who's down there?"

Jeremy doesn't answer, too busy turning back around.

She manages to cram herself in between them, looks over the bow towards the dock below.

If not for the railing she'd drop right where she's standing. Each of them looking down at her, but she not coming to. In her mind praying that she'll never.

She'd turn her head if she could, or run back towards the stern if there was blood enough in her legs. But there isn't any blood, all of it drained out of her.

Kent's waving up at her.

She doesn't wave back. Couldn't even if she'd wanted to. Lifting an eyebrow would be too much now.

Hospital greens underneath his open jacket. An arm in a sling. Blackened eyes. A blood-flecked bandage around his forehead. The same boots on from yesterday though. The only things not cut away and torn from him no doubt. "Careful with those boots," she imagines him having said. And, "Do what you want with the clothes." Hard to get a pair to fit his feet, that's why.

Even though she's told him not to, Jeremy leaves the railing and starts running.

She makes a grab for him, but he's too fast. "No! Come back!"

Lynette makes to move too, but Emily manages to reach out and stop her before she can. "Stay with me, okay baby."

"But I want to see Daddy."

Emily looks down on him.

How strange.

To look down on *him*.

5

SHE'S RUNNING – LYNETTE RIGHT BEHIND HER – towards the parked cars. She stops, then says, "Do you see Myles's?"

Lynette stops beside her.

"We have to find Myles's."

She grabs her daughter's hand and starts running again.

The sounds of turned ignitions, pumps of gas, the gangway lowering, echoing voices.

"There," she says, pointing to a cancerous billow of exhaust coming from a car near the back.

She increases her pace.

"Too fast, Mommy."

"Come on."

She can barely make out his face through the cigarette smoke when she gets there. She bangs on the window and tries opening the door, but it won't budge.

Myles lifts himself over the gearshift, then shimmies his way to the passenger side. Bangs open the door with his shoulder.

A plume of smoke escapes.

"It doesn't open from the outside," he says.

"Get in," she says to Lynette. She tries pulling the front seat forward so that her daughter can crawl into the back, but it won't give.

"I've been meaning to fix that too," he says.

"Squeeze in," she says.

Lynette does.

She throws the suitcase into the back and then gets in the passenger side.

"Changed your mind, did you?" Myles says.

"Drive off the gangway and keep going."

Myles pumps the gas. "What?"

She grabs his thigh with her good hand. "Drive off this boat and keep going."

He puts out his cigarette.

"Are you deaf? Drive off and don't stop. Ever!"

Myles grips the steering wheel. Doesn't so much look at her as he does through her. "What's the matter? Where's Jeremy?"

The gangway's completely down now. Up ahead, a dwarfish man with a wild beard starts directing off the few vehicles and walk-on passengers.

"With Dad," Lynette says from the back seat.

Emily grips the collar of Myles's jacket. A stab of pain shoots into her hand.

"Jesus!" His eyes are on the hanging bits of skin. "What happened?"

More vehicles driving off the ferry. A few horns and break lights. Rolled down windows and some lit cigarettes.

"It's nothing." She's almost whispering. "Nothing compared to what *he'll* do."

Myles looks out the driver's side window, then in the back at Lynette. "You're scaring the little one." He turns back to her, his voice lower than Emily's had been. "Who? Who'll do?"

She lets go of his jacket but keeps her face close to his. Body odour on his unwashed clothes, in his hair – breath like spoiled milk. She breathes. Then breathes again. "You're going to see my husband up ahead –"

"Kent – "

"Let me finish." She looks towards the front, then back at Myles. "You're going to see him up ahead. Jeremy will be with him. But you can't stop. Or roll down the window even. You have to drive. Just drive –"

"But – "

"And if he follows, you have to keep driving. Except faster. So much faster. All the way to Gander airport."

"Why can't I see Daddy?" Lynette says.

The man behind them is honking his horn.

Myles slips the gearshift into drive, but keeps his foot on the break. Looks at her. "Who'll do?"

She says, "You know."

"How would I?"

More honks from the car behind them.

She looks in the rear-view mirror; the man's waving them forward.

The dwarfish man is approaching them now, ushering them along with a pudgy finger, and mouthing something she can't make out.

Myles lifts his chin. "There he is."

She looks. It's Kent. Not fifty feet away and staring right at them; Jeremy pressed so close to his father's side that he looks attached.

"But he'll want me to stop," Myles says, edging the car forward at a trickle, yet enough for the man behind them to stop pressing his horn.

"Just keep your eyes ahead. Pretend you don't see him," she says.

"But he's looking right at us."

"Just drive."

"He knows it's me – "

"Just DRIVE!" Then, "Please!"

Twenty-five feet away.

Twenty-two.

Nineteen.

"What about Jeremy?" he asks.

Fifteen feet.

She fights the urge to reach out and press the brake herself. Throw open the door and run to him. Take her boy into her arms. "This wasn't how I planned it."

Lynette starts rolling down her window.

Emily turns back to her. "Roll it back up."

"I want to talk to Daddy."

"Do as I say!"

"Why?"

"*Do it!*"

Lynette winds the window back up, crying now as she does.

Twelve. Twelve feet. Kent battered and tired looking, but waving nonetheless. And smiling. Him probably thinking, "They've come after all."

She says, "He'll never let me have Jeremy now."

Nine feet.

Myles applies the brake.

She grabs his shoulder. "No!"

"She wants to see her dad for God's sake."

"No! Please!"

"He'll come to my house," Myles says, "tear me a new one."

"Daddy!" Lynette shouts.

Kent's saying something.

Myles slowing further, almost stopped.

"He'll kill me," she says.

"What?"

191

"He'll kill me."

"No –"

"He will! He's tried it before."

Kent tapping on the driver's side door. "What a surprise," he says.

Lynette knocks on the window. "Daddy!"

Kent says, "I didn't expect to see you, Myles."

Myles looks up at him. Brings the car to a stop.

She feels something inside of her let go. Wear away. Her life, she thinks, her desire to live it.

Kent reaches for Myles's door, grips the handle, but before he can open it, Myles suddenly jams down on the accelerator. Screeching tires, the front of the car swerving as if on a sheet of ice.

She turns and looks through the back window, their figures already growing smaller, falling away, like waking up and slowly forgetting the dream you've had.

She turns back around.

After a moment, Myles says, "What do you want me to do?" His foot is like a brick on the gas peddle. The engine rips into the morning like a motorboat on a lake.

Stop. Turn around. Go back. I have to get my boy. Go back. Please!

She doesn't look at him, just fixes her stare ahead. "Keep driving."

"You sure?"

She doesn't answer him.

"Are you sure, I said?"

She hesitates a moment, then says, "Yes, I'm sure."

A long silence falls over them.

Had to let him go, she thinks. To protect Lynette. Herself.

"I just wanted to say hi to Daddy," Lynette says then, her voice breaking.

6

SHE DOESN'T KNOW HOW LONG IT'S BEEN since either of them has said anything. Twenty minutes maybe. Half an hour.

She looks again in the side mirror, expecting to see Kent speeding towards the back bumper, forward in his seat, his chest almost touching the steering wheel, bruised face against the windshield. But there's nothing. Nothing at all since they got on the highway. Nothing speeding towards them in the oncoming lane, nothing behind them. The last three people on the planet it feels like.

One hundred and thirty kilometres an hour since they pulled away from the ferry. If Myles's clunker were a person, it would be on the verge of a massive coronary by now.

Jeremy in her head. Him alongside his father as Myles sped past. Only a second or two, yet she was able to see his face. Something in his eyes. Unsure if losing one to gain the other is all it's cracked up to be.

She's deserted him. No other way to put it. Left him behind like old clothes in a box.

She remembers her husband's smile, the way his hand had stayed up in the air. Probably saying to himself, "Don't you see us standing here?"

Myles takes a hand off the wheel and flicks on the radio and presses in the lighter and reaches inside his coat for his smokes. "I'll die if I don't spark one up," he says. "You mind?"

"Roll down your window, sweetheart," she says to Lynette.

Lynette does.

"I'll roll down mine too," Myles says.

"Can you spare one?" Emily says.

"Didn't know you smoked."

She shakes her head. "I don't, not really." She rolls down her own window.

He takes out two and hands her one. Offers her the lighter first before using it himself. Puts it back in. Hauls out the ashtray. It's overflowing with butts, the stink alone enough to cause lung cancer.

She sucks in hard, her throat on fire. Blows out in the throes of a strong head buzz. Looks in the side mirror. Nothing. Now that his truck is all smashed up what would Kent be driving anyway?

Them just smoking now.

James Taylor barely coming through the crackling radio.

Myles flicks his cigarette ash on the floor instead of out the window or in the ashtray.

Smokes finished and another song on the radio. Blue Rodeo. An old one she hasn't heard in a while. Something about seeing the world through rose-coloured glasses.

Myles switches it off.

Lynette's dozing in the back. Too much for a little one to take. A long silence.

Finally, he says, "It's hard to imagine."

She turns to him. "What?"

"Him beating on you." He runs his tongue over a tiny cold sore on his top lip, then nibbles on it. Rubs his forehead, his eyes. "I mean, Christ, I've known him for years."

She doesn't say anything. Turns away and stares at the shoulder of the road, at the scattered patches of yet-to-melt snow, and the blur of trees whipping past. Hard to focus. Like her life.

"It's not that I don't believe you or nothing, cause I do. I do. It's just that he doesn't seem like the type, you know. I mean, he's so big and you're so tiny, right?"

She looks again in the side mirror. Nothing.

Another silence.

She turns to him. "I shouldn't have gotten you involved. I'm sorry."

He lets out a big breath. "A lot a good that does me now." Then, almost immediately, "I didn't mean that."

"It's okay."

To prevent the car from exploding, she thinks, Myles eases up on the gas.

"Not far now," he says.

She nods, then turns back around. Just empty road behind her. She wonders where they might be now, Kent and Jeremy. On the ferry back to Lightning Cove probably. She remembers not having bothered to put the tarp back in place. What will he think? Clothes strewn about their bedroom. The middle drawer of their dresser nearly pulled out all the way. Just wait until he withdraws from their bank account. She can see the receipt balled and suffocating between his clenched fist.

"He's never hurt the kids," she says.

He looks over at her.

"I can imagine what you must be thinking. But he hasn't."

He doesn't say anything. Offers her another smoke from his pack. She shakes her head.

He lights up another for himself. Rolls down his window again. Chilly air streaming in.

"He's a better father than I've been a mother. Lately anyway."

He blows smoke out through his nostrils. After a while, he says, "Where are you going? *Really?*"

"Away." That's all she'll allow him.

The sun is shining directly into their eyes now. She reaches up and lowers the visor. Myles doesn't bother with his.

"Are you coming back?" He says.

Again her face is pointed toward the passenger side window. Not looking. Hard to with her eyes squeezed shut.

"You're not, right?"

She takes a moment before she speaks. She says, "I really appreciate the ride, Myles, but can we just be quiet for a while?"

More smoke through his nose. A clearing of his throat. The slightest of nods. His foot heavy on the gas again.

7

SOMEONE'S SHAKING HER. A voice calling in the distance. She opens her eyes but has no idea where she is.

"We're here," the voice says.

Myles. It's Myles. Everything comes back like an old pain: running away, Jeremy left behind.

Myles smiles. "One minute you were looking out the window, the next you were slumped over."

The codeine, she thinks. Stronger than she'd expected. Numb in her body now. A perpetual pulsing in her hand, but it isn't painful.

"Go inside and get a cart, I'll get your suitcase," Myles says.

Lynette's yawning when she turns around.

"Come with me, sweetheart."

They get out. Walk towards the sliding doors, Lynette through first, she next, her feet like warm bread. Bright lights inside. Passengers mingling. Some children gathered around an outdated video game beside the restaurant. The smells of french fries and stuffing and gravy.

"There's one," Lynette says, pointing at an abandoned cart beside a row of padded chairs.

Emily goes over and takes it, pushing it with her good hand back outside.

Myles has their suitcase waiting beside the car. He picks it up and walks in their direction. Loads it on.

They stand looking at each other afterwards: Myles with his hands in his pockets and the brim of his Maple Leafs' cap down low; Lynette pushing the cart back and forth as if she were trying to hush a crying baby.

Finally, he says, "What should I say when I see him?"

She breathes in deep, then looks beyond his left shoulder at a parked taxi, the engine still running. A fat man stands near to it, an unlit pipe in his mouth, reading *The Telegram*.

She looks back at Myles. "Tell him to blame me."

He nods. Pulls the brim of his cap even lower. Coughs a phlegmy cough, but doesn't bother covering his mouth. Swallows a ball of mucus before saying, "You aren't coming back." It isn't a question.

She says nothing. Looks at her watch. Not even ten. An hour of waiting. Thinks of Jeremy again. His face. Hadn't the whole point been to get him out too?

Myles has said something but she hasn't heard it. "What did you say?"

"I said, Irene'll be wondering where I am."

"Of course," she says. "Go. Give her a hug for me."

"I will."

Before he can turn to go, she grabs him. It's an awkward hug, but a hug nonetheless. She pulls away, wishing she could run him a warm bath and make him some soup, shave his face and let him know that better times are to come. "Thank you," she says. "You've risked a lot, I know."

He loops his fingers in his belt like a cowboy. "Breathing's a risk."

She nods, then unzips her purse and pulls out some of the money. Hands it to him.

"What's this?" he says.

"For the gas and everything."

"By the looks of that wad you'd think I was driving a transport truck."

She holds it out.

He pushes her hand away. "I bet you could probably use that more than me."

"Please take it."

"I won't, Emily. Thanks all the same."

He lifts the bill of his cap so that he doesn't pluck out an eye when he bends down to kiss her cheek.

She lets him.

He bends over and gives Lynette a hug, then starts walking back to the driver's side of his car.

Emily's voice stops him.

"What?" he says.

"I said that I haven't been honest with you."

"About…"

"The fish plant."

"Oh."

"It's finished. By Christmas, Kent says."

He nods. Gives her a look that says he'd expected as much.

"I couldn't find a way to tell you."

The slightest of pauses before he waves and gets in his car. Waves again as he pulls away.

8

IT FEELS LIKE SHE COULD MELT INTO HER CHAIR. Wonders how she'll get up when the call comes to start boarding the plane. The 747 out on the tarmac is being refueled, two men loading baggage.

She brings hers, Lynette's, and Jeremy's boarding passes close to her face, wondering if they're real. What about the plane outside, is that real? How about the seats beneath them? Or the smell of Lynette's half-eaten french fries?

Seats A, B, and C in row nine for what were supposed to have been the three of them. Can she really do it, she wonders? Leave without her boy? She puts the boarding passes in her pocket. It's bad enough that he has to lose his mother, but his sister too? The same for Lynette, she supposes – a father and a brother.

She reaches out for a french fry. It's soggy from all the vinegar Lynette dribbled on top. Still, she manages to chew and swallow it, wondering when it was she'd last eaten.

She tries moving the fingers of her injured hand, but only the thumb and pinky work, the rest like frozen sausages, barely any feeling at all. She'll take that though, over the pain she'd felt before taking the codeine. Two more tablets in her pocket. For the plane.

So tired. So bloody tired. She tilts her head back, letting the chair take its weight. Closes her eyes. How easily she could envision her new life out west before this morning. Every day for weeks she'd seen things so specifically, down to the smells in the air, to the colour of the paint on Jackie's living room wall. Not now, though. Nothing but blackness behind the lids of her eyes now. Sleep without dreams.

A pre-boarding announcement – those needing assistance or traveling with small children.

She decides to stay put, not quite ready to lift her head, not quite ready to go forward in all of this. Not yet. Besides, Lynette isn't a small child. Not anymore. Eight in January. Only ten years younger than she herself when she married Kent. She resists opening her eyes and telling her daughter that there's plenty of time and no need to rush. *Fight to stay young, my sweetheart,* she imagines saying, *for as long as you can. All the time in the world to become a woman.*

She hears passengers sauntering up to the gate, whispers and laughter. A young child is crying softly.

"I need to use the bathroom," Lynette says.

She doesn't open her eyes. "Be quick. We're boarding in a minute."

Lynette's steps on the floor fade into the white noise of coming and going, into the things we do to say hello, and those we must in order to say goodbye.

He's standing in front of her when she opens her eyes. Near enough to touch were she to straighten her legs, point her toes.

He looks worse close up, like starving wolves have had their way with him. His eyes like a bare canvas, telling her nothing and everything.

So still. She wonders if he's even breathing.

It occurs to her that, for the first time, she's unafraid. How funny not to be. Is it possible to use up too much of something so that there's nothing left? A tear duct can only release so much water. A heart can only beat so much.

"It's you," she says. She doesn't bother straightening up in her seat.

"It's me," he says.

They're quiet for a moment.

"How'd you get through security?" she says.

He reaches inside his coat pocket and hauls out a boarding pass. "I got the window seat in row 12." He looks at her. "You?"

She doesn't answer.

"Bloody expensive though, eh? Better off booking in advance." He puts the boarding pass away. "That what you did?"

A long silence.

"I didn't see you following us," she says.

"I wasn't. Not at first. Boarding the boat when Jeremy told me you were going on a plane."

"I thought you'd still be in the hospital."

"You *hoped* I would be, you mean."

She doesn't deny it.

"I thought I'd come home and surprise you."

She says nothing.

"Surprise!"

She looks beyond him. "Where's Jeremy?"

"In the truck."

"What truck?"

"The one I rented."

"You shouldn't leave him in the truck."

"No? You shouldn't *leave* him."

"He wanted to go with you."

"What did you expect?" He pauses and then says, "Where's Lynette?"

She doesn't say.

He edges closer.

"That's far enough," she says.

He grabs hold of her upper arm. "Get up."

"Let go."

He squeezes. "Take my kids away, will ya?"

"I said, let *GO!*"

A few in the distance are staring. A child points its finger.

"We're not at home now you son of a bitch."

He holds on a moment longer, then lets go. Stares at the gate that she and Lynette will have to pass through. Turns back to her. "Halifax, eh?"

She nods.

"Then where?"

"None of your business."

"It is if you're taking my daughter."

"Is it?"

"That's right."

Silence.

"How long?" he says.

"How long what?"

"Have you been planning this?"

She doesn't answer.

"No return date on your ticket, I bet."

The child's still pointing as her mother passes ID to the attendant at the gate. Those who had been staring earlier still are, turning their heads away whenever Emily's gaze goes to them.

"Come home," he says.

"What?"

"Come home."

"What's at home?"

"Everything."

"For *you.*"

200

"For you too."

"You're blind."

"I don't understand."

"I didn't expect you would."

The general boarding announcement, everyone in rows sixteen and higher. Some passengers close books and reach for bags, walk lazily to the gate.

"I could have *died*," he says.

She says nothing.

"What about our trip? We can stay longer, you know. I'll need the healing time." Something resembling a smile on his mouth.

She sees Lynette approaching, stuffed giraffe in her arms. She starts running when she sees him. "Daddy!"

Kent turns. It causes him pain to lift her. "How's my girl?" He kisses her on the lips.

"Mommy drove past and I couldn't say hello."

"I know, baby."

Lynette leans back, eyes all large. "Your face is bruised."

"It's worse than it looks, sweetheart."

"What happened, Daddy?"

He looks at Emily. "Mommy didn't tell you?"

"No."

He looks back at Lynette. "Daddy had a little accident in his truck."

"You did?"

"Yes. But don't worry, I'm okay."

Lynette lightly touches one side of his face. "It looks like it hurts."

"Does it?"

"Yes."

He kisses the tips of her fingers. "It does hurt a little."

"Are you coming with us, Daddy?"

"I don't know. Where are you going?"

"On the plane, Mommy says."

"Does she?"

"Yeah." Then, "Where's Jeremy?"

"Waiting for us."

"Where?"

"Outside."

Emily leans forward. "Come sit with me, honey – "

"She's fine where she is. Aren't you baby?"

Lynette nods, then touches the bandage around her father's head.

He gently removes her hand and then says, "You've got to make a decision, sweetheart."

Emily goes to stand but doesn't. "She's just a youngster."

"Old enough to make up her own mind if you ask me."

"She shouldn't have to choose."

He laughs now – loud with an open mouth. Then says, "At least *I* give her the choice."

She says nothing. Watches the last few passengers in rows sixteen and higher filter past the gate and then looks back at him. His eyes are right on her, have been the whole time, she bets. "You don't see me here, do you?"

"What are you talking about?" he says.

"What choice have you given me?"

It's him now who says nothing. Bounces Lynette lightly in his arms.

"You think my being here has nothing to do with *you?*" She struggles to keep her voice down, to keep her eyes, despite them burning, from watering. "Everything's because of you. All of it."

Another announcement, the remainder of the passengers can board now.

She looks at the gate, then back at him. The gate. Him. Their boarding passes in her pocket, their suitcase already on the plane – freedom just outside the window, close enough to breathe in, to taste.

"Don't want to miss your flight," he says.

Him. The gate. Him.

"You can go, but not with her."

"But I want to go on the plane," Lynette says.

"Give her to me, Kent."

"No."

"Please."

"No."

"I'll scream, I swear to Jesus I will."

"Go ahead. You still won't get her."

The final boarding call for Air Canada flight 8535 to Halifax.

"All you're good for is bagging groceries. What can you give her?"

"I want to go on the plane," Lynette says again. "I want to go with Mommy."

"There," Emily says. "She's chosen."

"I've changed my mind. What kind of father would I be if I gave her to a woman who can't make any more than minimum wage?"

Lynette starts to cry softly.

"And don't think I don't know what you've been up to with that Terry Hodder either."

She needs a moment to process his words. "*What?*"

"I'm surprised you didn't ask him to go with you."

"I don't know what you're talking about – "

"Or maybe he's waiting for you on the other end already, is that it?"

She nearly laughs out loud. "The shit you dream up."

"No wonder you were always in such a hurry to get to work." He pauses for a second, then says, "Frankly, I'm surprised that you would stoop so low. Not the best looking fella' on the block, is he?"

"You're crazy, you know that. Terry's been nothing but a gentleman. You're not even in his league."

"Is that right?"

"That's right."

"Well, perhaps I'll pay him a visit when I get back."

She remembers her nightmare from the other morning: Kent standing over Terry's body, blood all over Terry's shirt. She shuts the image out. Doesn't say anything. Can't. Cold all over. Sweating, but cold all over. Empty, that's how she feels, a pumpkin with a scooped out centre. Finally, she says, "I'll call the cops if you so much as touch him."

"Protecting your boyfriend now, are ya?"

"He's not my boyfriend."

"Call the cops, will ya? And what do you think they'll say when I tell them that you were trying to kidnap my kids?"

"They'll say I should have done it ages ago."

"Is that right?"

"That's right, once they hear what you're like."

Lynette rests her chin on her father's shoulder.

"A slut's all you are. A slut in high school and a slut now."

"Don't say that in front of my daughter," she says, the words coming from somewhere outside of herself.

The pale attendant at the gate looks in their direction.

"Oh," he says, "it's *my* daughter now, is it?"

"You can say what you want to me, just not in front of her."

"I think this is something that a daughter might like to know about her mother."

"Kent!"

Lynette lifts her head in order to wipe her eyes, then looks at her father. "Put me down."

"Give her to me," Emily says.

"Stay with your dad for now, sweetie, okay?"

"Will passengers, Emily Gyles, Lynette Gyles, and Jeremy Gyles please come to the gate for boarding. Passengers, Emily Gyles, Lynette Gyles, and Jeremy Gyles. Thank you." The attendant's looking right at her, charcoal eyes in a milk-coloured face.

She can hear her own breathing. There's a thumping in her inner ear, as if the pulse in her neck has relocated there. Those wandering behind him have gone blurry, out of focus, their movements slowed, their voices metallic. All that's clear is him: the colours of his clothes like fresh paint, bruises seemingly darkened, cuts suddenly re-opened and gushing thick blood, even the few hairs in one of his nostrils are visible.

She lays her good hand, palm down, on one side of her, tries to suck in enough breath to speak. Nothing comes.

She manages to unclamp her jaw. Perhaps some words will come now. Nothing does though. That's when she sees Jeremy standing just outside the security gate. He lowers his eyes when he sees her watching, his hands in his pockets.

Kent calls out to him. "I told you to wait in the truck."

"You were taking forever."

Kent puts Lynette down. "Take your sister out to play the video game."

"That game's ancient, Dad."

"Then buy yourselves something at the restaurant." Kent squats down and hands Lynette ten dollars. "Go on, sweetheart," he says. "Go out with your brother."

Lynette takes the money, but doesn't go. She stares at her mother.

Emily stares back, wishing there was some way to scoop her youngest into her arms and run to the plane without Kent catching them.

"Go on, sweetheart," Kent says. "All sorts of yummy things in the restaurant."

Stay, baby, stay! She thinks to herself. *Mommy can't lose you too.*

"Come on, Lynette," Jeremy says.

Lynette looks at her again, then goes and joins her brother. Jeremy snatches the money from her hands as soon as she gets there. He heads to the restaurant. Lynette follows.

The terminal is practically deserted now. Emily looks at the plane, then at the attendant, the plane, the attendant, resisting the urge to get to her feet and burst through the gate. How can she though, without her children?

Kent's looking down at her.

The attendant's staring too.

She turns towards the window. A man wearing a backwards baseball hat stands beside the plane holding what looks to her like an orange baton. The now-empty baggage car goes past him, its driver lifting a few fingers from the steering wheel as if to say, *The show's all yours.* The baton-holding man cocks his head and gives the 'thumbs up.' She imagines the captain and first mate in the cockpit putting on headphones and talking into little mouthpieces, pressing buttons above and in front of them. Then the captain looking out his window directly at her. *What are you waiting for?* she hears him say.

She thinks it's Kent speaking to her first, but when she looks up, it's the attendant. Taller close up, longer face too, a twig-like neck. Hardly any breasts.

"Sorry, what did you say?"

Kent's standing in the same spot. Looking at the both of them now.

"I said the plane's not going to wait forever." She looks at him, then back at her. "You're Mrs. Gyles, right?"

Emily nods.

The lady looks at Kent again, then bends over and puts her mouth close to Emily's ear, breath like peppermint Certs. Whispering now, she says, "Is everything all right?"

Emily nods.

"All's I need to do is make a call, you know. He can't stop you from getting on board."

Kent's still looking, big pupils, and a grin so slight that she doubts anyone other than herself can see it.

For a second she considers getting the lady to help get the children on board, but then changes her mind. No sense in it so long as Jeremy wants to stay with his father. And Kent's already warned her about trying to take Lynette. *You can go, but not with her.* Besides, he's right, taking the children *would* be kidnapping. Even if she did manage to get away, how long before the cops tracked her down? How long can you hide two youngsters? Stick out like boils the three of them would in Vancouver. What does she know about city life, anyway? She thinks that *St. John's* is too big. All those cars and one-way roads, the crowds down on George and Water Streets. Never off the island in her whole life and yet, somehow, she was silly enough to convince herself that she could make her way in a city like Vancouver. Over two million people. Four Newfoundland's.

"Two minutes and I won't be able to stop it, Mrs. Gyles," says the thin attendant. She straightens up to full height before adding, "Decide quick." Another look at Kent before walking away: blue tights and flat bum beneath a blue skirt, hair bobbed and bouncing, heels too long for skinny, on-the-cusp-of-breaking ankles.

How could a plan that had seemed so practical a few short weeks ago now feel as likely as changing the colour of her skin? She can't think straight. Something else Kent has taken from her. In her mind, all she'd wanted was to get away. So far away. Off the island and past Halifax and P.E.I. and Toronto and Manitoba and Saskatchewan and Alberta. And farther still. Even Vancouver seemed too close. She'd have chosen Japan if she could have. Another planet. Away. That's all she'd desired. Desired it so much in fact that she didn't stop to consider the consequences. And now here she is with the plane about to take off without her and him standing over her. Always over her. A prisoner now. Forever. If he doesn't kill her, she'll lose her mind. Or perhaps she has already.

Kent comes closer so that he's standing between her parted legs. She lets him.

"Come home," he says.

She doesn't speak.

"Won't you?"

All you're good for is bagging groceries. What can you give her? He's right. What can she offer? No trade, no university – nothing. And what happens when the money runs out? Cause it will, eventually. What then?

"Or else they'll be picking up pieces of Terry Hodder all over Lightning Cove."

"They'll be anyway whether I do or not."

"Not if you come back."

She manages to hold his gaze for a second before turning to look once more at the gate, into the eyes of the Air Canada attendant, eyes longing to give her more time even though there isn't any.

"I love you," he says.

She turns back to him.

"I said I love – "

"Yes, I heard you."

"You don't believe me?"

She goes to say something, but stops herself.

"Say it," he says.

She breathes and tries again. "Love me one second, then hate my guts the next."

"What?"

"Grip my throat with the same hand that you lay over my belly button."

"What are you talking about?"

"I'm so sick of being *scared*..." She almost cries, but manages to stifle it. "...when I hear your truck in the driveway, when you twist the handle of the door, when you lie down beside me."

He just looks at her.

"I'm so stupid, so *fucking* stupid."

He takes half a step forward, but she brings her knees together, stopping him.

He stares at her for a long time before turning to look at Lynette and Jeremy. They're near the security entrance again sharing something from a greasy paper bag. Onion rings, Emily thinks.

After a while, she says, "She had fries not ten minutes ago."

"What?"

"Lynette, I bought her french fries not long before you got here."

"Oh."

Kent takes a few steps towards them.

She watches.

He stops. Then says to them, "Go wait in the truck."

Lynette takes the onion ring that she was just about to chew out of her mouth. "We're not going on the plane then, Daddy?"

Kent shakes his head. "No honey. Not today."

Jeremy's mouth is stuffed. He's licking the grease from his fingers.

"Go on," Kent says.

"Mommy's coming?" Lynette says.

Kent gives Emily a look over his shoulder, then focuses back on his daughter. "Yes, sweetheart; Mommy's coming."

Emily watches the children leave.

Kent comes back.

She looks at him.

"Let's go," he says.

She doesn't move.

He holds out his hand. "Come *on*."

Still she doesn't move.

He stares right into her. "When you decide to give up this foolishness, I'll be waiting in the truck." His eyes linger on her a moment longer, then he turns and walks away, his strides older, more of an effort to lift his feet. The accident, she thinks. Kinks in his armour. A man after all. Just a man.

A sound of engines to her right.

She looks out onto the tarmac. The baton-man is guiding the plane into a wide circle towards the runway. No other planes in sight.

A voice behind her then. The Air Canada attendant. "Too late now," she says.

Emily turns away from the window and looks up at the woman. It takes everything inside her to stay seated, not to stand up and go outside to him. She stares harder into the woman's eyes.

"What?"

Emily says nothing.

The woman sits beside her.-

A long silence.

"Is there something I can do?" the woman says finally.

"Let me just sit here for a minute?"

"Okay."

Emily's tears are dripping onto her own hands.

The Air Canada attendant hands over a tissue.

"Thank you." She dabs at her eyes. Blows her nose. Dabs at her eyes again because the tears won't stop. After a long time, she says, "All of this waiting, and the farthest I could get was the airport." Laughter then; tears are running down her face, yet she's laughing.

The Air Canada attendant stares at her.

Emily stops. Breathes. Breathes again. "What good is running away if I have to keep looking over my shoulder? Or through the window above the door? That's not freedom."

The thin woman just stares at her.

"Perhaps I was never *meant* to go. Do you think?"

The woman doesn't say anything.

Emily dries her eyes for the last time. Puts the tissue in her pocket. Another moment passes.

Emily starts to get to her feet.

The Air Canada employee helps her.

They walk a little ways, then stop in time to watch the plane speed off down the runway and slip up into the sky.

"That's my favourite part," Emily says.

"Take-off?"

Emily nods.

Neither speaks for a moment. Then the woman says, "It's coming down, for me."

Emily stays watching for a long time. Then she leaves the security gate and goes toward the waiting truck. Walks through the sliding doors.

THE END

ACKNOWLEDGEMENTS

To my first readers: Richard Hynes, Lori MacLean, Trona Balkissoon, and Gerri Hynes, thank you so much.

Gil Adamson, thank you for reading and offering such valuable editorial direction. Thanks also for your guidance and friendship. I am truly indebted.

Joel Hynes, your good word on my behalf was very much appreciated, as was all your sound advice.

Ed Kavanagh, your honesty made this book better.

Annamarie Beckel, thanks for giving the manuscript a thorough read. Your helpful comments and insights undoubtedly shaped this novel.

The Humber School for Writers, thank you. Especially, Michael Helm.

Wherever you are, Paul Quarrington, thanks for the wings and Guinness and shoptalk.

A special thanks to: Eileen Morrow at The Ontario Association of Interval and Transition Houses for the taking the time to talk to me about domestic violence.

Thanks a million, Paul Rowe, Sherry White, Brian O'Dea, Dawson Oake, and especially my mom, June.

To Donna and Janine and the whole crowd at Creative Book Publishing, thank you for taking a chance on a first-time writer, and for believing in this book.

And finally to my love, Michelle. It's only possible because of you.

The second youngest of eight children, Darren Hynes was born in Fogo Island, Newfoundland, but grew up in Labrador City. He has a BFA (Theatre) from Sir Wilfred Grenfell College, Memorial University of Newfoundland, and a Post-Graduate Certificate in Creative Writing from the Humber School for Writers in Toronto. Darren lives in Toronto and is currently at work on his second novel.